THE WIDOW KNEW TOO MUCH

With one eye around the door, he could see her outlined in the discreet lighting from the pool. She fumbled at the light switch, and he expected her to go directly to the bedside lamp near him, which he'd unplugged. But instead she hiked up the skirt of her robe and flopped down by the end of the bed, sliding it beneath her shoulders....

A car door slammed. "Oh dear," Mildred groaned. "They're back and whatever will they think—" She edged out, stood up, frantically brushing at the front of her housecoat. As she turned toward the door he grabbed for the marble lamp. Unaware, she pushed at the screen, and he swung its base at her head. It slammed into the bone behind her ear....

Bantam Books offers the finest in classic and modern American murder mysteries
Ask your bookseller for the books you have missed

Rex Stout

Broken Vase
Death of a Dude
Death Times Three
Fer-de-Lance
The Final Deduction
Gambit
The Rubber Band
Too Many Cooks
The Black Mountain

Max Allan Collins

The Dark City

A. E. Maxwell

Just Another Day in Paradise
Gatsby's Vineyard
The Frog and the Scorpion

Joseph Louis

Madelaine
The Trouble with Stephanie

M. J. Adamson

Not Till a Hot January
A February Face
Remember March
April When They Woo
May's Newfangled Mirth

P. M. Carlson

Murder Unrenovated
Rehearsal for Murder

Ross Macdonald

The Goodbye Look
Sleeping Beauty
The Name Is Archer
The Drowning Pool
The Underground Man
The Zebra-Striped Hearse
The Ivory Grin
The Wycherly Woman

Margaret Maron

The Right Jack
Baby Doll Games
One Coffee With
coming soon: Corpus Christmas

William Murray

When The Fat Man Sings

Robert Goldsborough

Murder in E Minor
Death on Deadline
The Bloodied Ivy

Sue Grafton

"A" Is for Alibi
"B" Is for Burglar
"C" Is for Corpse
"D" Is for Deadbeat
coming soon: "E" Is for Evidence

Joseph Telushkin

The Unorthodox Murder of Rabbi Wahl
The Final Analysis of Doctor Stark

Richard Hilary

Snake in the Grasses
Pieces of Cream
Pillow of the Community

Carolyn G. Hart

Design for Murder
Death on Demand
Something Wicked
Honeymoon With Murder

Lia Matera

Where Lawyers Fear to Tread
A Radical Departure
The Smart Money
Hidden Agenda

Robert Crais

The Monkey's Raincoat

Keith Peterson

The Trapdoor
There Fell a Shadow

David Handler

The Man Who Died Laughing
The Man Who Lived by Night

Marilyn Wallace

Primary Target

MAY'S
NEWFANGLED
MIRTH

Mary Jo Adamson

BANTAM BOOKS
NEW YORK · TORONTO · LONDON · SYDNEY · AUCKLAND

MAY'S NEWFANGLED MIRTH

A Bantam Book / May 1989

All rights reserved.
Copyright © 1989 by M. J. Adamson.
Cover art copyright © 1989 by Kam Mak.
No part of this book may be reproduced or transmitted
in any form or by any means, electronic or mechanical,
including photocopying, recording, or by any information
storage and retrieval system, without permission in writing from
the publisher.
For information address: Bantam Books

ISBN 0-553-27908-4

Published simultaneously in the United States and Canada

Bantam Books are published by Bantam Books, a division of Bantam
Doubleday Dell Publishing Group, Inc. Its trademark, consisting of the
words "Bantam Books" and the portrayal of a rooster, is Registered in U.S.
Patent and Trademark Office and in other countries. Marca Regis-
trada. Bantam Books, 666 Fifth Avenue, New York, New York 10103.

PRINTED IN THE UNITED STATES OF AMERICA

O   0 9 8 7 6 5 4 3 2 1

In memory of my mother, Frances M. Dauw

ACKNOWLEDGMENTS

My thanks to Sergeant Felix L. Cintrón Herrera of the Puerto Rican *Policía*, stationed on Vieques, and to Sr. Ramon Ruiz-Cox of the Esperanza Beach and Tennis Club. I extend my continuing gratitude to Tamara Escribano and Ed Poullet. I shall never forget Investigator Irving Lugo of the San Juan Homicide Section—the real-life Balthazar Marten.

BEROWNE: Why should I joy in an abortive birth?
At Christmas I no more desire a rose
Than wish a snow in May's newfangled mirth.

The Globe edition of
Love's Labor's Lost

1

EVEN IF HE HAD NOT been wearing transparent surgical gloves, the outfit of the man walking purposefully down the somnolent Vieques beach would have attracted the attention of the most incurious tourist or resident. Not because of his jeans, so faded by frequent laundering that they resembled the expensive acid-washed ones, nor because of the sea-stained yachting cap of the type often seen on nonsailors protecting or disguising bald spots. But mornings on the small island, while fresh, were never cool, and the long sleeves of his frayed plaid shirt were buttoned at the wrist. Instead of beach sandals, he had on shabby high-topped sneakers. The narrow hems of his denims were carefully tucked into these. A well-used blue canvas backpack was slung over one shoulder. A pair of splayed plastic sunglasses, child-size, were perched uncomfortably high on the bridge of his nose.

But he was quite alone on the shore. The Caribbean beach was as deserted as it might have been the moment God scooped up a handful of dust with Adam in mind. The shining sand ahead of him was just rinsed by the slow withdrawal of the sea. Since he was striding on the firm surface near the water's edge, even his footprints would soon be washed away by the returning waves. The sky was a uniform blank white, still empty of birds. Because the sun had not yet burned through the haze, Puerto Rico's bulk, six miles to the west across the channel, was invisible. He had picked the time, and the day, to ensure this solitude, but that was not difficult.

1

Vieques is shaped like an elongated dragon with fleshy hindquarters and a swollen tail, dragging itself out to sea. Part of the Commonwealth of Puerto Rico, it is twenty miles long and from three to six miles wide. The U.S. Navy owns both ends of the island—the small reptilian head and sloping shoulders on the eastern side and the fat haunch of the western end. In the middle, scattered on separate hilltops, are the opulent homes of continental snowbirds—residents who winter there and return to the States when the lilacs bloom. A few small hotels can be found in Isabel Segunda, the only town. A fishing village on the south coast boasts several guest houses, as well as an agreeable resort, the Esperanza Beach and Tennis Club. The miles of virgin beaches are uncrowded.

May is an especially quiet month here. The winter visitors have gone and Puerto Rican families, who seek the peace and safety of the neighboring island for brief vacations, still have children in school. It is, however, a popular time for the American navy to bombard the western end of the island. Cruisers and destroyers steam across the narrow channel from their Roosevelt Roads base on Puerto Rico's southeastern shore, and direct their heavy firepower at this unpopulated area—for practice. Unexploded ammunition booby-traps certain stretches, and that sector is strictly off limits. But Green Beach, where the man was currently hiking, is only used for training in assault landings. Marines scramble ashore, under the guns of an "enemy" presumably already weakened by naval barrages. Victorious, the troops then return to their ships, and tourists are allowed to invade the quiet sands.

Since this was the Thursday before Memorial Day, these would be the last maneuvers until after the holiday. But, in any case, Green Beach is only open to the public after three o'clock. At this hour in the morning, the intruder would have been turned back at the military checkpoint. He'd slipped unobserved through a fence.

The full-time residents of Vieques bitterly resent the navy's shelling, and in 1978 an enraged flotilla of outboard motors was launched against the cruisers to protest the interruption of fishing. The wildlife, however, infinitely prefer the occasional explosion to man's actual presence.

Land crabs the size of dinner plates scuttle across the clearings and vanish in the glossy-leaved underbrush. Snowy-feathered egrets perch on the back of the contentedly munching Brahman bulls, allowed to graze in certain areas. In the deserted mangrove swamps, the natty, two-toned loggerhead kingbird flaunts its crest, and the black-masked mangrove cuckoo flicks a sable tail stenciled with white butterfly wings. Mourning doves coo and breed undisturbed, and yellow-legged sandpipers quickstep along the shore. The hawksbill turtle, whose speckled shell is too much in demand for ladies' combs, swims safely through crystal water and above him, the endangered brown pelican swoops fearlessly.

Some of the early-rising birds had now begun their dawn songs. The man stopped abruptly on hearing one particular call. *Whee-a-wit-whee.* He cocked his head to listen to the plaintive whistle. Perhaps it was the kingbird, whose notes sometimes sounded like an unenthusiastic version of the Puerto Rican flycatcher's. Again, he heard a rollercoaster *whee* and smiled. The flycatcher had become almost extinct at the turn of the century when every field was plowed for sugar cane. With the destruction of the forests in the American Virgin Islands, it had disappeared there too, but apparently it'd found refuge in this preserve. He was tempted to catch a glimpse of the shy, inconspicuous bird hidden in a thick-leaved cóbana tree. But he wasn't sure how long his task would take, so he hurried on.

Besides, now the haze was thinning into gauzy sheets, with scraps of blue topaz appearing. A helicopter or two might be sent to sweep the area, for form's sake. While he had no intention of disturbing the navy's games, he did not want his own plans interrupted. If he were spotted, everything would be halted until he was removed. Later, someone might remember he'd been in the area. He'd have a plausible excuse for his unauthorized presence, but even that slight risk meant he would have to change his method of killing. And the symbolism of this particular plan appealed to him.

The crumpled sunglasses slid down and he tried to tuck the small hooks more firmly over his ears. Since everything he had on should best be buried after he finished, he'd gratefully picked up this pair yesterday where he'd found it washed ashore, rakishly snagged on the handle of an empty Clorox bottle, which was also useful. That had been rinsed and filled with clear water and thrust into the backpack. His careful mother's habit of reusing all items had remained with him. Also, he regarded these provisions from the sea as another symbol. Nature was conspiring with him to dispose of Luttrell.

Humanizing the universe in this way, imagining that there were sympathetic cosmic forces, was a habit of mind he'd acquired in his youth, studying the English Romantic poets. Later, living on the banks of the Amazon shook such a sentimental belief. There nature is man's adversary. Dangers come in all sizes and amazing varieties. Disease-carrying mosquitoes jostle each other for a place on bare arms and legs. Some South American bees have no sting, but these "eye-lickers" delight in human sweat, clustering at the corner of the eye, the lip, the nostril. As fast as they are pulled away, others attach themselves. While the human system can adapt to the infections of the mosquitoes in a few weeks, the bees are a plague. And the swarms of tiny blood-sucking flies make survival a matter of indifference. One bite is painful, ten excruciating. Plunging into the water to escape the infestation of insects puts the sufferer at the mercy of the small, terrible-toothed piranha. Even as they gasp, flopping in the bottom of a boat, these fish are capable of slicing off a toe.

Large wild pigs go in bands of fifty or more and if one of them is killed or wounded, the angry herd will make a mass attack on the hunter. The jaguar's size alone makes it lethal. But it is hunger that most often destroys Amazon inhabitants. Despite the lush abundance covering tropical earth, the jungle provides man with very few edible plants. In England's green and pleasant land, humans view natural forces differently.

And the intensity of his own desire to be a poet was entangled with the works he'd read early. He'd never lost the passion: in his mind he turned words like jewels, admiring the luster of each. As a child, he'd savored his own name. When he'd learned his first name meant his last, with the spelling slightly changed, he'd been delighted. In college in the nineteen-sixties, he'd always gone by Le.

Yet he wasn't particularly good with languages—it'd taken him rather a long time to become fluent in Solveyo, the Brazilian tribe's tongue. His Spanish had come back slowly here, and his whole vocabulary was tinted with English connotations. *Negro*, the Spanish word for "black," always had a warm brown sheen, with none of the bleak depth of the English word. The softness of *verde* called up summer's lush fields more readily than the generic "green."

Hearing the ventriloquial note of the Key West quail dove in a nearby thicket, he tried to catch a glimpse of its green head and rosy back. Its breeding season lasted until August and the plump bird was probably near its nest hidden in the underbrush. Ground nesters were vulnerable. Rats found their eggs tasty, and mongooses, imported a century ago to control the sugar-cane-gnawing rats, preyed on the young doves. Briefly, he contemplated moving near the shore trees where he'd be unseen by aircraft. But slogging through the deep sand there would slow him down, and he intended to be well away before the exercises began. It couldn't be much farther.

Checking his whereabouts, he made the mistake of gazing at the sky. Even without the sun's full glare, the dark glasses, which he normally never wore, did not prevent an effect of snow-dazzle. He closed his eyes gently, irritated at his own carelessness. Now he might be plagued with the recurring problem: those abrupt, startling shapes he glimpsed out of the corners of his eyes. They were possibly caused by a trick of light. When he'd first returned, he'd jerked his head continually to see what they were. Although he had the impression of dark, menacing mammals or even crouching men, there'd been nothing there.

During these last weeks, he'd speculated about the hallucinations obsessively. While he was now drenched in the open sunlight on this island whose forests had long ago been razed, all those years in the Amazonian jungle he'd been dependent on his peripheral vision. There in the greenish half-light filtering through the trees, any slight movements in the surrounding foliage might signal danger or the nearness of the animal being sought. His keen sight had served him well. Always, he spotted the prey before the sharpest-eyed adolescent, the most experienced Indian huntsman. Partly because of this skill, the tribe had been willing to listen to him, to follow him when he told them they must leave their home site long before the soil was exhausted, move much farther back into the jungle to preserve themselves.

While the tribe was on the move, as they often were, finding meat was essential. If the men returned tired, silent, and empty-handed, the Solveyo women reached into their plaited bamboo baskets for the miserable minimum. They would draw out a few orange-colored palm fruits, a large and poisonous spider or two, a lizard, a bat, a handful of locusts, another of little nuts. The fruits were crushed into a water-filled gourd, the nuts broken open, and the rest scattered in among the ashes of the fire. Altogether, it was not even food for one, but everyone had a morsel. Early Amazonian explorers had disgustedly labeled the Indians "gluttons" because of the way they would stuff themselves on a gloriously roasted pig. But anyone who'd shared the contents of the baskets understood the impulse.

Since he'd been a slight, unathletic boy, an outsider condescended to by the muscular sons of lumberjacks in his northern California high school, his own talent at hunting amazed even him. Then he'd realized why. Not only did he have highly-developed peripheral vision, he was partly color-blind. Certain orange reds were muddy brown to him, and shades of green were lost. In the jungle, most animals, birds, and even butterflies depended on their intricate hues for camouflage from predators. Freed of the charm of color, he saw their shapes instead. The persistence of this genetic mutation in a civilized society testified to its previous value, he mused. Finding explanations seemed a part of his own genes.

Perhaps an ophthalmologist could tell him why he was troubled by these apparitions at the edges. It might be common at the onset of one's middle years, just like the miniscule wavy lines, called floaters, now forever present before his pupils. Panicked when he became aware of the first one, he'd spent the better part of three days bathing his eyes in boiled stream water. He'd been unable to understand why he'd had no tears, no feelings of irritation from that intrusive mote, why he hadn't felt what he could so clearly see. Then he'd discovered floaters were common minor distractions, and everyone learned to look past them. They did not affect his normal clear vision or his still unerring aim.

A crunch, as of gravel, beneath his rubber soles made him pause, stoop down with pleasure. Just here the shore was littered with the shells of tiny bivalves, marking the nearness of the grove where he would turn slightly inland. On his palm he held a perfect specimen, the diminutive body gone, the rosy, mother-of-pearl shell butterflied open. Flipping it over with a plastic-encased finger, he marveled at the outer exquisite deep pink—a hue he was sure he could identify. A vision from Spain surfaced. It was his junior year at Harvard, and he'd taken off a semester, and traveling alone, stopped one night at a fishing village for dinner. A fat señorita, laughing, scattered heaping hand- fuls of small cockles on a grill sizzling with fresh olive oil and garlic. They crackled like popcorn, and she scooped them into a bowl. Prying out each hot morsel quickly with greasy, greedy fingers, he'd piled up a mound of shells, mopped up the juices with coarse bread.

A flash of movement to his left interrupted the re- membrance. He peered at the packed sand at his feet and then, a half yard away, spied the almost transparent three- inch crab, motionless with fear. The little creature, fooled by the man's stillness, had begun its daily, desperate race from the safety of its hole in the loose sand toward the sea for food. Its color melted into that of the flecked sand, but he could even make out the dark pinpricks of its protuber- ant eyes. Relieved, he moved briskly away, careful to drop the seashell where it would not further alarm the crab.

Fortunately, he reminded himself, he had none of the infirmities that he'd heard others complain of as they grew older. No needlepoint arthritic pains in shoulders, wrists, or knees. No digestive problems. After twenty years, he could still run tirelessly. Because of the constant exercise involved in getting food, he knew he had the unclogged veins and the heart of a young man. In the jungle, without clocks and calendars, the days and years had passed seamlessly and he'd never thought about his age. Now he thought the mirrors lied.

As for this growing tendency of his to pick angrily over his history, to grieve over the major defeats, no doubt his contemporaries here who'd led more routine existences did that as well. Like him, many of them probably resurrected those occasional shining moments, artifacts that the sad dust of later experiences couldn't tarnish, and bitterly buried those that seemed covered with the green film of egoism and naïveté. There were those who might see losses as experience. Some might leave the past undisturbed and concentrate on forging the future—their own or their children's. A few might stoke the furious furnace, fashioning revenge. Like him.

Neither the festering passion—nor the analysis—would be possible for the Solveyos who'd been his companions for most of his adult life. The events of yesterday were recalled on a daily basis, of course. The tribesmen, swinging in the hammocks looped in the Hut of Men, would endlessly go over hunting episodes, giggling over their failures, boasting of their triumphs. If a jaguar with coveted skin killed a man instead of being killed, if a handsome child drowned, even if an old man passed away, they took action. No fists were shaken upward at the mismatched twins who, their myths said, created the universe. Instead, they exacted immediate revenge. Nature herself was held responsible. A death was an injury to the entire group. The tribe, on behalf of the bereaved family, organized a collective hunt and went out and killed some sizable creature. Nature must pay her debt to their society. The last time he saw them, the Solveyos were filled with enormous confusion and despair, but they did not know what to do. How could one avenge oneself for the death of the spirit? They had not cast a reproachful glance at him who'd come to save them.

Blaylock's betrayal—of the Solveyos and himself—had made executing him *first* only just. Blaylock had been his friend, and he himself had played fair—sent Blaylock a warning. Yesterday he'd even scrupulously notified Luttrell. Although the message would alarm the retired helicopter pilot, he probably would not leave the island. Not that it mattered. He would find him. When Luttrell had arrived in Vieques unexpectedly, it'd merely simplified his task. Now they were all here on this gentle volcanic upthrust in the Caribbean. Luttrell had only seen him briefly years ago, and the others had never met him. He would kill them all.

Douglas Blaylock had understood the message, had moved, cowered in his isolated house on the main island much of the time after receiving it. Perhaps because of the once-strong bond between them, Doug had known all these years that he was still alive, waiting for retribution. He'd brooded over confronting Doug, envisioning the leap of terror into the fine-fringed eyes, the flaring of the nostrils of the elegant nose. A fearful Doug he'd seen many times. What words, he'd wondered, would Doug have chosen to explain his actions?

From the beginning, even in the buoyant 1960's, hope for his and Blaylock's mission had been anchored grimly. Most of the Indian tribes of Brazil had been wiped out as a result of both government policy and individual effort: The clothing of smallpox victims was collected at hospitals and gleefully distributed in the villages. Because of their remoteness and wariness, the Solveyos had so far avoided the holocaust. The two young graduates were recruited to try to gain their trust in order to make the Solveyos even more suspicious and to teach them a few civilized survival skills. The Indians, for example, had no concept of numbers. Capitalism required that—they were always cheated. Camp near them, the trainers in Puerto Rico had advised, but offer them nothing, make no overtures, simply observe and be observed, perhaps you will succeed. In those heady days, such doubt was rare, but this assignment was outside the Peace Corps' purview. His elders' misgivings had not affected his own keenness.

But neither the rigors of the Outward Bound instruction in Arecibo—which quickly began to seem a version of summer camp—nor the strength of their enthusiasm had prepared the two volunteers for the jungle's corrosive inhospitality. The struggle for daily food sapped them. The threats from without and within, the cruelties of insects and isolation, devitalized them, Doug in particular. After only a few weeks, he'd talked of a quick return, begun concocting explanations for their superiors. Yet Doug's chiseled features, his clear-eyed gaze into the future, had been reproduced on countless posters, in the brochures distributed on selected college campuses, and even on the red-bordered cover of a national newsmagazine. Giving up would therefore exact a price from his friend, and he tried to use his vanity to persuade him to stay. His own commitment burned undimmed, but the jungle was no place for a man alone. More than that, he wanted to be with Doug—just the two of them. Later, he'd understood that Blaylock needed people to impress, satellites to make him shine. A devoted comrade was not enough. To be strong, Doug had needed to appear so to a group.

True, when he'd first become ill, Doug had played conscientious nurse. But as one feverish day melted into another, his inability to help in getting their necessities made Doug increasingly tired and petulant. The portable radio in which they and headquarters had put such trust hadn't survived its baptism in the rapids of the brown river. Their small stock of medicines could not repel whatever alien virus had attacked him. His flesh seemed to be evaporating until he was only a brain shimmering with vibrant words. They were mirages he managed to capture, whenever he had the strength to scribble. But he became so wasted that he could not hold a pencil, and a languid indifference set in. If the cup were put to his lips, he drank, but stretching out a hand, lifting his own head was too exhausting. When Blaylock began insisting that he be taken to the mission six days' travel from their site, he repeatedly refused. Being carried on his friend's back for some distance and then jounced in the rapids while lying in the canoe's floor seemed intolerable.

Then, perhaps because of his delirium, he began to see relief in Doug's countenance and interpreted that as a sign that he was dying. If that happened, Doug could not be expected to remain, could return a hero. He was almost relieved when, leaving him food and water, Doug decided to undertake the treacherous river journey alone to the nearest point a helicopter could land. But he'd never returned, nor sent anyone else.

For some time afterwards, while recuperating in the Solveyo camp, he'd assumed Doug had drowned. He mourned him wrenchingly. Then he discovered what Blaylock had taken from him, and what he'd stolen from the Solveyos. The Indians had not told him, perhaps not sure how it happened; but the day they'd paddled him down the noisy river to that tranquil cove, showed him their appalling loss, he'd known. Together, the two young volunteers had earlier found the Lagoon of the Dead. Moreover, when no one from headquarters ever came, a different interpretation of Doug's failure to return occurred to him.

Pulling the trigger had not caused him any regret. Doug was already dead; it was not his weapon that'd killed him. It was true that his friend's second death was no less painful. But he was satisfied that his aim had been so sure, that he'd accomplished what he'd set out to do with dispatch, without arousing the *Policía*. He had left immediately thereafter for Vieques.

Being found guilty of murder would spoil the symmetry of his actions. He'd envisioned each step, just as he had when stalking even the harmless brown paca, a sweet-fleshed rodent. One left nothing to chance, lest one be surprised by danger and act without due consideration. His education as an anthropologist also influenced his method since he understood a community's structure—the way each regulated behavior provided for basic needs, such as food supply. In a large and complex capitalistic society like the United States, the closest equivalent of the huntsman would probably be the entrepreneur: the risk-taker who created jobs that led to obtaining food. But the function of the police dictated that on occasion they needed some of the skills of the hunter. Some of these men were no doubt quite good at what they did. He had covered his spoor.

The aptness of the image made him glance backward with a grin at his own footprints. For some six feet behind him, the bare outlines of his sneakers were lightly sketched in the arched pattern of his stride. But beyond that, the lapping waves had erased them. Even as he applauded himself for such caution, he found it difficult to see a real necessity for it.

There seemed little cause for concern after the event, either. Only one Criminal Investigation Corps officer was assigned here. Sleepy Vieques was considered semiretirement; a man about to collect his pension was rewarded with this post. While the detective was required to appear at the scene when the cause of death was in question, those occasions were rare. The islanders still excitedly talked of the shooting of a meat market owner by one of his in-laws three years previously. As for auto accidents, one had to be not only drunk but determined in order to find another car to crash into at high speed. The tourists who rented the few available cars were usually staid family men. Couples often preferred the shiny little rental mopeds. The drivers of the *publicos*, vans that served as buses, tended to drive too fast, but they knew the roads.

He'd checked on Luis Carillo, the current CIC investigator. Carillo had apparently long ago succumbed to the soporific atmosphere, anesthetized in the process by rum. Divorced, the policeman rented a beach cottage some distance from the town of Isabel Segunda, but he could usually be found on the deck of his small sailboat, rocking at anchor, or on a back porch of a lady friend, if he could be found at all. His frequent trips to his headquarters in Humacao, on Puerto Rico's south coast, were perhaps spurred by a need for the camaraderie of his fellow agents. Carillo presented no threat.

The uniformed branch of the *Policía* handled Vieques and Culebra, an island to the north with even fewer people, by capably preventing crime. Sergeant Augusto Mulero, referred to as Gusto by all, was the ideal peace officer. He directed the traffic of people's affairs with foresight. Obstreperous drunks were pointed homewards, unruly adolescents detoured back to watchful mothers. Every day he could be seen, lounging at the dockside as the ferries from the main island arrived. His always crisp uniform shirt tucked neatly in the belt below the gentle swell of his stomach, Gusto picked his teeth, one hand politely cupped over his mouth, and ran an experienced eye over the passengers. His primary target was the *pillos*, sneak thieves. Young males without families were from that point on carefully observed until they left Vieques. The small airport didn't require vigilance. Those poor enough to try to steal a little hadn't the fare.

Although Gusto was conscientious, he undoubtedly had his priorities based on his community's prerequisites— saw the importance of protecting those on whom Vieques' flimsy economy depended. All policemen, the walker reasoned, noticing that the risen sun was glittering the sand, must have their rough hierarchy of crimes: those that were never permitted, those that were sometimes overlooked, those too common to worry about. Here theft from the rich would be shoved into the first category because the affluent residents would raise an enormous fuss if iron grillwork became as necessary for their homes as it was in San Juan, and because the tourists might eventually refuse to return. One of Vieques' chief attractions, since it had none of the diversions common in the Caribbean, like gambling or shopping, was that it was a sanctuary. Women could stroll alone in the balmy night, children could stray from their parents, and even car burglar alarms were not necessary.

Furthermore, Gusto would be anxious to avoid disturbances of any kind. The edgy truce between the navy and the islanders must be preserved. Confrontations, indeed almost all meetings, between residents, as well as tourists, and boisterous young marines stationed at Camp Garcia on the eastern end, were kept to a minimum by the free movies, cheap drinks, and other recreational activities offered on the base itself. A few shopkeepers had hand-printed signs to the effect that the servicemen's business was unwanted, but the camp had a glorious PX. Would a sensible policeman, therefore, want to raise a question in the investigation of the accidental death of a retired military man? Especially when a slight difficulty would go unnoticed, unless mentioned?

Pushing the bridge of the sunglasses against his nose, he stopped to turn over the idea once more, trying to ferret out any element of rationalization in his deductive process. The only flaw in his plan to dispose of Luttrell centered around a certain inconsistency, one that would only occur to a man with an eye for detail and some insight into Luttrell's habits. Carillo's years in the Criminal Investigation Corps would give him the first, but there was little likelihood he'd ever met the planned victim, who was a recent arrival. But Gusto would know something about Luttrell simply because his drinking habits had made the man widely disliked as soon as he'd arrived. An unpleasant, surly drunk, Luttrell's company was avoided in both the tourist and the native bars. No, an accident that removed him from the scene would be regarded with equanimity.

If Luttrell's wife Mildred were at present on Vieques, however, a policeman would be certain to cast an oblique eyebrow in her direction. But for the last ten days, Mildred had been visiting her sister on St. Croix. His timing for Luttrell's demise had been precise. Not only would having suspicion directed at her injure his sense of justice, the poor woman needed no further burden. She'd been here alone for some time, perhaps preferring to live away from her alcoholic husband. Although she traded orchid cuttings with fellow gardeners, she had seemed content to live by herself in the wide-bodied mobile home nestled above a steep slope in an unfashionable section near Isabel Segunda. Her husband had brought a jeep, but until then Mildred had shyly accepted lifts or ridden in one of the public vans. A thin, narrow-faced woman, she walked hurriedly through the streets with downcast eyes, a beribboned basket holding a small white poodle always on her arm. He felt a great deal of sympathy for her, although he'd disliked Joan Blaylock on sight.

But even if Luttrell's death was officially stamped a homicide, he himself would never be on a suspect list because he, too, was officially dead. Moreover, his new identity made him invisible, despite the fact that he was well-known in this small society. Some occupations, some functions are disguises. And, although he'd settled in on Vieques, ultimately he was regarded as an exotic bird of passage.

He began to move briskly. As usual in the tropics, the dawn had appeared with little color and less drama; sunsets made the grand gesture. The sun in a cloudless sky was creating rivulets of sweat under his shirt and the plastic gloves were sticking to his skin like cellophane tape. But he now saw the grove whose location he'd marked earlier, and veered away from the shore.

Sheltered by the high branches of the soft-needled pines, there was a *manzanillo*, sometimes called a manchineel, tree. Although a sleek black chango cocked a white encircled eye at him from a pine, he did not think that cagey cousin of the crow would perch on the *manzanillo*. It was said that even rainwater dripping from the shiny, leathery leaves was injurious. Cattle brushing against the tree suffered skin irritation. Although the wood was employed in furniture and cabinetwork, the caustic milky sap oozing out produced severe blisters on the skin, so that the bark must be burned before felling. Should the sap come in contact with a man's eyes, it caused prolonged pain and temporary blindness. The fierce Carib Indians dipped their arrows in the *manzanillo*'s toxic liquid. Commonly found growing in coastal woods along the shore, its fruits were disseminated by ocean currents. The most poisonous tree in tropical America, unless eradicated by man as it was in Florida and in many populated areas, it flourished. In his youthful training, he'd been repeatedly warned about the tree.

The odd thing about the *manzanillo*, which means "little apple," is that its fruits are sweet-scented and very palatable. They are round, yellow-green tinged with red on the outside, and resemble a guava or a largish crab apple. The outside of the fruit is deceptive. Unlike the leaves, its satiny feel is soothing. The white mellow flesh is delicious and quite deadly. If even a small quantity of the fruit is eaten, serious nausea and diarrhea are followed by shock and an appalling muscular weakness. Arrowroot starch must be given liberally and immediately as an antidote.

Luttrell's groceries, in his wife's absence, were delivered from a small local market. Either because the slim Hispanic youth who brought them had been so instructed by Mildred or because he'd experienced Luttrell's bad temper, the food—usually staples and canned goods—was left near the gate on the road by ten o'clock. It was often noon before Luttrell heaved the sack up the hill.

One of the produce bags used by that *colmado* was now pulled from the blue backpack, which he set at some distance from the tree. Squatting down, he took the Clorox bottle from the canvas bag and, opening it, laid the fat blue cap on the ground. He removed a used spice can labeled ground ginger, its bottom rusted, from his shirt pocket and tapped white arrowroot powder from it into the Clorox lid, mixing this with a bit of water from the bottle. He stirred it carefully with his gloved finger. Should he feel any stinging on the unprotected part of his face, he could smear the paste on right away.

Stepping carefully over the squashed, fallen fruit, he smoothed his plastic gloves well over the cuffs of his shirt. He shoved the sunglasses up so that the top of the frames touched his eyebrows. Then he studied each fruit on the lower branches. As he did so, he trilled the melodious slide of the flycatcher. *Whee-a-wet-whee*. Not quite right, he thought. *Whee-a-wit-whee*. Better.

Still whistling, he plucked five ripe, unblemished apples. Detecting a brown spot on one, he tossed it into the underbrush. Carrying the others to the Clorox bottle, he rinsed off the slight dusty film, polishing each on his sleeve until they reached a waxy perfection. As he did so, Miltonic echoes rolled majestically through his mind: ". . . the fruit of that forbidden tree whose mortal taste/Brought death into the world, and all our woe,/With loss of Eden." The memorization of poetry while young, he decided, should be required. Besides the civilizing effect, it returned in one's later years at appropriate moments. One by one, he slid the four delicately into the bag to avoid bruising them. As he closed the plastic top tightly with a paper-coated wire twist, his eyes behind the dark glasses were merry.

2

NAKED, HE LAY SPRAWLED face down across the pink-flowered sheet. An elasticized corner had come untucked, displaying the neat white quilting of the mattress pad beneath, but the sheet itself was stained and strewn with sand. A thin pillow in the same floral pattern loosely covered his head. The body hair sprouting from his thick shoulders was rather dark, considering the fairness of his skin, and it furred his back down to the thumbnail-size dimples in the fat near his shoulder blades, spreading again down his spine to the top of his bulging buttocks. Even darker pubic hair curled up between these. His arms were stretched out limply by his torso, the matted forearms beneath the gray crinkle of his elbows as wide as the flaccid biceps, the palms of his hands out. Although the flesh of the fullback thighs hung loosely, the calves were tight, powerful. The upturned bottoms of his feet were grimy but uncallused.

Dust motes danced in the narrow strips of sunlight angling through the rolled-down bamboo blind, but the only other movement in the darkened, cluttered room was that of a mosquito buzzing over the unprotected back as if judiciously considering the opportunities offered. A brown gecko clung to the pink wall near the top of the white wicker headboard, but not even a flicker of its dainty lizard eyes betrayed its intense interest in the mosquito. The insect's faint drone was drowned out by the soothing swish of the ceiling fan in the adjoining living room. In the nearby kitchen, the refrigerator motor abruptly came on

17

with a clatter, with the loud complaint of metal corroding in the tropics. But the man didn't move.

Suddenly, just as the mosquito had settled comfortably to feed on the back of a knee, the heel of the huge hand squashed it, leaving a slight splotch of blood. The fragile remains were smeared on the pillowcase, the pillow was lifted carefully off the unstirring head. Then the man groaned, pushed the thick graying hair off his sweat-prickled forehead.

If Mildred had the sense God gave fucking fruit flies, Luttrell swore to himself, *she'd have had a ceiling fan put in this goddamned bedroom.*

A portable oscillating fan, the cage protecting the blades already pitted with rust despite the shiny newness of its plastic base, stood on the crowded chest at the foot of the bed, although a pair of gray boxer shorts with a paper-thin crotch draped it. But he was not yet willing to risk opening his eyes. His hair follicles smarted, he could feel his eyelashes growing, the sweat stung his skin, as tender as if it were sunburned, and his tongue felt like a fat foreign lump in his parched mouth. He imagined the tart sweetness of a cold Seven-Up, fizzing over clear ice cubes, and again cursed his wife and her sick sister in St. Croix. While there might be some soda in the sack of groceries broiling at the bottom of the hill, fetching it himself would mean at the very least finding a pair of canvas shorts, thongs, and above all sunglasses, and then stumbling down the gravelly hill and back up with the heavy bag. And he was sure there was no ice.

The rum evaporating from his pores had the pungent odor of nail polish remover. The reek, mingling with his stale perspiration, offended his queasy stomach. His bladder ached. But in order to alleviate his suffering, he would have to expose his eyes, raise his head, feel the familiar vise-clamp of the morning hangover digging into his temples. He stared glumly at the insides of his eyelids, knowing it had to be done—slowly but immediately. *Fucking noisy refrigerator.* He manuevered onto his side, swung his legs to the floor, and levered his body into a sitting position on the edge of the bed. His hairy belly, as tight and distended as a pregnant woman's, almost touched his thighs. Massaging it gently, he fought back the lurch of nausea. Pain spiked into his temples, jabbed behind his sockets. As he reluctantly pulled his eyes open, he turned away from the threads of light allowed by the blinds.

The pounding in his head recalled nightmare moments in the past when the helicopter's rotors thudded noisily above as he'd lifted the craft from the jungle's grasp, and had on occasion heard the worse sound of the blades faltering. Death was, one of his buddies had cracked, the ultimate hangover. He settled bitterly into the swamp of self-pity. *Man's entitled to something now. And she's off tending Helen who has plenty of bucks to hire some nurse, when she damned well should be here, giving me a little help. Who pays the fucking bills? Me. Captain Chet Luttrell, who sweated off his butt in those choppers, the poor sonofabitch that nobody can bring a goddamned aspirin to.*

The barrage in his head, he suddenly realized, was not all in his head. Morning maneuvers were being conducted by the U.S. Navy on the island. Bombs were actually bursting in air, cannons roaring, although at this distance they sounded rather more like a superior fireworks display.

Sweat itched down his chest. The heavy noon air wrapped his body like a woolen blanket. Grimacing, he contemplated the slight comfort of the shower. While the clear water of Vieques originated miles away in Puerto Rico's cool rain forest and was piped under the channel, it was unpleasantly warm by the time it trickled out of his showerhead. *Like the fool woman to buy on top of a hill where the water pressure sucks. A shitty little trailer. Told her white folks don't live in shitty trailers. Said she liked the view, the space around it for her fucking garden, place was easy to keep up. Bullshit. Probably knew I wouldn't like it, get pissed off and leave. Bitch.*

Heaving his body up, he took one step and the sharp plastic of the glass he'd left by the bedside scrunched under his bare foot. A fragment sliced the tender pad. Yowling, he kicked the frame of the bed, sending it shuddering into the night table. The lizard next to it flashed ceilingward, and the small bedside lamp teetered and tipped onto the floor, smashing its delicate oriental shade. Somewhat mollified, he strode into the bathroom.

But a few minutes later he had to admit the shower had helped. Ignoring the now grubby embroidered towels mildewing on the floor, he let his body dry while he lathered up. He narrowed his protuberant blue eyes so the red veins were less conspicuous and studied the effect in the mirror. Not bad, he decided. He still had all his hair, no wattles along the chin. Jutting his tightened jaw forward, he expertly slid the razor from the base of his throat to his chin. Getting rid of the stubble made the day begin, he'd always thought, not that today had much going for it. What was it—Thursday? Memorial Day coming up.

Bastards won't invite me on their fucking boats, to their fucking parties, wouldn't even sit next to me at a fucking bar. Some business partners! All Mildred's fault. Get her in a crowd, she clams up, fidgets at any joke she thinks is 'dirty.' Won't ask people over, says she doesn't know how to entertain 'those' people, how to dress. Who dresses out here? Boring piece of rock. No action at all. Every decent-looking woman trying to hook an unmarried marine. He rinsed his soapy razor in disgust.

And yet last year when Mildred had mentioned buying a place here, he'd thought it a great idea. Their marriage had survived because he was frequently gone on long tours of duty. The desire for comfort would overwhelm him, but after only a few days at home, the massive irritation of living with Mildred returned. So he'd welcomed the idea of getting rid of her. He'd stayed behind in New Jersey to sell the house.

Besides, then he'd had a good thing going with Joycie. Mildred said she'd been thinking about this island for fifteen years, ever since she'd read one of Clay's pieces. Vieques was safe, quiet, and she'd be near her sister Helen on St. Croix in the American Virgins. But she didn't want to live *on* St. Croix because Helen was "social," and might feel like she'd have to invite her along. Said she didn't think it'd be too expensive and they ought to save their money. Said they had to be careful since even though his writing paid well, it wasn't a regular income that you could plan on all your life.

He grinned at himself in the mirror as he checked for any missed spots by his right ear. She still thought his money came from writing. Woman hadn't a clue. It was a pittance, and his military retirement pay wasn't that much either. But writing provided a few deductions, and the accountant took care of the IRS, never cracked a smile when he showed Mildred where to sign all the pages of the tax form. Joycie would have been a lot more curious where the money came from and how much there was. She'd gotten bitchy when she finally figured out that he wasn't going to dump Mildred and marry her. Why should he? Once you married 'em, that was the end of the fun. Got laid once a year on your birthday. And Joycie wasn't about to crack an egg for your breakfast or fry up a steak. Mildred hopped to it, kept the place clean. Shut right up when you gave her the look.

But even Jesus couldn't live with the woman without itching to strangle her. Going at a half trot all day long, her slippers flop-flopping, fool dog at her heels, his toenails going clit, clat, clit on the tile. Out to the garden and back. Fussing over orchids and herbs and damn-all. Buying all kinds of little crap for the house and then dusting it every day. No way you could set a drink on a table without knocking over some frigging plant or the crummy junk made here on the island. And you had to have the sun glaring in all day for the fucking plants.

He'd taken care of all that as soon as she'd left, he thought with satisfaction. Pulled the blinds and dumped all the shit on the tables in the garbage. Every damned day some new piece that she'd ordered from catalogs came in the mail. Hummingbird feeders, needlepoint canvases, packets of seeds, a soap dish shaped like a poodle, a butterfly in a plastic case, a peanut tray, paper doilies with poems on them—unbelievable crap. He'd thrown those in the trash can, along with the note she'd left reminding him to take his vitamins and water the garden. He'd shoved the hose in the corner so he could get to the hammock under the big trees without tripping. Hammock was the only decent thing in the whole setup. Tossing the razor down, he leaned his elbows on the white tile counter and pressed the heels of his hands against his temples. *Mother-fucking headache!*

After breakfast, he could mix up a Bloody Mary, crawl in the hammock. Maybe drag a fan out, plug it into the long cord on the patio. Not a damned thing on the island was air-conditioned and you couldn't have a phone unless you lived right in the middle of the stinking town. Leave it to Mildred to find the hind end of the universe to move to, and then think she was in paradise, going on about how pretty it was, how quiet, and how nice to have this beautiful weather all winter. Splattering lukewarm water on his face, he wiped it with the crook of his arm. He squeezed some minty toothpaste onto the brush and jerked it quickly over his large white canines. Good teeth, he congratulated himself, not a cavity in years. Finishing his side teeth with a flourish, he ran the brush over his coated tongue. Breakfast. He liked a big one. That was the way to separate drinkers from alcoholics. *Alkies don't eat*, he thought smugly, moving toward the tiny kitchen.

Three frying pans were piled on the small, apartment-size electric stove, dead gnats embedded in the layer of congealed fat in the bottoms. Tilted on the fourth burner was a soup-encrusted saucepan. But on the grease-splattered surface was an almost full bottle of vodka. He brightened and began rummaging in yesterday's grocery sack shoved amid the clutter of dirty glasses on the gold Formica counter between the stove and refrigerator, praying for a can of tomato juice. But there was only a loaf of French bread, some desperately limp celery, and a dozen brown-shelled eggs.

He swung open the top door to the freezer. It needed defrosting, and the compartment was narrowed by thick white coils of ice. It contained nothing but six empty ice cube trays. Viciously slamming the inner door, he cursed trailer manufacturers who designed cramped kitchens and benighted islands without ice makers. Yanking open the refrigerator itself, he saw two dried-out limes, several jars of homemade jelly, a bottle of ketchup, a half stick of margarine, and a brown-edged casserole dish, now furred with gray mold, that he'd stuck back in after he'd run out of counter space. The smell of spoiling fruits and vegetables discouraged him from even opening the produce bins. As he hung on the open door, he looked over his shoulder at the counters on the sides of the sink. The entire space was overflowing with egg-streaked plates and glasses holding the dregs of various liquids. Jammed into an ice bucket was the wadded-up plastic bag that had held disposable glasses.

He pressed his aching forehead against the bedewed surface of the freezer compartment. He hated going out for breakfast, especially before he'd had his life-preserving Bloody Mary. It would mean putting on a shirt as well as a pair of long pants because the seats of the jeep would fry his thighs, driving down the winding hill in the sun's brutal glare, parking, and finally getting eggs that were either runny or hard. Then he lifted his head, wondering if that Chink nearby could do eggs over easy.

A Chinese restaurant, against all the laws of commercial sense, was located on the next hill, far from the business district. It might not be open for lunch, he considered, but the guy'd be there, chopping up stuff. And he'd be bound to have eggs, maybe a slice of ham, definitely a bar with tomato juice. Mildred was always going on about the place. Guy was a friend of hers— probably keeping the fool dog for her. Such a nice man, she'd repeated, and doing so well with his new restaurant, even though he found it hard to find good help here. She'd gotten take-out food from there a time or two, remarking that she'd like to eat there someday because it would be nice with the open-air tables all laid out under bamboo roofs. She was always nattering about how good Chinese food was for you—all those crisp vegetables. And the owner was so nice about taking her into town in the mornings when he went for his produce. *Nice.* He could hear Mildred's flat Midwestern voice, using the word as the ultimate compliment.

When he'd first met her, a clerk in one of the marine PX's, he recalled with a sour grimace, he'd been pleased that she was a "nice" girl. He'd watched his language around her, chuckled when she'd slapped his straying hands. The stories about the wars, his life, rounded the gray eyes in her thin face. A slight, delicate woman, sure that much worse things than bears lurked behind every bush, she'd aroused his protective instincts. *But, Christ, she was chicken shit about everything, even driving. Said it made her nervous—maybe later on when she got used to the island. So, she goes into town in the Chink's truck. No wonder nobody asks us any place.*

His eyes focused on the egg carton. If he only had the ice and the tomato juice, he could do his own eggs. The right way. Ice. He pulled open the freezer door and eyed the opaque formation on the coils of the freezer. Anybody who'd lived through Vietnam and the jungle could improvise, he thought with a smirk, further pleased by imagining Mildred's horrified protest about how "germy" the ice was. He'd chip some of that off. And there should be some juice in the groceries at the bottom of the hill. Leaving both doors of the refrigerator open, he hurried into the living room. A pair of canvas shorts were slung on the glass coffee table, and he pulled them on, looking around for sunglasses. He swept the piled-up mail on top of a carved teak desk onto the floor, then began jerking out the drawers. In a bottom one was a pair of his old marine-issue aviator shades. He pushed them on his nose, stepped into a pair of shower clogs by the door. Shoving against the screendoor, he bravely stepped into the midday sun.

Ten minutes later, he dumped the sack on the desk, then staggered back a bit, leaning against the laminated paneling of the living room wall, catching his breath. The steepness of the hill made him rethink the instructions he'd given the loudly whistling delivery boy regarding leaving the groceries by the fence below. As he gasped for breath, Mildred's warnings about heart attacks at his age, his drinking and eating habits, rose troublingly. But fifty wasn't old, he reassured himself, and even if he was panting a bit, he could still swim a good mile. The dryness of his mouth reminded him that he'd certainly felt some small juice cans in the bottom of the brown bag. He unsnapped the shorts, wiggled out of them, and kicked them and his flip-flops under the coffee table. Tearing down the side of the bag, letting the contents spill out on the desk, he grabbed a V-8 can and headed for the kitchen.

In an open cupboard he spotted a washed mayonnaise jar, scooped up a sharp knife from the counter, and began gouging fat, white chunks of ice from the sides of the freezer compartment. Cramming these into the jar, he filled it half full of vodka, emptied the juice on top, and gave it all a stir with the knife. Taking a long swallow, he smacked his lips, then decided it needed a squirt of Tabasco sauce. He remembered seeing a thin, red-capped bottle roll out of the torn bag. Mildred was good about ordering the necessaries, even if she'd also told them to bring the fruits and vegetables he never bothered with. He went back to take a look.

Tucking a tall disposable bottle of club soda in the crook of an arm, he lifted a blue cardboard container of salt and a clear plastic bag of small fruit. Under that lay the brown sauce bottle. He carried all four items to the kitchen. He turned the small cap of the Tabasco sauce between his strong side teeth and spit it out, adding a dollop of the liquid to the jar's contents. Looking around vaguely for a place to put down the groceries he was holding and finding none, he finally shoved soda, salt, and plastic bag into the open refrigerator. The plump yellow fruits slid out of the bag onto the rack-like shelf. *Had to be starving to eat tropical fruit. Mango was like a watery peach and papaya tasted like squash. All of it was mushy.* He thought of the satisfying crunch of the autumn apples in his youth. Then he shut the door and, after taking a long swallow from the jar, turned to the business of cooking his eggs.

A late afternoon breeze swung the hammock, cut through the electric fan's smooth hum, and disturbed a pleasant dream in which a soft saffron hand was stroking his groin. Luttrell sighed and settled more comfortably on his side, but the image wafted away. In an effort to lure it back, he flopped over and tried to recall some of the stunning Oriental bar girls he'd known in Vietnam. Although her features eluded him, one in particular came to mind because as one of his buddies had said, "She could suck the chrome off a trailer hitch." His lips twisted into a smile— he could use that expression. An editor had rejected his most recent work on the grounds that his writing was "trite, unimaginative." *A guy's name, too, on the slip. More likely some bitch using a guy's name. What'd the idiots want? Porno's porno. Point was to get turned on.*

He'd had some things published, enough to deduct

the Memorywriter. Even if writing didn't pay, sometimes when he'd had a few and was bored, he enjoyed clicking on the machine and letting it all out. Sometimes he'd get on a roll and then stuff the printout in an envelope and send it off. Usually it'd come back with a pink slip. Mildred wouldn't even glance over it. She called it "filth" and said she couldn't imagine why anyone would read it. If he really wanted to make her flinch, he'd remind her they bought food with money from that. But then everything made Mildred flinch. On the other hand, it'd spoil the fun to tell her that the major part of their income was based on stock in an aluminum mining company. Besides, it might give her ideas, get her thinking about living alone—permanently. He liked having a home base. Some place to come back to.

Pillowing his hands beneath his head, he swayed the hammock with his hips, reflecting that the only good thing about a hangover was that it caused an almost constant hard-on. His writing did that, too. Vivid images from his past sprang up behind his closed eyes—busty South American girls beckoning from shaded doorways, and the Oriental girls, always eager to please. They knew all the tricks. As he wrote, he remembered it all. And still the magazine editors were always writing snotty notes to the effect that he needed to use more description. *Christ, no way to tell somebody how something feels. Only so many words, anyway. A cock's a cock.*

Not, he thought, as he gazed with real satisfaction at the bulge beneath his own belly, that some guys even seemed to have one. Take Kimble for example. Probably the only thing that wasn't stiff about that guy was his cock. Even when he'd first met him and Kimble was only in his forties, even then the guy walked like he had a poker stuck up his backside instead of his front. Horsy New England face and his wife looking like she'd come out of the same stable. And it always was costing you somehow if he smiled. But for all Kimble's business know-how there wouldn't have been *any* company without good old Chet Luttrell, yours truly. But Kimble knew that. *Probably why he avoids me, gives me his no-mouth look. Guy needs some woman to sit on his face.* The idea of Kimble's wife Virginia, her

gray hair carefully sprayed in place, doing that made
Luttrell's body and the hammock shake with laughter.

But Grover Clay, now, he was different, different
altogether, he considered. Funny that Grover and Kimble
were friends as well as partners. Clay had that high fat ass
you saw on kids that sucked up to their grade school
teachers. Fleshy face. Wore big turquoise rings, waved his
pudgy white hands, just like a woman's, when he talked.
Lately all he could talk about was a museum on Vieques,
but Grover liked a good joke as well as the next guy, had
the kind of laugh that oozed out of him. Clap you on the
back and sit down if it was just the two of you. But if he
was with Kimble, he'd just nod, stretch his lips at you.
Hadn't seen a lot of Grover over the years—never married,
always traveling off somewhere. Said there was decent
money writing up his articles on Sri Lanka, Morocco, or
whatever. Not that he needed the money, either.

Blaylock had been the worst, though. *A pencil-prick if
there ever was one.* Going on and on about his nightmares
over what they'd done. Whining that he regretted more
than anything taking the stuff. *And why the hell not? Not any
fucking use to a bunch of Indians!* Quoted poetry—how could
you trust a guy that spouted poetry? But old Doug had his
hand right out for his share of the money at the end.

Luttrell brushed an officious fly from his nose in
exasperation. He remembered screaming at Blaylock over
the sound of the rotors to get him to climb down the rope
ladder. Later on, the guys in Nam had done it all the
time—had more guts. After Blaylock had come back up,
he'd started to cry, sniveled for hours on the way to the
Amazonian port of Belem. But there'd been no sign of the
skinny, wimpy kid he'd taken out with Blaylock the first
time. No camp. Nothing. Indians took everything, probably pitched his body in the river. Had to be dead. So why
not take the goodies, and just tell everybody we'd buried
the kid ourselves. No point at all in sending people back
out there. Guy was dead, dead, dead.

So was Blaylock now, for that matter. Had an accident
a few months back, Grover said. Drove his motorcycle off
a mountain in PR. About that time, Grover'd started to
tell him some junk about getting a letter from Blaylock, said

the man was scared shitless his friend had lived and come back. But then Kimble'd walked over and Grover'd gotten right up. Blaylock probably started to believe the stuff he was always spouting about those Indians. Probably rode motorcycles because it was the only hot piece he could get on top of.

Yawning, Luttrell threw a heavy leg out of the hammock. It occurred to him that in this piece he was writing he'd mentioned his business partner. He sniggered. Maybe he'd just get himself a rum, turn on the machine, write about the girl who'd been in his mind earlier. Then he could go and eat. Maybe at the Beach and Tennis Club, get some sautéed Caribbean lobster and cornmeal cakes. He was already hungry. Stretching, he stood up and went into the house. He ambled over to the word processor in his den, and clicked it on. As he slid in a floppy disk, he chortled again, recalling his description of Blaylock. *Now for the rum.*

Hacking off more ice and stuffing it into the jar, the vague remembrance of the Oriental girl sharpened in his mind. *Ought to go back there. Not to Nam, but maybe Hong Kong. Grover'd be able to tell him quite a bit about what was doing there, where the action was.* He poured the dark rum over the ice and took the club soda out of the refrigerator, leaving the door open. *Sure. Tell Mildred I had some investments there to check on—tell her I'd gotten a wire to come quickly.*

Adding some soda to the top of the jar, he took a quick sip as it fizzed up his nose. Turning over the pleasant possibilities of Hong Kong, he opened cupboard doors in search of a snack. Mildred had outlawed his favorite jars of cashews as too fattening, and he aimlessly moved the cans of soup around, hoping at least to spy the dry-roasted peanuts she occasionally allowed. Nothing.

Taking another satisfying swig of rum, he peered into the refrigerator again, stared at the salt and the fruit. His grandmother had made crab apple jelly and sometimes, after picking them for her, he'd sit on the porch and sprinkle salt on them, take a bite or two. Hadn't been bad. Idly, he picked up a fleshier one, hefted it, thinking that if Mildred were here, he'd die before he'd let her see him eat it. She'd give him that half-assed hopeful look. The color was that of a Golden Delicious apple. Running a thumb over the cool grape-peel softness of the outside, across the bulging vertical cleft on the skin, he thought of Hong Kong. He took a tenative nibble, then, surprised, pleased at the taste of the fruit, sank his teeth into it.

3

HERMAN VILLAREAL, Chief of the Homicide Division, was seated on the second floor of the marble-based, antenna-laden building in San Juan that housed the Puerto Rican *Policía*, staring benignly at the muddled mass of paperwork on his desk. That functional piece of furniture, whose glass top was personally Windexed once each day by Villareal himself, had never been in that state, in any of the detectives' experience. No one, not even Montez, had expected the chief to return yet. Although the hospital had released him last week, it was expected that he would still be convalescing. A stab wound so near the heart, even if the knife had been deflected by the sternum, was serious. Fondo, the agency that oversaw the health of the public labor force, would have been generous in its assessment of the time needed to recuperate from such a work-related injury. Moreover, it was the Friday before the Memorial Day holiday.

So, although everyone was pleased that he was recovering, all the agents had sanguinely hoped Villareal would be recovering at home for at least another week. Everyone, including Montez, who was nominally in charge, had been sure they'd have a few more days' grace to straighten things up—to write reports, for example, that would already have been finished if Villareal had been on the job. And Oscar Montez, a man of massive proportions and placid disposition, had a tendency to believe that some paperwork improved if allowed to age undisturbed. Thus mellowed, memos from administrators on the upper floors often slipped gently through his thick fingers into the wastebasket. Villareal, whose perceptive, hooded eyes saw territory-threatening nuances in such communiqués, was punctilious in this regard and, on his cool days, was inflammable. The men of both Homicide One and Homicide Two anticipated unmuffled explosions whenever he came back, but they'd planned to be on the streets fighting crime early that day.

And, astonishingly, without comment, he had sent them out to do just that. Almost all of them had immediately gathered in the basement cafeteria and over coffee, speculated on the dosage of the prescribed tranquilizer.

Villareal had not taken any medication, despite the fact that his healing chest itched annoyingly and sent quivers of pain toward both arms if he moved quickly. Moreover, since the hospital stay had finally weaned him from nicotine, he no longer had that soothing drug to ward off daily irritability. But in April he'd met Thea deGroote, a tenderhearted spinster in budding middle age, ten years younger than he. His inner man wore a new suit of clothes, was turning shyly, awkwardly before the mirror of her admiration, surprised at how good he looked.

Too, time off from his job, as it sometimes does, had made returning to work desirable. Bored at home, confined to bed both by pain and by the necessity to be near the fan, he'd found that even personnel problems that could never be solved, only diluted, seemed less tiresome. And even the morguelike chill of the Homicide Department, which he was sure was responsible for his continual sniffles, was welcome in May's sudden, outrageous heat. Certainly, the thermostat's setting did elicit quicker statements from those prisoners, stripped to their underwear, who occupied the concrete holding cells around the corner.

At ten o'clock in the morning, the large outer room was hushed. The familiar smell of old linoleum soaked in that pungent yellow cleaner surrounded him. The morning stretched out reassuringly. Feeling safe from interruptions, he'd left his door open. From his office, he could see across the empty reception area, which consisted of a Formica-topped coffee table and a square of welded-together molded chairs in an annoying color he thought of as pond-scum

green, to another small office where a Homicide Two agent
was writing steadily. One of the frosted-glass cubicles that
lined both walls, used by agents coming in from the field
to write reports, was occupied, since he could hear brisk
two-fingered typing. But if the phone remained still, the
task of restoring order to his desk seemed satisfyingly
possible. Any second now he intended to wave away the
peace and tackle it.

A sleek paper airplane shot across the room over the
green plastic chairs. Streamlined, it went arrow-straight to
the opposite compartment. A startled Villareal leaned over
his cluttered desk and saw Balthazar Marten standing in
the doorway of one of the cubicles, preparing to launch
another, with the closed eye and outstretched arm of a
concentrating dart player. Since it was that particular
detective, Villareal leaned back and ran one hand over his
neat eyebrow mustache and mouth, as if physically
suppressing hasty sarcasms. Not only was Marten a former lieutenant on the New York police force, a rank that
the chief suspected was superior to his own Agent Four
status, but he was pleased to have this competent man as
the Criminal Investigation Corps' newest investigator.

While bedridden, Villareal had pondered Marten's
decision to stay in Puerto Rico and join the Homicide
Department. To give up his rank, his pension—it was an
extraordinary thing for Marten to do. And Villareal knew
that Marten was a cautious man. The difference in pay was
enormous, and it was not cheap to live in San Juan. That
Marten must have some money of his own was apparent.
Although his assignment was finished and the City of
New York was no longer paying, he was still staying at the
Condado Plaza Hotel in the Tourist Zone. Very nice, very
expensive, the chief reflected now. No doubt they were
giving him a rate, of course, but an apartment, easy to find
now that the tourist season was over, would be much more
economical.

He knew little about Marten's personal life. The New
Yorker had only arrived in January and part of his time
had been spent on a Drug Enforcement Administration
assignment. A man of his experience, in his late thirties,
surely could have commanded quite a good salary in

Florida or California, if he simply wanted out of a cold climate. His idiomatic Spanish would no doubt have been an asset in those states as well. He did have the injured knee, not yet healed, but a waiver was no doubt obtainable there as well as here. Yet he was in San Juan and had settled in. An agreeable, if reserved, man, he got along well with the other agents, except for Angel Negrón. But then, Villareal reflected, no one got along well with Negrón.

The reminder of that ongoing problem jiggled Villareal's tranquility and, opening his top right-hand drawer, he shook two yellow Chiclets into his hand. He began chewing the gum slowly and deliberately, wondering where Marten's partner was. Perhaps Marten was just waiting for Cardenas now, instead of looking like a man, for all the airplane business, who had something on his mind. Something that would require consultation and might interfere with the necessary desk-ordering. Still, he soothed himself, when Cardenas showed up the two of them might just go about their business in their usual efficient manner.

By chance, Marten had been paired with young Sixto Cardenas from the first, a combination that had proved very successful. One day in April, as they sat in front of his desk, it had occurred to Villareal that the two men rather looked alike. Although Marten was taller and had the blue eyes and bonier features that marked him as an Anglo—as well as an enviable assurance—he also had the thick dark hair, olive skin, and lean intensity of his partner. Marten was no doubt attractive to women, Villareal considered, with the comfortable generosity of a man in a happy relationship, and then he paused. He had heard that the widowed Marten himself now had a *novia*, a good-looking woman professor at the University of Puerto Rico. Yes.

A third airplane, as carefully aimed, sped by. Seeing the chief's bemused glance, Balthazar turned back into the cubicle and, carrying a file, came into Villareal's office. He lowered himself into a metal chair, started to add the folder to the desk's confusion and then thought better of it for fear it might be returned smartly before an explanation could be given. Flipping the manila edge with a tentative fingernail, he asked, "Do you remember the Blaylock case?"

For a protective second, Villareal's memory refused to jog. "Blaylock?"

"A writer—a poet—lived in the mountains near Barranquitas? He was killed in March in a motorcycle accident."

"Sí." The chief drew out the vowel. "But it *was* an accident. So the Ponce investigators said. As I recall, it was only the widow's insistence—based on no evidence—and, of course, her close friendship with the Education Secretary that involved us at all. The Education Secretary is a most . . . determined woman. But Negrón went up to talk to this Señora Blaylock. All she had to say was that her husband had received a threatening letter—which incidentally she herself had never seen—and that he then became very frightened." Villareal relaxed a little, seeing no harm in this discussion, despite a certain grimness around Balthazar's mouth. "If true, that the man was disturbed, an accident is more likely."

Swiveling in his chair as if that ended the discussion, the chief neatly deposited his gum on a crumpled envelope in the wastebasket. Since he no longer smoked, plastic liners were unnecessary. He added, "Negrón concluded that the widow was . . ." Here Villareal edited carefully, remembering Negrón's terse obscenities regarding gringo arrogance, ". . . unsettled by grief, and that there was in fact a nail in the tire."

"She didn't give up. While you were in the hospital, Montez finally sent me." Balthazar recalled Joan Blaylock's anger, thinking then that her reaction to her husband's death was like a robbery victim's. A slim, elegant woman in her forties with thin penciled eyebrows and a bitter mouth, she'd complained about her loss as if he personally could remedy it. Yet it did not seem the grief-induced sense of abandonment that the recently bereaved sometimes suffered, even if the loved one's death was accidental. Very little grief, at all. Beneath her fulsome praise for her husband's poetic gifts, there was an unmistakable current of resentment against the dead man. Intelligent and articulate, she'd firmly insisted that her husband had been killed, while admitting she had no idea of how it could have been done. Nor could she even suggest a motive. The short recital of her husband's career—a few years as a Peace Corps administrator, then a highly praised poet, lecturing at the university—made the idea of homicide even more implausible, which she seemed to understand. Reading Negrón's laconic report, Balthazar could sense that detective's sharp distaste for the woman. Mrs. Blaylock had a habit of interrupting and contradicting the most noncommittal remark. But she'd aroused his own curiosity. He'd kept the interview brief, however, because he'd assumed this was a police public relations chore, rather than a serious inquiry.

Regretting that judgment now, he continued, "The circumstances of Blaylock's death were straightforward. A blowout at high speed on a curve. Loss of control. Bias ply tire with worn thread. Looking at it, anyone would assume the accident was caused by a nail, with the tip ripped off on entry. But the widow now has something to confirm her suspicions. I brought the rear motorcycle tire into the lab. They say it's a piece of tempered steel, piano wire. That rules out nails. What's more, it's sharpened—honed to a point. Probably a dart."

Villareal's lower lip first nibbled his mustache, then met his upper lip with a tentative smack. "So a dart lying in the road, rather than a nail?"

Balthazar continued remorselessly. "While Blaylock was thrown off and tumbled quite a distance down the rock face at a curve—broke his neck—the vehicle didn't go far down. A big Kawasaki. At the widow's insistence, it was taken to the Barranquitas Headquarters, kept there. Even if she had wanted to tamper with the tire, and I can't see why she would, she had no chance. And that piece of steel is firmly imbedded in the tire's opposite rim. It went right through—driven in with great force, they say upstairs."

"The dart was thrown?" Villareal's heavy-lidded eyes widened skeptically.

"Not even," Balthazar replied with a rueful grin, "if the guy was the British pub Olympic entry. I thought about it, but not likely. Couldn't have been shoved in manually, either, because of his location at the time of the accident. Mrs. Blaylock said he was so fearful he'd been avoiding everyone. He'd only leave the house late at night and then, she thought, only to roar around the mountain roads as if whatever had spooked him was right behind. But even if he had stopped to talk with someone he trusted on a deserted mountain road late at night and that someone shoved the dart in while chatting, Blaylock would have noticed the problem in time. The tire'd go flat before he got to speed on the upgrade where he went over. Skid marks show he was going seventy-five. So we checked out air rifles. The fragment in the tire matches the forty-caliber Mega MX Seven dart. Too big for the twenty-two-caliber. The sporting goods stores say that this dart travels at seven hundred twenty feet per second and it'll go through a half-inch piece of plywood like cheese. Probably what it was. Gun has a range of fifty yards plus."

Villareal picked up an unopened letter and tapped it aggrievedly on the edge of the desk. "So you are saying that someone hid himself on the side of the road and shot—"

"Not quite. The dart went right through the tread in the back—which was pretty worn—not the sidewall. He must have stepped out as soon as the motorcycle went by and aimed at the rear reflector. As I say, it was late. Quite a marksman."

"*Sí*. Still, this occurred near Barranquitas and that puts it in the district of Ponce," Villareal said, referring to Puerto Rico's second largest city, located on the south coast. He was already formulating a semitactful phone call to their CIC, mentioning that one of his investigators picked up something *they* missed, thinking about the arrangements for sending them the motorcycle tire and the problem.

"Ye-es," Balthazar agreed hesitantly. "But the Blaylocks only recently bought that house—they lived for quite a few years in San Juan. The wife was not at all happy about moving away from her friends, said her husband insisted. Given the remoteness of the area, the house he chose, I wonder if he hadn't been concerned about his safety for some time. Mrs. Blaylock doesn't know *when* he received the letter, only that he'd recently told her about it. That would mean checking out his circle here. We'd at least have to cooperate with Ponce."

Villareal grumpily revised his version of the phone call. After all, Ponce, too, had heard from the Education Secretary, and if he wasn't careful, they would smoothly suggest to her that the entire affair be transferred to San Juan, and that woman would probably talk to her good friend, the Governor, who'd undoubtedly grant such a small request. And she would call here for updates. A difficult case, best left in Ponce's primary jurisdiction. He only caught the end of Balthazar's next sentence.

". . . don't know where she is. They're sending the uniformed branch out to check with the neighbors. Mrs. Blaylock might just have gone to visit relatives over the Memorial Day weekend. But I thought I'd better give this file with the current information to you, since technically it'd be Negrón at this end. He interviewed her first." Marten put the file carefully and finally on top of the clutter.

Villareal sneezed, then opened the second right-hand drawer and took out a tissue. After blowing his nose, he asked, "Why did you bring that tire back to be tested?"

With a half shrug, Balthazar replied, "A very determined woman, but I couldn't figure out what she wanted. Telling her that's what I was going to do got me out the door." And he'd been thinking—which he did not add— that if he'd hurried back to San Juan, he could try to interest Maira in a late dinner, at least pick up fresh shrimp, lobster salad, a Spanish white wine, and take it to her.

Villareal nodded, calling to mind that Marten had been a detective in Manhattan, where he was used to dealing with those who demanded that attention be paid, people who not only had complaints, but connections. Negrón's prickly ego unfortunately did not allow for such distinctions. He lowered the used tissue into the wastepaper basket. "What have you and Cardenas got now?"

"Missing girl. May have left for New York, though. And the man that was shot while he was barbecuing in his backyard. But that looks now as if it'll go to Homicide Two. Likely suspects. Neighbors gave a good description of a couple of kids from the housing project nearly. They were seen running away, and the victim had chased them from the neighborhood in the past."

"Señora Blaylock would have to be found and reinterviewed?"

"Looking at our reports, I'd say that neither Negrón nor I asked enough questions. But we have some names of their old friends here in San Juan. Ponce uniforms are checking on her whereabouts."

"Where *is* Cardenas?"

"Sixto's outside checking with one of the mechanics. Car's stalling."

"But that Ford is quite new!" When the *Policía* had switched from the Chevrolet Novas to the Fords, Villareal had assigned one of the first LTDs to Cardenas and Marten, telling himself that he had done so because Sixto was a careful driver.

"Carburetor may just need adjusting." Balthazar stretched out an unconcerned palm.

The phone jangled. Peevishly, the chief picked it up, and before speaking into the receiver, thrust the file back at the New Yorker. "You take this."

Tossing the file on the empty gray metal desk in the functional cubicle, Balthazar sank into the swivel chair. He pushed his hands against the metal edge of the desk as if pressing back the unwelcome thought that he had another long weekend to fill. Maira would even be on a separate island, staying with friends on Vieques, a duty visit, she'd insisted. He could do something with this odd, troubling case, use up the time. Abstractedly, he spun the thin manila folder with his index finger. Yesterday afternoon when he'd picked up the lab report that ruled out a simple puncture, he'd been surprisingly unsurprised.

Yet going to Barranquitas last Saturday he'd been convinced that Blaylock's death was an unfortunate accident. There'd been a moment, after he'd seen the dead man's study, when he and Joan Blaylock had been sitting in a living room all open arches over the canyon that was half sunlit, half cloud-screened, her hard, dark gaze intent on him, when he'd almost believed her. But if he'd examined that impression thoroughly then, he'd have attributed it to the force of the widow's conviction or even to the rapid change he'd experienced from San Juan's pulsing heat to the cool, pastoral mountains.

Now he wondered if an ignored detail hadn't also niggled at his consciousness, and he mentally reviewed that day's activities. He'd planned to make the trip a semiholiday, to lure Maira with him, order a sumptuous lunch basket from the hotel restaurant. She'd said she'd like to visit the Muñoz Rivera Library Museum in town, so he'd intended to drop her off, make a brief stop at the Barranquitas police, a perfunctory visit to the widow, and then picnic with Maira. But on Friday she'd gestured toward her own weekend plans—a teetering pile of semester's end student papers. With disappointment like a metallic taste on his tongue, he'd collected a Thermos of coffee and a sweet roll from the restaurant the next morning and left at seven-thirty to avoid the summer heat that came so early to the city, and munching on the *quesito*, a delicious version of cheese Danish, had driven through the quiet suburbs.

As the squat shopping malls and the Americanized Spanish tract houses faded from his rearview mirror, as the four-lane highway rose upward, the curtained sky had opened to bright sun and his spirits had lifted. The larger houses here, still white with pastel trim, were scattered on haystack hills, their windows' door-high curves letting the outside in, their fences draped with bougainvillea blossoms in a rainbow of pink from salmon to fuchsia. Even though he knew it was too far for a commute, he'd begun imagining which house he'd choose for Maira and him. These maneuverings of hers, the ways in which she ensured they were never quite alone, unless late in her own house with her small nephew asleep down the hall, would end. Despite the desire that made his own pulse throb in his ears, he'd not pressed her. A black New York policewoman had once told him, "Smart sisters who live alone learn to keep seven deadbolts on the door. Last one don't even open from the *inside*. Key to that's down the hall with your momma."

He didn't know how Maira had imagined her future

before they'd met—they'd never discussed any future at all. But she had her career, her ordered household. He'd made his decision, and she would have to make hers, which was harder since her pilot husband had never been declared dead in Vietnam. But the waiting was harder for him, he'd reflected, knowing he would do it if it took months and at the same time keeping an eye out for the perfect spot because university classes did end in a few weeks.

The road narrowed; the landscape became more rural. Black-and-white Jerseys stood belly-deep in lush grass. The heat dropped away like a discarded woolen sweater, and the freshness of the air was exhilarating. Trumpet trees, whose umbrella leaves were two feet across and silvery underneath, starred the breezy hillsides. Clumps of small unripened bananas, tilted upward like thick green fingers reaching skyward, grew along the roadside. The bushes with upside-down lilies, pale orange-honey-colored, were so spectacular that he wanted to uproot them, take armloads back to Maira. As he drove, since he'd already decided the task ahead required only patience and a little tact, his mind was as centered on her as if she were present, next to him in the passenger seat.

Together in the car, she was always oblivious to the surrounding traffic or the route to their destination, absorbed in their conversation, gesturing animatedly. If she asked a question, she'd lean forward to see his face even though his eyes had to be on the road. Quotations zigzagged through her sentences. "But," she'd added once, "My memory—unlike yours—is fickle. Whole Shakespearean sonnets fall out of my head, while truly awful lines of poetry are Elmer-glued. For example, when I'm the oldest inhabitant in the nursing home, I shall still be able to quaver out this stanza by a deservedly anonymous writer: 'O never, never she'll forget/The happy, happy day/When in the church, before God's priest,/She gave herself away.'"

Her soft sunwashed hair was always pinned up haphazardly, tendriling down, requiring much adjustment of combs, because not only her face but her whole body moved as she talked, as she listened. Her skin was so white it reflected light, the kind that bruised impossibly easily.

When he'd comment on a purplish-blue mark on an arm or leg, she'd grin. "A passing piece of furniture knicked me." Her eyes were sea-colored, changeable. . . .

Tapping the file he held in his hand, he reminded himself wryly that he was supposed to be recalling the few *relevant* thoughts he'd had on Saturday. Barranquitas, he'd reflected as he had drawn near, with its outlying villas clinging to the steep San Cristobal Canyon, seemed to have been miraculously transplanted from the rocky sides of the Pyrenees to these green-covered Puerto Rican slopes. The indecisive sky, one moment filled with huge lakes of blue, the next hiding these beneath whispery mists, had heightened the mirage impression. When the sun would briefly disappear, the air felt like unfallen rain on one's face. The town, whose neat houses pressed up to the narrow streets, the small flowered squares in the residential areas, looked like a European village.

At the police station, the laconic CIC agent, whose drawl transformed his common Puerto Rican name—Cintron—into the Spanish word for "seat belt," showed him the motorcycle Blaylock had been riding when he died. Although dented, the frame twisted, it looked repairable. Running his hand over one crushed chrome fender, Balthazar commented on the size.

"Kawasaki KZ Eleven Hundred. They call them superbikes." Cintron paused. "Also call them crotch rockets."

The flat rear tire had been removed, a section sliced open, showing the sharp steel jutting from the rim.

When asked if he had any ideas at all about the widow's adamant assertion of homicide, the Barranquitas man, his eyes heavy with patience, had given the full Hispanic shrug, with his shoulders raised to his ears and both palms expressively out.

Leaving the station, Balthazar asked about places to lunch. First, Cintron mentioned that several roadside stands would now be roasting pigs. He became suddenly eloquent, describing the seasoning, the succulence of the white juicy meat done best some distance away near the Toro Negro forest. Sketching a map in Balthazar's notebook, he pointed out that visiting this particular open-air restaurant would save time because, in addition to taking in the cloud forest and its waterfalls, Balthazar could then drive south and pick up the fast toll road back to San Juan. Before waving him off with a friendly hand, the agent had provided directions to the Blaylocks.

Without these, Balthazar soon realized, he'd never have found the house. It stood isolated on a shelf plateau, with no visible roads leading to it. Although flat-roofed, it called to mind a remote castle: its white walls insubstantial because of looped arches trimmed in pink all along the sides, low-hanging mists surrounding its base like a moat. Arriving at the front door required going down into the canyon and then up to the mesa on an overgrown, one-lane byway. While following it, he'd had to adjust his thinking. He'd speculated that the woman might feel herself also endangered, that her persistence was really an indirect call for help. Like most people, she wouldn't understand how little the police could do to protect them, even from a known threat. But she surely would have moved from this house if she were frightened.

The attractive woman who'd opened that door resembled a noted film star, sparse eyebrows over heavily-lashed slightly bulging eyes, broad cheekbones, a wide mouth. The actress's name lingered just out of recall. Her evenly tinted chestnut hair was a shade too dark for her clear skin. With her brisk woman-executive manner, she was, he thought, wholly miscast as the wife of the poet living in this secluded retreat. The decor, however, fit her rather than the house. The spacious living room contained the spare, expensive glass-and-steel furniture of a modernistic Manhattan penthouse. He accepted the offer of coffee, and as he lowered himself into a soft-leather black chair with a stiff back and chrome base, mused that the poor always seemed to have more possessions than the rich, probably because the rich had bigger closets. There were none of the tropical plants that might soften the crisp high-tech lines of the lamps and angular chairs, the cold solidity of the gray marble coffee table. But the spectacular view and its greenery did seem to fill the room. Perhaps she liked that cool effect.

Returning with a polished candlewood tray holding a functional dark blue pot, a squat creamer and matching mugs, she mixed the hot milk and coffee in his cup without asking for his preference. As she seated herself across from him, lifting an almost non-existent eyebrow, she asked, "You're a New Yorker?"

Nodding, he tried to decide if that was a social opener to which one responded with a polite inquiry as to her home state or a question that would dictate the phrasing of her next statement.

Apparently it was the latter because she'd continued bluntly, "I do not feel as if my life is in any danger. And I do not need soothing. I simply cannot accept such a coincidence. My husband believed he would be killed; then he died. I have no evidence, but I want this investigated."

As if this, too, were an explanation for her insistence, Mrs. Blaylock had referred several times to her husband's international renown. The Nobel Prize, she implied, would one day have been his, had he lived to produce a larger body of work. But she turned aside even routine inquiries with asperity, as if the detective were a plumber asking *her* how to fix the drains. She maintained that her husband was faithful to her, shrugging off the girls with the moon in their eyes, as she'd put it, who always clustered around a handsome writer/professor, and stated primly that she herself had never had a lover in the fifteen years of their marriage. They had no children.

Regarding finances, she proved very sensitive. She made a blanket statement that their affairs were in good order since the proceeds of her husband's first book had been well-invested, but when Balthazar began asking for particulars, she stopped him in midsentence with the flat remark that she did not have any figures. And that seemed to be what bothered her. Twice she found it necessary to retuck her gray silk shirt into her linen skirt, before leaning back in her chair.

"Naturally," he'd said, "you went through his papers for this information after—"

"Hardly necessary. I knew where his will was, and that his executor is an old lawyer friend in New York."

"You are familiar with the contents?"

"I'm the sole beneficiary, but as yet I don't know the amount involved."

"Copies of your tax returns would help determine—"

"We had to use the long forms. They're very complicated. In the past I just signed the appropriate places. My husband didn't like dealing with what he called the 'sharp pencils of life,' and didn't want to go over the accountant's figures with me. He said that's what he paid such high fees to the man for, and he apparently expected our copies to be filed there. There were none in his study."

She'd clearly gone through everything. But since this was only to be expected, why not say so, he'd wondered. Why these circumlocutions? If her husband had not been open about their finances, why refuse to admit it? His very reticence made it a promising area of investigation. If she genuinely wanted the police to find the person who'd made Blaylock feel his life was in danger, why was his widow blockading that avenue?

Had the man really been threatened? Perhaps her husband had suffered a small stroke. He'd read that these short-circuited the brain, led to certain kinds of irrational behavior that often went undiagnosed. Now was not the time to mention that, however. Later, when he had to tell her that an investigation without evidence of wrongdoing was impossible, then he could bring it up, if she seemed able to hear it. Or possibly he'd just suggest a private investigator.

In response to his questions about their pasts, their present, she'd built up rather a vague picture of an acquiescent husband, forthcoming in nonfinancial areas, a man who spent a good part of his day in his office at home but who had enjoyed socializing until their move here. She'd been his student at the university where he'd been writer-in-residence for some time, a post she was surprised that he would resign. The implication was that she regarded the position as a joint effort and he had—not surprisingly— failed her. Balthazar found himself increasingly frustrated. He did not doubt that she believed in her suspicions. But if Joan Blaylock imagined the police might find hidden assets or even unpleasant bones, she was not willing to give any pointers as to what she suspected, either hoped or feared to unbury. At a loss, he asked to see her husband's study.

He was immediately struck by the room's order and sterility. And this latter impression was not changed by the fact that the room contained two of everything. A pair of beige filing cabinets stood against one wall next to a small walnut desk with an electric typewriter. A much longer matching desk contained a new computer keyboard, screen, and printer. By the desks were two swivel chairs in a rust brown leather that picked up the hue of the thick earthen floor tiles. Identical fluorescent lamps arched over the typewriter and the computer. A diptych—two oriental paintings in muted greens and grays separately framed—flowed into each other above the smaller desk. On the opposite wall, two darkwood bookcases served as brackets for a life-size portrait, presumably of the writer as a much younger man. And the head was that of a poet. The light hair, in a 1960's length, unkemptly framed an aesthetic face with a strong jaw and a soft mouth. The sensitive blue eyes were focused somewhere over the viewer's shoulder. Although done in oils, it had the wash effect of watercolors.

The widow gestured toward it. "They took that for his book jacket." Reaching up, she took down one of the copies, all of the same book, that filled the top shelves. "Published in 1967. It was wildly successful—Robert Penn Warren, John Crowe Ransom, all the major poets—gave him ecstatic blurbs. *The Sepia Mirror.* Poems about nature and man," she added almost regretfully.

At his request, she handed the slim volume over, but as carefully as if it were a Fabergé egg. "He used this copy when he read before an audience—with notes to himself in the margins," she explained. The poet's scribbled memos were so expansive that it was impossible for Balthazar to read the text itself. Every change in intonation had been rehearsed, every gesture scripted. "Throw head forcefully back—hold five seconds," one direction read. "Wince painfully here," another admonished. On the dedication page, Blaylock had printed in block capitals, "Tone—quiet solemnity." The dedication read: "Poetry is King. *Vive la poésie, vive le roi.* The first is the last."

Peering over the detective's arm as if anxious to censor

a previously overlooked jotting, Joan Blaylock pursed her lips. She translated the French, " 'Long live the poetry, long live the king.' " Her lip trembled a little as she read the last sentence. Turning away, she commented, "A little trite perhaps, but he was only twenty-three at the time."

Balthazar closed the book without comment and as she replaced it, he noticed a butterfly transfixed in a lucite case set among the many copies of that volume on the second shelf. The dazzling blue wings shone in that otherwise colorless room.

A glowing clump of amber was nestled by the typewriter. Moving closer, he picked it up—the transparent gold of the fossil resin had been carved into the shape of a stringed instrument. Six small strips of dark thread were stretched tautly and delicately knotted across the center hollow. The widow took the small gem from his hand. "I don't know where my husband came by this." She stopped, then added a little sourly, "Of course one of the early poets wanted to sing to his lady on a lute of amber, presumably imagining her lying on a bed of plucked rose petals meanwhile."

He'd had a sudden vision of porcelain skin against dark red, white breasts firm and soft, the nipple itself almost rose-colored.

Mrs. Blaylock pulled out a desk drawer, allowing him only a glimpse of pencils, pens, paper clips arranged neatly in a tray. "There are only supplies in these drawers. He did his lectures and business correspondence on the computer. I've printed out everything—there was nothing of importance. And," she continued, moving almost protectively toward the filing cabinets, "he kept no personal correspondence in his files. Annual reports on the companies he owned stock in and so forth. I can give you a note to our accountant, who will have copies of our tax returns, if you find that necessary. You will need his passport." She retrieved that from the top of the cabinet.

"You're sure that the threatening letter he mentioned isn't still—"

"Absolutely." She remained standing in front of the files.

"And you're sure, after thinking it over, that there's

nothing you can add to what you told the previous investigators about that letter."

"I didn't want to move here." She walked over to stand in front of the computer, her back to him. Outside, the taller trees looked as if they'd snagged trailing clouds for decoration. "At first he said he'd be inspired by all this beauty—that he could write again—after all these years. At last he admitted he'd received a message from someone who had cause to kill him. He insisted he had to feel safe. That's all he said. Every day he sat in here with the door closed. On the few occasions when I interrupted him, he was always playing solitaire. Shuffling, dealing the cards out, then almost immediately reshuffling. He was genuinely frightened." She turned to face him, and added bleakly, "He said he deserved to die."

Imagining her anxiety, her loneliness, Balthazar had felt genuine pity. And, as if she knew that and rebuffed it, the corners of her mouth had twisted down, and she asked drily, "Is that all?"

In the living room, he asked for the names of several long-time friends of her husband. He'd told her he'd take the tire to the lab, check the site where the motorcycle had gone off the road. As he drove off, she remained standing in the doorway, looking up at the not far distant cliff where her husband had died. Framed rather theatrically between the open double doors, her back straight, she looked as if she felt that, since the one thing she'd feared had already happened, life held no further dangers. He could imagine the film star that she resembled in just such a pose, but he hadn't been able to remember which one it was.

He'd stopped at the accident scene, but by this time all traces had been covered by the tropics' eager growth. The motorcycle had spun into a thick tree, but the man had apparently hurtled off, crashing down into the wedge-shaped canyon whose bottom seemed to go to the center of the earth. Did he, falling, reach out for a handhold, one foot arched as the ball still vainly pressed on the brake, the last sound in his ears the fruitlessly spinning front wheel above him? Or did he just plunge as straight as Lucifer thrown furiously downward? The detective turned away. No action could be taken now. But he'd picked up the tire, and on the way back he'd begun wondering if Blaylock wrote about velvety beds of rose petals. *The Sepia Mirror* hadn't looked as if it contained that sort of poems—the cover showed a tangle of rather menacing trees and vines.

Now, leaning back in the desk chair and staring at the ceiling of the cubicle, he thought about where he could buy a little lute of amber for Maira, maybe as a pin. She'd know what he meant. The kind of music he had in mind from a pliable instrument, the sighing of pine needles long imprisoned, as they sometimes were, in the shining resin before it hardened. Since she'd be gone this weekend, he could wander around all the jewelry stores in Old San Juan, see what he could find. She'd promised months ago, she'd said, to spend a few days with an old friend who wintered in Vieques, who would soon be leaving for Connecticut. Even so, she'd have to take her essays to grade with her. Someday he'd take her there himself, having heard of that island's deserted beaches, its slumbrous beauty. In fact someone had said that you could find beaches so empty that—

"Car's fixed," his partner said, coming through the entrance with both hands jiggling his shirt back to dry the sweat. Not only did Sixto Cardenas's mother send him off immaculately pressed each morning, the smell of a warm iron still clinging to his shirt, but he also seemed to have an antiwrinkle gene, Balthazar mused. He smoothed the ridges in his own tan *guayabera*, itself just back from the hotel laundry but already crumpled, and said, "Have you noticed that thinking about women keeps you from thinking about your work?"

"Other way around," Sixto replied, grinning, energetically lifting his hair off his damp scalp with spread fingers. The sideburn shaved in March because of a bullet wound had almost grown in, giving his thin, handsome face its usual symmetry. He jerked his head toward Villareal's office. "You tell him yet about the Blaylock case?"

Balthazar shot a gun finger toward the file in front of him. "Gave it to us."

"We cannot do much at the moment," Sixto retorted cheerfully. "We might catch a few people on the list the widow gave you, but today is the Friday before a holiday weekend. Alvalos told me on the way in that Ponce had called, saying Señora Blaylock's friends reported she'd gone to Vieques. If she does not come back after Memorial Day, we can go there and find her. It's a small island."

"Vieques?" Balthazar began to smile. "I think we'll have to go there right away. We've got important new evidence. Flight only takes twenty minutes, I've heard. We'll call the Air Link. Probably be best if we leave as soon as we can."

Sixto collapsed into the chair across from him. "Not this weekend, *Baltasar*. Not this weekend," he implored. "It is truly hard to get a dentist to take off two full days. She is most conscientious about Saturday hours because she says her patients are working people and that's the only day they've got. But I have things lined up for Sunday and Monday."

Seeing his partner's expression—his appalled raised eyebrows, his dismayed widened eyes, his horrified upper lip—it occurred to Balthazar that to really look aghast one had to be Puerto Rican. He thought of the lovely Dr. Inez Silva Casas, her rounded figure continually threatening the professional look of her white jackets. "Well . . ." he paused, as if deliberating. "Given the current depressed state of the Commonwealth's economy, I see no reason why the *Policía* should have to send both of us, do you? Since I have never been to Vieques—and since it just happens that Maira will be there visiting—I'll go."

Sixto bounced as lightly out of the chair as if he'd been lifted. "Here is the plan. I will go out and ask Alvalos to call the Isla Grande airport. Much easier for you to fly from there than from Muñoz Marin International. We will go by the hotel and you can get a shirt and your bathing suit. Also the snorkeling mask. The ocean on the Caribbean side is as clear," he stopped, groping, "as . . . water. A little bag only, though. These airplanes are very small and they weigh you and your luggage. I will also get the travel forms for your expenses from Alvalos. The island hotels may be crowded, but Police Headquarters there has a dormitory. We will tell them you are coming. I am certain you will enjoy yourself."

Just before zooming around the corner of the cubicle

on his way to the front office of the CIC, he skidded to a stop and added, "Since I will have some time this afternoon, and even tomorrow, I will interview any of the victim's friends at the university, if they can be found. Check the ones I should start with." He slid out, humming happily.

Hastily spreading out the file's contents, Balthazar glanced up and saw that Villareal's door was now closed. But from behind it, he caught the loud rasps of an angry Spanish obscenity, followed by an explosive English one, both in Negrón's distinctive unaccented tones. By coincidence, Angel Negrón—although a native Puerto Rican— had also been a detective in the States before joining the *Policía.* In New Jersey, Balthazar remembered. This circumstance did not improve their relationship, however. From the first, Negrón had not viewed him as a colleague, but as a competitor—a gringo who, by his very existence, asserted his superiority over the islanders. On his side, Balthazar, considering as he searched for the list of Blaylock's friends to give Sixto, regarded Negrón as a complete asshole.

Pendejo. A versatile Puerto Rican insult, whose literal meaning was a pubic or anal hair. But it was a stretchy vulgarity that included anything demeaning that you wanted it to convey, including the idea of a real loser. Invariably directed at a person, it was an apt description as well, Balthazar thought irritatedly, of the case in front of him. The Blaylock file, no matter the number of shrill phone calls from politicians, would probably be pushed relentlessly back in some metal drawer. Not by choice. But there'd be no internal pressure because it looked like an isolated event. And not enough time to chase after a loose end. On average, each pair of detectives caught two new cases each week. Over eighty percent of all homicides were solved, but that was known homicides, usually committed by enraged family members, whose very passion kept them from making an effort to cover their tracks.

There were a few smart murderers. This one merely was unlucky in his choice of a victim's wife. But Joan Blaylock might yet help by hindering. If she were determined to guard her husband's reputation, the motive would be obscured, if it wasn't already buried in thick ledgers three accountants would have to pore over.

And the reason for Blaylock's murder might be one she was hiding from herself as well as the police. Some unsavory incident involving a woman student, perhaps. For years, the handsome poet had been standing in front of a classroom that must include willing, unwise virgins, whose eyes were right at the level of his belt buckle. Such fresh temptations might make desert hermits cry for saltpeter. Joan Blaylock had once been his student.

Worse, even if a motive like a directional beacon transfixed an individual, located him firmly near the scene, the case would be flimsily circumstantial. Should some sharp-eyed, credible sporting goods store clerk be found who remembered selling an air rifle, should that suspect's marksmanship be proven, what judge would indict on that evidence? What detective would want this case? A *pendejo*.

With so little chance of success, Negrón would not want to get within smelling distance of it. But he would see the reassignment to the New Yorker as a putdown, a slur on his own abilities. Yes.

The door to Villareal's office was wrenched open so abruptly that the lock's tongue screeched against the wood frame. Cleated heels pocked the linoleum tiles, then the sound stopped at the cubicle's entrance. Trying to clutch at the good humor of a moment ago, Balthazar nevertheless noticed that he was shoving the loose reports back in the folder with what Maira, quoting Wodehouse, had once described as a "nasty, wristy motion."

"As usual," Negrón addressed him always in English, "gringos stick together. The Blaylock cunt told me nothing. Nothing. Now you imagine you've nailed me."

Looking into the obdurate eyes set in the bearded, impassive face, Balthazar wondered if the man were capable of punning. He wondered why some doctor had so incompetently stitched the scar which slashed Negrón's left cheek, leaving a shiny white excrescence suppurating through the sallow, heavy-pored skin. And he wondered if he himself were capable of a neutral answer. "Prick," he enunciated carefully, "to your self-esteem?"

Without shifting his eyes, or a flicker of expression,

the Puerto Rican ran the back of his right hand along his trimmed beard. It was against regulations to have one, waived in this case perhaps because of the scar, although the dark whiskers did little to conceal it. He allowed the silence to lengthen, and Balthazar reflected that Negrón's success, especially in dealing with street punks, was due to his aura of leashed menace. Although he lacked Montez's trucklike frame, he was powerfully built, the big head set on a thick neck, with bull shoulders and a weightlifter's chest beneath the tailored *guayabera*.

"*Acaso*," Villareal, his approach hidden by Negrón's bulk, cracked the Spanish word like a whip, "I could find a very small piece of wood even in this room of plastic, and you, Angel, could put it on your shoulder. Perhaps he'd try to knock it off. You both seem to have much time—" The chief broke off and barked, "Cardenas!"

Sixto, apparently braking to a stop before the two men in the doorway, managed to insert a silken innocence in his "*Sí?*"

"What are *you* doing?" Villareal demanded. But before Sixto could finish rattling off an explanation involving the presence of Señora Blaylock on Vieques, and the necessity to conserve funds by sending only one agent, he was interrupted by the chief's snap, "You yourself planned an enjoyable early start to the holiday?"

Scooping up the top sheet of paper, Balthazar rose and came around the desk, suppressing the desire to give his ailing knee a hearty squeeze to relieve the stiffness of sitting. Negrón stepped aside, but gave only an inch of space. Near enough to catch the heavy odor of the dark cigars, the chemical whiff of deodorant, the New Yorker reached across him, handed the list to Villareal, pointing out that Blaylock had old friends in San Juan that his partner would interview.

Villareal skimmed the typed sheet, then fastened his exasperated eyes on Sixto. "You have a young woman?"

Confused, the young detective obviously swallowed his first response. Then, his eyes clearing, he replied, "Oh . . . *sí*. Missing from home for three days."

"Go find her." Villareal handed the sheet to Negrón. "You, Angel, were on the case from the start. You do this.

Marten can go to Vieques. When he returns, the two of you can . . . confer."

The chief wheeled, went into his office, and closed the door, pushing the knob behind him with a hard, outraged click.

4

ALTHOUGH IN A CRISP U.S. Marine uniform, the young
Puerto Rican was slouching negligently, with his
right knee jutting out, foot resting against the Plexiglas
side of the roofed shelter, in an unmilitary stance. He
seemed as patiently waiting as the three older people on
the bench inside—a man of sixty and two plump matrons.
They sat with their backs wearily pressed against the clear
rain shield, surrounded by numerous overflowing plastic
supermarket bags and one cardboard suitcase with rusty
metal corners, staring mutely over the sun-lit sea at the
approaching Vieques ferry, just visible in the distance. But
the serviceman's back was arched with the suppressed energy
of the young, as if he might, at any second, push off on that
braced foot, spring forward. A single medal—the colorful,
orange-tipped United Nations bar given to all new recruits—
was pinned to the knife-pressed shirt. The dark khaki pants
were somewhat bunched around his narrow hips, as if he'd
recently lost weight. In profile, he was rather handsome,
with a high-bridged nose and a clean jaw, his longish hair
falling in oiled ringlets from beneath his spruce visored cap.
However, the left side of his forehead sloped downward, a
mushy boneless ridge over a drooping eyelid.

He was not looking at the ocean, but at a very
attractive woman standing alone some ten feet away, rummaging in a fat, ginger-colored leather purse. As she
searched for something at its bottom, she leaned forward
and the scoop neckline of her blue-green blouse gapped.
He could see that although her throat looked as white as

skin ever got, the tops of her breasts were even paler. Two-tone skin, he thought, imagining first pulling out the turquoise and silver combs glinting in the back of her upswept blond/brown hair, yanking off the silk blouse to expose milky breasts, see a light arm only a shade darker trying to cover them. She was taller than he was, even in her barefoot sandals, good legs beneath the swirl of a soft cotton skirt. She had to be over thirty, he thought, but not at all bad for old. And she was probably too healthy to be bowled over easily in a snatch and grab.

By her feet, there was a rather worn leather briefcase and a maroon canvas suitcase. She would, he considered, slip the shoulder strap of the purse loosely over one shoulder soon. The timing here would therefore have to be rather close. He'd have to snatch it away before she picked up the other two pieces. He never took his eyes off her purse. Once he grabbed it, he would have no trouble. He was fast, and he knew the seedy side streets near the Fajardo docks well.

Somewhere in here, Maira Knight thought anxiously as she dredged in the bottom of her purse, was that tube of sun block she'd need in Vieques. She was sure that she'd had it when she and Lena had taken the boys to the beach last week. Her fingers closed over a something round and plastic, but it proved to be a sample of eye cream she'd picked up in an expensive store in Plaza Las Americas. Scrounging deeper, she turned over the boys' vaccination records. She and her housekeeper had from the first settled into patterns of duties that encompassed both Lena's son and her own nephew. Medical records were Maira's responsibility, and she rather guiltily eyed the dog-eared cards that held the lists of shots the two youngsters had had from their births five years ago. On the margins she'd scribbled in the dates they'd had mumps and chicken pox, a few notes on odd stomach upsets that might be caused by food allergies. Really she ought to file these, she reflected, but it was handy to just keep them in her purse in case a visit to the doctor was necessary.

The purse was older than both the boys. She'd always wondered how Puerto Rican women not only managed to have matching purses for their many different pairs of shoes, but how they faced transferring all their belongings every day. And their handbags were usually small, too. She eyed the fraying strap on her own enormous pouch ruefully.

Pricking her thumb, she stared down with pleasure at a pink coral comb she'd thought she'd lost. But no sun block. The number thirty lotion she needed would probably be hard to find on Vieques and she'd not brought much money. It was so near the end of the month that the balance would be wickedly low, and she hadn't had time for a stop at the bank, anyway. Impatiently scooping in the purse, she thought that making even a short trip at the end of the semester was the worst idea. She had to make every second count just now, even parceling out her thinking time so that she could come up with the right essay questions for the finals, talk to panicked students, and grade the interminable term papers in her briefcase. Had she remembered to cram her favorite red erasable pen in the litter bin that was her purse?

Her fingers pushed aside all the crumpled Kleenex and used gum wrappers, most of which enclosed a wad of equally used gum, that the boys faithfully deposited in her bag when there were no available trash baskets. She looked vaguely around now, deciding it would be worth it to cart all her luggage to the nearest one and dump out some of the detritus. Looking up, she noticed the stare of the young Puerto Rican, who quickly shifted his gaze to the horizon.

When she'd first arrived on the island, the teenage wife of a marine pilot, the open, admiring look that all the Puerto Rican males trained on women had intensified her shyness, even alarmed her. She ignored it now, distracted by her own thoughts, although sometimes she found those bold eyings irritating, sometimes flattering. There was often an eager guilelessness about such stares, and many of the men, with their dark eyes and fine features, were extraordinarily handsome. The intermarriage of Anglos, Hispanics, and blacks had produced an attractive array of skin colors in the islanders.

The charm, the good looks of one young man had entranced her visiting fifteen-year-old sister, Diana. The news of the ensuing pregnancy, following so closely after their parents' death in a plane crash, had overwhelmed Maira. By then, she had adjusted to her status of semiwidow, grown used to solitude, burying herself in her work, accustomed to her independence. But Rico's birth had proved an unmixed blessing. The tie between the sisters had narrowed the twelve-year age gap between them, and Diana, now in graduate school at Cornell, had cheerfully become the doting aunt, Maira the mother. Still scrabbling at the bottom of her purse, she recalled the thousands of times she'd crept anxiously into the baby's room, held a small mirror with fierce love to his sleeping face to make sure he was breathing.

For the first few weeks, Rico had cried nonstop, unable to adjust to any of the formulas the pediatrician had recommended. When she'd started falling asleep standing up, a university friend had recommended a neighbor's daughter as a live-in. Only a little older than Diana, Lena had stood at Maira's door, with desperate hope in her eyes and an illegitimate baby of her own. Lena had had plenty of milk for two, and although at first the older woman had turned away from those swollen breasts, sometimes with envy, sometimes with a slight repugnance she was ashamed of, Rico had prospered. He thought of Juan as his brother, and Lena even-handedly dispensed love and justice to them both. She'd become an excellent cook, a fastidious housekeeper, and a member of the family.

It was to this settled matriarchy, with its busy tranquility, that Maira now wanted to add a man. No, she told herself, be precise. She wanted him, rapt in an emotion that she'd hoped—and not hoped—she'd left behind, a desire that made her mind wander when he was absent, and narrowed her vision to take in only him when he was in the room. Balthazar Marten. Was he, as his name suggested, one of the three Wise Men? For much of her adult life, she mused, she had not thought there were even three of them. Pausing, hand still in her purse, she examined that idea, a little surprised at her own asperity.

Certainly she did not dislike men. Two of her married male colleagues were her most trusted friends, and she found some of her men students, just as some of the women, endearing. But to uncloister the heart? In newer, larger quarters, there was more room for pain.

Men's susceptibility alarmed her. They were so easily

entranced by a delicate curl, a summery cheek, an elegant ankle, all the while maintaining that women were the romantic sex. Thoughtful women, she knew, feared romance, even as they themselves adjusted flowered combs in their hair.

As men's dazzled eyes cleared, they saw so many different ways to leave love's community. Maira remembered her mother watching as her father, in happy absorption, packed boxes for yet another anthropological expedition to the Amazon that would last for months. Her mother would sweep up the excelsior, clean out the refrigerator, weep quietly that night. What drew a given man and woman together had nothing to do with how they filled their days, with balancing the checkbook, with rinsing out the bathtub, with teaching children not to slurp their soup.

Her own first marriage, had it not ended after a few months by his disappearance, might have ended in a few years by hers, a possibility she'd often brooded over. At seventeen, she'd met Michael Knight and was instantly subject to all her beguiled senses. He had blond eyebrows, adventurous eyes, a careless laugh, a quick, burning touch. "You cannot put a Fire out—/A Thing that can ignite/Can go, itself, without a Fan/Upon the slowest Night—." It was part of an Emily Dickinson poem that she'd appreciated then and her students seemed to grasp readily now.

But, occasionally, after finishing the champagne they couldn't really afford, Michael would deliberately smash one of the crystal glasses she always handled with such care. He'd forget to call when playing poker until the early hours. Much too often he gulped his Scotch, laughingly telling her the morning-after fumes made him retch at the black rubber smell of his oxygen mask, grow dizzy in the stifling cockpit. But he'd thrown his jet boldly into the sky, never mentioning fear, and she'd been afraid all the time. And here was another man, darker, quieter, warier, but one who had also chosen a dangerous occupation. And the choice had been his. Here, Balthazar could easily have an administrative post comparable to the lieutenant's position he'd given up in New York. She wasn't sure she could trust herself to understand.

The guilt she'd suffered for the previous failure to do

that, since the jungle swallowed Michael, couldn't be reasoned away. But she was honest in acknowledging to herself that her current situation satisfied her, kept men not too distant, yet at arm's length. She realized, too, that she was pushing Zar Marten away with one outstretched palm, beckoning with the other hand. There was a confidence in his patient waiting that both provoked and enormously attracted her.

He wasn't vain, if one could judge by the wry shrug he turned on the setbacks, the small ego-puncturings of daily life. And he only grinned at the raillery of his closest friend, T., a New York bookie who mocked Zar's occupation in that incomprehensible male form of comradeship. Of course, they *had* known each other from boyhood. On the other hand, there was Zar's partner, Sixto, always looking at him with shiny younger-brother eyes. But Balthazar was, she felt, strong and self-reliant. That was reassuring— and worrying.

Zipping her purse closed as she brooded, she quite unconsciously tightened her stomach muscles, straightened her shoulders. Her women friends had been supportive, she thought. But one of them might, carefully clearing the throat before speaking, comment that, after all, a number of other wives of MIA's had married again, that one shouldn't wait too long, that one's looks didn't last forever. And another, she recalled, hearing the name of Balthazar's hotel, became downright passionate about the wisdom of encouraging a suitor with some money, especially given the paltry salaries of untenured professors. Maira recalled how that had stiffened her resolve to go slowly. She had no intention of making any decision in the foreseeable future.

The elderly man emerged from the shelter and paced briskly by her on his way to the end of the pier, as if anxious to be the first on board. His thick gray hair was brushed upward into a neat, almost dandyish, pompador. Tufted eyebrows gave him a look of wild surprise, but his bright squirrel eyes cast an alert glance in her direction. Then he smiled with that warm, unintrusive acknowledgment of strangers that was habitual on the island. Smiling back, Maira thought that Puerto Ricans newly arrived in New York, confronted with the absence of eye contact, the tight lips with which those citizens ward off the press of too many people, must find it cold indeed.

Patting her skirt pocket to make sure she'd put her ticket in an accessible place, she turned herself to check the ferry's progress. Wide-bellied, with rounded puffs of diesel smoke like dirty cotton balls floating up into the clear, gull-filled Caribbean sky, the old steel-sided boat was steaming nearer at a dowagerly pace, now passing the gleaming condo towers on a tiny outer island. The Fajardo port area here resembled a seedy Italian dockside, with crumpled concrete streets, a crowded sidewalk bar; but the high-rises and the hundreds of trim pleasure craft, some layered in rows out of the water in neat four-story cubicles to save space, looked Californian.

Impulsively, glancing at those sleek boats, she pulled out her back combs, letting her hair fall, planning with pleasure the way the wind would catch it on the open deck. As she slipped the ornaments in her purse, she admired the carved turquoise insets in the silver. One evening Zar had picked one of these up from the coffee table, staring at it with his customary attention, turning it gently. She'd shivered as she watched his smooth fingers.

Now, running her own fingers through her hair as if to brush away the thoughts that circled the detective's mental presence like light-besotted moths, she resolved to concentrate on the exam questions while en route. Once on Vieques, she'd have some time to work, but that island's very air seemed poppy-laden, conducive only to languorous thoughts. And she wanted to talk at length with Virginia Kimble. Her hostess was in her seventies, an intelligent, reserved woman who perhaps knew a secret or two about long marriages. Although there was quite an age difference between them, the two women had taken graduate classes together, had never tired of discussing books. It suddenly occurred to her that she and Virginia had rarely talked about men.

The older Puerto Rican had stopped at a heavy, rusty trash barrel, eying its contents. Then he passed Maira and a little further on, picked up the steel-laced loop that would soon anchor the ferry, hefting it with a wiry arm, looking closely as if to check for flaws in the workmanship.

She envied his leisure, the freedom to let his thoughts wander to whatever caught his glance, to—Trash barrel. She'd clean out her purse. Clutching the top loosely, she strolled over and began piling wadded Kleenex on top of the empty Burger King soda cups, the greasy french fry envelopes, the flimsy white packages smeared with the remnants of orangey sauce.

Sorting painstakingly so as not to also throw away the paper clips, bobby pins, and loose coins mixed with the gum wrappers, she did not see the outstretched hand until it jerked violently on her purse strap. As quickly as it grasped, it let go and a khaki-clad arm encircled the container and slid downward. She heard an astonished "*Ooof.*" The young marine lay sprawled on the other side of the barrel, his legs entangled in the steel docking cable, his cap still arcing slowly, Frisbee-like, over the oil-stained ocean.

With a metallic clunk, the elderly Puerto Rican let the rest of the cable fall on the wooden pier, calling out an insincere, faintly boastful, apology. Rising on his knees, the young man responded with a volley of furious obscenities and just before he turned toward the other man, Maira saw the feral anger in his eyes. Steadying himself with one hand, he was clearly ready to launch himself at his attacker.

In quick panic, she shoved the unwieldly barrel forward sharply with the heel of her hand and her knee. It caught the marine on the forehead with a dull *whang*. He collapsed as the oil drum tumbled hard across his shoulders, spilling its pungent contents down his back and over the splintered boards.

In the brief, shocked silence, the waxed cardboard cups skittered in the breeze; the soiled napkins fluttered out over the water. Then the two older women erupted from the shelter, their exclamations loud and gull-like. The bar patrons from the back street hurried over with the instinctive ability of Puerto Ricans to form an instant crowd on any occasion. One of the older women turned immediately back to guard their luggage, the other began gesticulating and explaining to the recent arrivals. She spraddled her short legs, gave an underhanded toss, demonstrating the man's rope throw with the cable that had brought down the young thief. Only the legs and feet of the fallen teenager were clearly visible beneath the barrel, and they didn't move.

Maira let her purse sag to her feet and, still breathing too fast, noticed the older Puerto Rican was already talking excitedly into a small radio.

"What happened?" Two teenagers in cutoff sweatshirts and expressions of intense interest had materialized by her side.

"I think," she replied with a cottony mouth, "we'd better move that oil drum." Gallantly, they waved her aside and hefted its weight with a struggle. The back of the once-immaculate khaki shirt had been turned into abstract art, splotched with ketchup, cola, and special sauce. The wearer was quite unconscious, face down, nose mashed against the wooden boards of the pier.

Waving his radio, the older man walked carefully around the debris to Maira, nudging a crumpled cup aside with a polished loafer. Facing her, the top of his head came to her nose. "I am," he explained proudly, "a night watchman at one of those condos. I have access to any emergency police channel. They will come soon."

"But . . . you could have been hurt—"

"I," he drew himself up, obviously dashed by her remark, "am an ex-marine, a staff sergeant when I retired." With his left hand, he gestured toward his chest, as if there were rows of resplendent medals still pinned there. "I was trained to handle myself. One does not forget. In this case, I would have . . . side-stepped his rush. This *insecto* clearly was not in the Corps. Hair of such length, shoes not regulation issue—and not shined. Moreover, I could see his back through the glass. The pants did not fit. Wearing a stolen uniform, he must, I knew, have been a *pillo*. These young men, they hang about the docks, trying to steal whatever they can."

"I am so grateful. You were amazing!" Maira hastened to repair any ego damage, to express her thanks. "You know, it isn't the money in one's purse, but the credit cards, the driver's license, the documents. I would have been so unhappy if he'd taken them. Thank heavens you were such an observant man—and so quick-thinking."

"Well," the older man shrugged modestly, his eyes shiny with pleasure, "you were engrossed in your own thoughts, I could see. And you would not think anything of his marked interest in you." He tilted his head with an almost courtly gesture, and added with a murmur, "So lovely as you are." In a louder voice, he continued, "But you were very quick-thinking yourself. Normally, of course, I do not approve of litter." He did not smile as he said it.

Biting back a laugh she was sure would be high-pitched and inappropriate, she gestured with a still shaky hand in the direction of an arriving patrol car. "I hope this won't make us miss the ferry."

"Oh, not at all." His eyebrows were now really surprised. "An unfortunate accident. I had stretched out the cable, not seeing his rapid approach. Falling, he clutched at the trash barrel which fell over. I will, of course, point out the poorly fitted uniform."

"He may really be injured," she said worriedly. "I'd hate to think I'd—"

"That is not our problem," he returned, walking over to pick up her suitcase. "The ferry has docked. I will help you aboard and then come back to make my report to the police."

Unbidden, Balthazar's enormously reassuring image rose before her. Blinking it away, repeating to herself that this all was really quite minor, that she was fine, she began collecting her other belongings.

"I am sorry that you should have been so bothered," her companion continued. "At one time, such things would never have happened in Puerto Rico. The island was like a small village, a community. Now one must eye every stranger. You will forgive me for saying so," he reached out with a thin arm to escort her, cradling her elbow gently as the ferry ramp clattered down, "but you should have a man to protect you."

5

A RAKISH LEATHER flying helmet, with goggles on top, long sidepieces framing the jaw, would have better suited the man shouting at him over the washing-machine whirr of the little Jonas Islander's twin engines, Balthazar thought queasily. He was seated next to the pilot, a dashing, gregarious Hispanic in headphones and a starched white shirt with dark epaulets, possibly because that front seat provided a little more leg room for a tall man, possibly because the Vieques Air Link personnel carefully screened the person in that position. Not that the small plane (ten passengers, counting the pilot) would have had the fuel for the long flight to Cuba. Nor would any hijacker have survived the wrath of the other travelers, miserably crammed into the fuselage, who would then have been asked to endure a flight longer than thirty minutes. The nearest person, and they were all very near, would have throttled him.

But the view did compensate for the assault on the ears, the crowding, the secondhand air, the plane's bucketing pace. They were not too high to see how whitely the waves broke on Puerto Rico's wide shores, the palms like stars, the flourishing green on hills and mountains. From here, man's interventions in nature seemed benign. Highways were sun-splashed ribbons, towns were charming oases in the foliage. A cruiser with its destroyer escorts, leaving Roosevelt Roads Naval Base, looked bathtub-size, a boy's armada. Directly below, the green transparence of the water seemed to afford a view clear to the ocean's floor, marred only by the occasional dark shadows of coral reefs. In the middle distance the wind crinkled the waves into shining reptilian skin, and toward the horizon, all was molten silver.

He found the pilot's enthusiastic commentary on things below a little worrying. If the man flew this route several times a day, as one hoped, how could he maintain such interest in history and topography? At present, the aviator was wondering at the top of his voice how they drew maps before they had airplanes, with a segue in the direction of the many coves on the island of Culebra, which they'd just gone past, and on Vieques, which they were nearing, that, he pointed out, the pirates had found ideal. He hooted with laughter at the idea that the Spanish had named these two the "Useless Islands," at God's little joke on the benighted sailors who'd found paradise and didn't recognize it. Abruptly, he stopped talking, swooped the plane lower and, with a pleasant bump, landed smoothly on a runway that Balthazar had only just spotted. They taxied up to a low cream-colored terminal, surrounded by a number of small planes and two bright ochre rescue trucks.

On the tarmac, stretching numbly and inhaling deeply, as did each deplaning passenger, Balthazar blessed the sudden silence of the stopped engines. Although he hadn't noticed any pines, nor even many tall trees as they'd approached, the air smelled of dried Christmas trees, with a salty scent of swimsuits hanging in the sun. Unfortunately, the sun seemed even closer than it had in San Juan and he picked up his bag, just unloaded from the rear, and hurried into the terminal, out of the sultry air.

Near the doors, the casually dressed departing travelers were lined unevenly before an industrial-size scale. First the baggage was weighed by a cheerful attendant, who called out the figure to another with a clipboard, then it was removed so that the passenger himself could step on. Besides the suitcases, each person seemed to have at least one shopping bag topped with sunhats and souvenirs woven of slick green palm fronds, all subject to the jovial comments of the weigher. A squat, mustached woman in a gathered caftan was eying the scale with dismay. Without a pause in his chatter, the young attendant swung her case

on the scale, pantomiming a hernia, and then invited her
to step on as well. He gave the total to his co-worker,
smilingly chiding the plump woman for transporting an
old sugar mill brick by brick in her luggage.

Although the front of the long, cool terminal was
crowded with tourists departing for Puerto Rico and other
islands, there was no sign of the officer he was told would
pick him up. Hoisting his bags, he reluctantly crossed to
the street doors. Outside, the heat and heavy atmosphere
immediately pressed against his skin with the weight of
water; as he strode away from the doors, he felt as if he
were wading, slow-motion, along the bottom of the sea. A
blue-capped driver, busily loading luggage in the rear of a
dusty Chevrolet van with a taxi insignia, asked for the
name of his hotel. Even his brief, negative headshake in
response seemed an underwater move. A row of mostly
older people, luggageless and almost motionless, except for
a lethargic fanning with a newspaper by one woman, filled
several green slatted benches in the narrow shade of the
building's roof. They had the mien of spectators paid to
observe, and they seemed bent on punctiliously fulfilling
their duty by inspecting, if it did not require much
head-turning, each new arrival.

But the cabman had loaded his fares briskly enough,
and as the van pulled away from the curb, Balthazar could
see a lone figure in white, previously hidden by the Chevrolet's bulk, standing in the middle of the road. The
driver of a metallic gray Subaru, intent on delivering a
passenger, swerved around him without a glance.

His knee-length thin cotton shift might have been
made in Mexico, might have been imported from India.
Two untied strings dangled along the V-neck opening of
the throat, the gauzy sleeves hung to the bony, interlaced
fingers clasped below his waist. The fabric was undoubtedly transparent, but the wearer's fish-white flesh blended
in without contrast. However, the faint red stripe in the
elastic waistband of fitted Jockey shorts was discernible
under the thin material. His cropped hair allowed the scalp
to show pinkly through, and the detective would have
assumed the man was an albino, except that the unblinking
eyes beneath fat lids were hazel and did not have the

characteristic reddened rims. His legs, as scrawny as a deer's, ended in skeletal ankles and huge, splayed-out feet. A hollowed-out gourd lay on the pavement beside them. If the black asphalt of the road seared his bare soles, he gave no sign of discomfort.

Occasionally clapping and exclaiming, a small group near the end of the terminal was much more animated. These travelers, surrounded by their clutter of bags and plastic carry-alls, were clustered by a T-shirted man with lowered head. Seeing no police driver yet, Balthazar approached. A singsong spiel drifted from the man in the center. "Han' made souvenirs, han' made souvenirs. An angel fish, a parrot in two sizes, and a grasshopper. And something new, a butterfly and a frog." Although his English was clear, the accenting and delivery were odd. He emphasized the "two" as if that were an amazing feat. The stress was on "hopper" instead of "grass," giving that word a more descriptive meaning. And "something new"—a phrase any pitchman would have belted out—slipped out as if he were as surprised as everyone else. The "frog" was rumbled with that amphibian's croak.

The salesman was weaving these souvenirs from long, pliable palm fronds, and as soon as he finished the words, he waited two beats and began again, repeating precisely, never stopping his work, never looking up. Although the detective had often seen craftsmen doing exactly these figures on San Juan streets, this man was clearly an artist. His fingers flashed with the speed and virtuosity of a pianist. He slit the long green leaves with a sharp razor blade, flicked that aside, braided the bodies, and zipped in threadlike strands to represent antennas, the filaments of the fish, or trailing bird feathers. Wings sprouted in his hands, eyes bulged magically from the heads. The jaunty insect he was just completing seemed ready to sail off the pole to which it was attached and land triumphantly on the nearest plant.

As quickly as one was done, it was paid for, snatched away, and the tardy passenger headed for the terminal. Without a pause, new fronds were carefully selected from a box against the building. More of the tall, prickly-pointed shafts jutted from deep baskets slung over the back of a glossy brown horse, muching the grass beneath the NO PARKING sign to which he was tethered.

Only the kinked mat of hair and the slight darkening of the elbows and knuckles identified the maker as a black man. His smooth skin looked merely tanned, the nose aquiline, the lips Anglo-thin. Dressed in stiff new jeans and high-top sneakers without a scuff, he might have been college-age, but his neck was lined, there was a stoop to his thin shoulders. He had the bowed legs of a speedy broken field runner.

Suddenly, in a preternaturally loud voice, the white-clad man in the road boomed out: "Brothers and sisters, we meet now for our noon prayers." Even the last two avid souvenir purchasers whirled around at the resonant organ voice coming from the withered, ascetic figure. "I speak with my mouth, you listen with your ears. Almighty God—who gave us both—wishes us to gather now, to bid farewell to those who are leaving us and to welcome those who have come from the sky. He wishes us to meet with acuity. How else can we be saved? We must greet lovingly, have the clear truth, perspicaciously spoken. So it is written. So—although they could not read—the Taino Indians, our forefathers, knew as they made their lovely pots, some of which are still on our island, although kept in a warehouse by the U.S. Government. Lest the Evil One win us, we must practice our faith with sagacity, put poultices on our sins, and study the Bible. The Bible—so it is interpreted—tells us that the devil roams the earth, trying to seduce our souls that would prefer going to heaven."

The palm-weaver's mantralike recitation merged with the preacher's garble. Balthazar strained to make sense of the sermon. Moving back, he could see that the senior citizens on the bench certainly enjoyed it. They nodded, now and then murmured an approving word in Spanish. Closing his eyes, lifting his skull-like face to the sun, the minister proceeded sonorously, "The rich man, we have been told, will find it much more difficult to enter heaven than a camel finds it to go through the eye of the needle. And the camel is much larger than the cow. The Lord Brahma loves the cow, some of which have birds on their backs waiting to eat the seeds in their defecation. God Himself protects the birds, noticing each sparrow's fall to the ground. Possibly He also loves the fly. On Vieques, we have flies, birds, and many cows growing fat. They will be eaten, which is not a desirable thing to have happen to you." Flinging out his arms, he paused, opened eyes that glistened troutlike, and looked significantly at two perspiring tourists who'd stopped to listen. Flustered at the attention, they escaped inside.

Those on the bench dipped their heads in agreement. Either, Balthazar decided, they were committed vegetarians, or their command of English was shaky.

It didn't look like his escort was going to show up. He planned to leap into the next taxi that appeared. The next air-conditioned taxi, he amended, finding that even his eyelids were heavy with sweat.

Two paragraphs later, he'd determined that he'd commandeer any passing car. The sermonizer had invoked a number of saints, as well as an entire pantheon whose names sounded vaguely Aztec in origin. He had exhorted his listeners to love the beasts of the field, the birds of the air, and the fish in the sea. They were to eschew beef although, the detective gathered, those Puerto Rican favorites—chicken and octopus salad—were not ruled out.

An old yellow Monte Carlo with a peeling black vinyl top threw itself around the nearest bend of the road, curved neatly behind the evangelist, and juddered to a stop five feet beyond. A jumble of small children peered through the back window, and a curly head popped out of the passenger side. Digressing along a route headed for an "Amen," the speaker arrived there with aplomb. Ostentatiously shoving the gourd forward with one dirty foot, he added as if following an arranged program, "Sister Gloria will now sing for us."

The woman who stepped from the driver's seat and joined him had a short brick-dust Afro, freckles that polka-dotted her nose, cheeks, bare shoulders and arms, as well as a great deal of self-possession. She was buxom, without a brassiere beneath her orange, spaghetti-strapped shirt. But her tight-fitting jeans encased a flat stomach and pleasingly rounded hips. Her short, grubby toes, shoved into battered thongs, were orange-tipped.

The people on the bench leaned forward expectantly as she spread her fingers before her waist and slowly raised her hands. As they reached her shoulders, circled outward, an astonishingly beautiful "Ave, Ave Maria" poured from her throat. This particular greeting of Mary by the Angel Gabriel expressed awe, admiration, and joy. Balthazar, as a small boy in stiff corduroys squirming on a polished pew, had heard the hymn many times, but never sung like this. In that soaring soprano, there were trumpets flaring in honor of a queen. The rendition did not call to mind all those carved and painted Madonnas in blue robes, eyes cast demurely down, an outstretched hand gesturing to a Son who deserved all honor. Indeed, the "gratia plena" described a woman full of her own grace.

The doors to the terminal were being held open, and the airline attendants and travelers stood grouped there, listening. The singer's unremarkable features were transformed into a particular beauty by her vibrance, the enthusiasm with which her whole body sang. Her eyes, beneath half-closed lids, shone as she entreated that queen's help. "Ora, ora, ora," she sang, her mouth a perfect O of supplication. And at the end, her voice ascended to heaven as her soul clearly desired, that she might meet that female source of goodness. After the last glorious "Amen," she shut her eyes completely.

No one stirred, as if by not acknowledging that ending, they could induce her to sing again. And she seemed prepared to, but on opening her eyes, she glanced at Balthazar.

"Are you the CIC from San Juan?" she asked abruptly, not a trace of Spanish lilt in her English.

At his surprised nod, she continued matter-of-factly, "I'm supposed to pick you up."

"Are you a policewoman?" he blurted in confusion.

"No." Her tawny eyebrows wriggled upward in amazement. "Of course not. I'm Gloria Mujero, Gusto's wife's cousin. We have similar names, but he and I aren't related."

"Gusto?"

"Sergeant Augusto Mulero." She elaborated the name

with a maternal patience. Seeing his hesitation, she added, "It's okay. I get paid. I taxi for a living." She took a step as if to tug him forward, but settled for a descriptive gesture toward the Monte Carlo that encompassed getting in, driving off, and arriving somewhere. "Everyone was busy, and I was passing by. Gusto's at the crime scene and can't leave. I am here to take you to the police station."

6

GLORIA'S CHILDREN, whom she introduced with a rattle of names and a proud wave of chipped-polish nails, could have been chosen for a commercial whose shrewd producers wanted representative skin colors. The oldest boy, now clambering over the front seat of the two-door car to make room for Balthazar, was very fair, with a splash of freckles and a tangle of red-gold ringlets. The other three boys, sprawling in a back seat cluttered with an astonishing array of toy cars, empty potato chip packets, and juice cans, covered the range from dark brown to café au lait. When he told them his name, they all returned his smile with shy pleasure, as if he were a favorite uncle whom they hadn't seen for some time. Settling in the front, he tucked his feet well under the dash to avoid the sticky, sand-encrusted mat and propped his bag on his ankles. The car smelled of pineapple juice and a too insistent perfume.

Ignoring the engine's stuttering start, the tires squealing as she forced the Monte Carlo into a reluctant U-turn, Gloria pressed her foot flatly on the accelerator, superbly confident that mere machinery could not impede her forward progress. They hurtled down the smooth two-lane blacktop, the loose head of the plastic infant Jesus on the dash bobbing frantically. Although the crackling energy of her wiry Afro seemed unwilted by the heat, she put her head slightly out the window and ruffled it in the breeze, her breasts jouncing firmly as she did so. The roadside was a blur of stunted trees, brownish green fields, and

72

patches of red hibiscus, but the moving air was so welcome that Balthazar decided to ignore the rocketing speedometer.

"The sergeant is at a crime scene?"

"Well," she replied, bringing her head back in, "I don't know what the problem is, but I thought everyone at the airport would appreciate that explanation." Her right hand sketched a picture of an officer, dramatically performing some important duty. "He certainly said he couldn't leave, and he did look bothered. He's up at this big trailer house outside town. The woman who lives there is a nice lady—Mildred Luttrell—always gives me a big tip. Her husband, though... well, I was singing at the fish bar a few weeks ago, and he sends over a drink. I wave thanks." Her fingers pirouetted gratefully. "Then I'm talking to Jorge—the guitarist—about the next song and now this Luttrell comes over, wants to talk. I smile but I'm busy—working. He grabs my breast." Her thumb and index finger formed a solid pinch hold, her eyebrows darting together in angry wings. Then she giggled. "Now he doesn't talk to me *at all*. Anyway, Gusto just said that I should look for you at the airport. He was going to come himself, of course."

Her perfume was now enticing, the spice diluted by sweat into a rich, female musk. Trying to cool off, she flapped the bottom of the orange top so high that the bottom swell of the breast showed. He leaned back against the cracked plastic of the seat, savoring Gloria. She was not being seductive; that would have implied the brain—that clever general—was deploying the body for effect. Instead, her whole body thought all at once. There was no distinction between the dancer and the dance, the singer and the song.

"You sing beautifully," he remarked. "Did you have voice training?"

"Studied at Juilliard before I got married," she replied. "I wasn't as good then. My voice hadn't matured."

"You didn't want to stay, pursue a career?"

"New York." She took her eyes off the road briefly, and their brown light faded to the bleak umber of wet concrete sidewalks, dark ice streets. Then her right hand made scallops that included the sun, bright air, and flowers of Vieques.

"Do you get to San Juan often? The Centro de Bellas Artes there is magnificent, and you could surely—"

"Oh, I get plenty of chances to sing here," she interrupted. "I do weddings, sing at the Beach and Tennis Club when they have a band, all the local bars, and I help Santo out."

"Santo is the evangelist?"

"He gives me a few dollars when he can. He must have had a good education, but his brain is fried. But, see, the poor people don't have television here, no work, not much to do. They like listening to Santo—he's got a deep voice, uses a lot of big words. But they don't have any spare change to give him. And—without the singing—the tourists get uncomfortable. The restaurant owners shoo him away. Still, if he keeps it short, and I'm there, he gets enough money to eat, buy some rum. Everybody likes 'Amazing Grace,' and 'Onward Christian Soldiers.'"

He nodded appreciatively, imagining the sweetness she could infuse in the first and the clarion bugles she could sound in the second hymn. "Santo's an alcoholic?" he asked.

"No." She looked at him in real surprise. "He's just nuts."

A sleek blazer-blue Mercedes zoomed past, the only car in either direction that the detective had seen. The lone occupant, the driver, raised a pudgy hand to Gloria. "That's Grover Clay," she said chattily. "Travel writer. Wants to put a museum on Vieques—Indian stuff. I like that idea. And he's all right, once you get past his toothy be-pleasant-to-the-peasant number. He's got the best car here." Balthazar heard no envy in her admiration. Perhaps Gloria was one of the truly saved: the earthly elect who wanted what they had. "Most people have jeeps," she noted. "More practical."

"Do you know many of the regular winter visitors here? I have a friend visiting a couple name Kimble."

Gloria whistled. "They've got the best house in Pilon, and that whole area is fine. Julio's"—she thrust a thumb backwards at the redhead, "daddy's second wife works for them, and I help her at a party once in a while. They've got a big pool, *two* guest houses, kitchen like a restaurant, microwave, even a phone."

"Most of the houses don't have phones?"

"Well," she shrugged. "The houses are pretty scattered up there, expensive to wire. And people have to come to town every day, pick up their mail. They see each other at the beach. It seems like you see everybody on the island twice a day at least. And a lot of the people in Pilon have horses that need exercise. They ride around. Sometimes they bring the horses to town to get the mail. Pretty little *paso fino* ponies." Her fingers trotted in an elegant quick step.

Ahead of them, a blond jogger clad only in boxer shorts loped on the shoulder of the blacktop, his leggy stride as vigorous as a teenager's. Gloria gave the gentlest of toots on the horn before passing and a quick wave. Balthazar noted the pink of the man's monkish tonsure as they zipped by and, in the side mirror, he could see he was quite bald in front, despite the youthful gait. The runner did not acknowledge their passing, his face scrunched in painful concentration. "Poor Mr. Templeton," Gloria sighed softly. "Every day he races all over the island, but it's never fast enough. He's trying to outrun himself."

"Another of the local eccentrics?"

"No, *he's* an alcoholic. He's only been here a couple of months. I wonder if he's not on a geographic."

"A geographic?"

"You know, alcoholics are always going somewhere else, thinking it'll be different in a new place. He gets all the poisons out of his system by running, I suppose, but every night he dresses up, puts on his toupee, and honestly it's so good you can hardly tell, and gets sopping. He just wanders from bar to bar until he's put in a cab. But he's always polite and very witty for the first two hours. You listen but after a while he rambles. He's just the opposite of Santo in a way. Santo starts making more sense the longer he goes."

They crested a hill. On their left was a modern elementary school, the worn grass of the yard brightened by the daisy yellow polo shirts, worn by boys and girls alike. Beyond that was a small, mellow brick building with a hospital sign. But on a higher hill, looming over the unseen town of Isabel Segunda, rose a huge chunk of a fort, its crenellated roof facing out to sea. The battlements, the blackened stones of the walls, one with a huge hole in the side, were ominous despite the sunlight.

"Never finished the fort," Gloria remarked, her fingers' clever prose suggesting the departure of tall ships. "Now sometimes they talk about turning it into a casino. Mr. Clay wants it for the museum. But it's a good place for the arts and crafts shows."

Although there were no cars to be seen, at the bottom of the hill Balthazar could make out a steadily marching pedestrian, wearing what seemed a replica of Santo's knee-length white shirt. The sun picked up gleams of blond in the pure white hair.

"Does Santo have . . . followers? Has he started a cult?"

"The heat affecting you?" she inquired.

He pointed at the man ahead, now reaching a cluster of shops.

"That is Santo," she said offhandedly, "he's good at getting lifts. And here *we* are." The Monte Carlo slid into a parking lot with a blue-and-white Impala with the logo of the Puerto Rican *Policía* on its door, next to a white jeep emblazoned "Tribunal General De Justicia." The gloomy fort, framed by flagpoles—one with Puerto Rico's white star on a blue triangle with wide red and white stripes, the other that of the United States—was directly above the pleasant dusty-rose-and-white two-story concrete building at the end of the parking lot. Landscaped with small palms and buttery petunias, had it not been labelled clearly, no one would have taken it for a police station.

7

"LUCKY THING for us you happened to come just now." It was perhaps the sixth time Sergeant Gusto Mulero had made the remark since Balthazar's arrival at the Luttrell house. And once again the sergeant, ruminating on his toothpick, stopped his pacing through the living room to stare at the plastic-encased lump on the patio. Although the succulents at the end of the surrounding brick-shelved wall shone greenly, with several cacti sporting thin, exquisite flowers, the other withered, dying plants drooping all down the terraced sides made it a rather appropriate place for a corpse.

"Eventually Carillo'd turn up, but—" He flipped the toothpick to the other side of his mouth without finishing the sentence. The absence of the resident Criminal Investigation Corps agent had also been explained several times. First by the young officer at the Vieques police station who'd worried aloud about the dead man—a straightforward case of accidental poisoning—in the hills outside of town. Such occurrences, he'd pointed out unnecessarily, did require the presence of a CIC agent before the body could be removed. Carillo could not be located—possibly he was on his way to headquarters in Humacao on the mainland. In the meantime the body was . . . deteriorating. In this heat, the officer had underlined, a matter of a few hours made a distinct difference. On cue, Balthazar had offered to go, plunking his bag in the upstairs dormitory at the station. Excuses were also made for Carillo by the older patrolman who drove him to the house. And, at the

77

scene, by Gusto. In addition, everyone had, at one time or another, expressed their thanks.

Then the body, wedged in the entrance of the foul-smelling bathroom, had been moved to the outdoors so that samples of the stomach's contents, splattered down the side of the tub, on the white-tiled floor, in the toilet, on the seat, and even the counter top, could be obtained. Three large dead cockroaches were mired in these remains. Photographs had already been taken by the officer who doubled as a technician. The doctor who doubled as a coroner had left before Balthazar got there. The island's ambulance, it was explained, was busy elsewhere, but the hearse was due to come at any moment. Everything was proceeding tidily now, although that adverb was singularly inappropriate in connection with that house and its contents. So why, the detective wondered, lifting his dark hair from his forehead under the welcome whiffs of air from the ceiling fan, was the pleasant, walnut-cheeked Gusto so edgy?

As the sergeant wandered by the coffee table, his squat brown hand would hover as if to gather up the sticky cocktail glasses with clustered flies on their rims, brush dried cheese crumbs off the copies of *Woman's Day* and *House and Garden* that had been used for makeshift appetizer plates. But halfway there, the hand would be recalled. Each time he stepped over the tipped rum bottle by the brown-and-yellow striped recliner, he'd restrain a tentative swoop aimed at picking it up.

Perhaps the messiness just grated on his sensibilities like an imperfectly tuned radio station. Balthazar guessed the Vieques officer was a fastidious man—even uniforms describe their wearers. Despite the heat, he was wearing his stiff cap, and the visor's gloss matched that of his regulation shoes. His belt buckle was positioned precisely beneath his shirt buttons. A policeman who might show an intelligent flexibility in enforcing a law, but one who, like Chief Herman Villareal, was cursed with a craving for order. The detective lifted his face to the fan's breeze as he noted Gusto's own appraising glance. It was also possible, Balthazar mused, that the officer was avoiding leaving his fingerprints, which could hardly have been a concern if there was no question of homicide.

The sergeant's account, which he'd delivered in a rather tight-lipped fashion to hide his picket-fence upper teeth, had been concise. Chet Luttrell, a recent arrival, a former helicopter pilot, had unwisely eaten green apples, poisonous ones, and died. This last snack, the doctor estimated, had been ingested some time yesterday afternoon or early evening. The body would, of course, be sent to San Juan for the autopsy. At ten this morning, Howard Yung, the owner of a nearby Chinese restaurant named the Lotus Garden, had come by to tell Luttrell that his wife Mildred was returning on the four o'clock flight from St. Croix. Not only was Mr. Yung a friend of Mrs. Luttrell's, but he had the nearest phone. Mr. Yung had not wanted to disturb Luttrell, who was a late sleeper, and he opened the front screen quietly to slip in a note. He'd seen a foot protruding from the small bathroom off the kitchen.

The coroner, Dr. Reyes, had said the last case he'd heard of involving the *manzanillo* had been thirty years previously on St. Thomas, one of the nearby Virgin Islands, where the fruit was called poison guava. Luckily, those apple-eaters had had their stomachs pumped promptly. Gusto himself had called the doctor's attention to the two fruits still on the refrigerator shelf. Since the policeman had grown up on Vieques, he'd been warned many times as a child about them, he mentioned. When he was young, there'd been quite a few of the trees on the beaches, but he had thought they'd all been uprooted. Dr. Reyes knew of a biologist stationed at Camp Garcia, and Gusto had gone to the Lotus Garden and called the man. Rather defensively, the biologist pointed out that last spring—a year ago—he'd notified his superiors that there was a blooming *manzanillo* near Green Beach, which tourists and residents often used. It took the fruit a year to mature, and he thought the tree had been removed. He had not noted any other mature tress on Vieques, and he'd been scrupulous in his note-taking. While he was not allowed on certain parts of the island because of unexploded ordnance, he insisted these areas were too far inland for the *manzanillo*, which was dependent on ocean currents to carry the seeds. An officer had been dispatched to check on the tree's location.

On his return to the house, the sergeant had continued, he'd emptied the contents of the overflowing kitchen trash container onto plastic bags, still spread out at the far end of the living room, and poked through with a plastic hanger. The apples in the refrigerator were the only remaining ones. Luttrell had apparently picked them after swimming, brought them home, put them away. Yesterday he'd turned on his word processor, which was still humming, gone to the kitchen and eaten at least one. Dr. Reyes had pointed out that the stomach erupted pretty quickly, but the body's muscles became devastatingly limp. Without a phone to crawl to, the unfortunate man had no way to summon aid.

"Seen ransacked houses that looked better," Gusto grunted as he and Balthazar picked their way through each littered room. "Wife's been gone ten days. I leave our kitchen like that, my wife'd shoot me, and a jury of island women'd let her off. Might as well invite the roaches to dinner. And once they come they want to stay."

Brooding on the bulk of those king-size tropical pests, Balthazar glanced around the tiny kitchen and wondered if they'd find room. He inspected the freezer and then the refrigerator, peering at the shining apples amid the spoiled contents and then checked the bottom produce bins. The odor of rotting fruit made him shut those compartments after a hasty examination. A vision of Maira's kitchen came to his mind. Baskets of fruits ripening on the counter and bowls of others ready to eat in the refrigerator, nestled next to plastic cartons of fresh celery sticks and scraped carrots. On the wall, rows of alphabetized spices in racks. The whole room smelled nostalgically of cinnamon. His spinster aunt, who'd raised him after his parents' death, had starched her white kitchen curtains every week, made Brown Betty dessert on Friday from leftover scraps of bread, butter, and that sweet brown spice.

Elsewhere in this trailer, the neatly folded bras and panties in dresser drawers, the blouses carefully hung above lined-up women's shoes in the closets, the china hutch with stacked dishes above and glowing hand-labeled jars of papaya jelly and mango chutney below, reproached the surface grit and jumble. "Retired military man—you'd think he'd be neater somehow." The sergeant dusted off his hands in finicky disapproval as they finished. Yet Balthazar recalled that the corpse had had a fresh shave, clean nails, trimmed cuticles. Enough dirty clothes were scattered on the floor to show the man had started each day fresh. There almost seemed a hostility in Luttrell's slovenliness, a calculated disruption of the household. On the other hand, he paused, considering what his own hotel room might look like after ten days without maid service.

They adjourned at last to the comfort of the ceiling fan in the living room. Resisting a sleepy impulse to remain leaning back on the cushions of the plaid maple-armed sofa, Balthazar watched the sergeant now peering through the sliding doors to the patio.

Addressing Gusto's back, Balthazar commented, "Those apples do look good."

"Smell good, too," the officer replied without turning. "No way to know they're poisonous. Unless somebody told you."

"These look fresh," the detective continued. "You figure he picked them up yesterday—Thursday?"

The policeman's back muscles tightened beneath his crisp blue shirt. "Not yesterday. Had to be Wednesday," he responded without turning, his sentences bitten off.

"Why do you think so?"

With his face still averted, Gusto answered, "Can't get into Green Beach before three. Not open. Be cutting the time pretty close, unless the doctor's way off on the time of death. It takes a while to get there. Have to drive. There's a military guard at the entrance—writes down your driver's license number. Patrolman's checking that, too. Luttrell could have gone with somebody else, of course. Had to, in fact. His jeep was in the driveway yesterday afternoon. I saw it myself."

"Could you get in any other way?"

Gusto wheeled around, took out his toothpick and scrutinized it. "Easy enough, but a long, long walk. Maybe three miles. Each way. And yesterday morning, the marines landed at eight o'clock. To practice taking a beachhead. Couldn't have missed him, you'd think. Could have gone earlier but Yung," he gestured toward the Lotus Garden on the next hill, "swears that Luttrell's jeep was here at seven A.M. yesterday when he went to town to get produce. Still there after nine when he returned."

"Observant man." The ceiling fan whirred lazily but effectively. And Gusto, too, was inching as surely toward prickly questions. Did he suspect the neighbor of having solicitously left a sack of apples by the door?

"Says he would have noticed if it *hadn't* been there. Small island. Luttrell kept to his routine. That's why I noticed the jeep myself in the afternoon. Because it *was* there. Not usual. By then, he'd usually taken off for Sun Bay."

"Same beach? Every day?" Was it the heaviness of the air that made this conversation slow-motion? If Carillo had been there, would Gusto have spit it out faster?

"You can drive right up to the beach. Unload beer, food, whatever. And nice clean showers right there to wash off the sand." He dropped his toothpick in a shirt pocket. "Tourists like it, so do the locals. You can walk down a ways to Half-Moon Beach, more secluded, if you don't want to socialize."

"It'd be interesting to know if he went to Sun Bay as usual on Wednesday."

"He did. As near as people can recall, he got there before one o'clock. Even when his wife was here, he'd arrive about then. He liked to visit, sleep, whatever. Then he'd shower, head for one of the bars late afternoon. Pretty regular. Sorry we couldn't pick you up," Gusto added. "Had everybody out asking around."

The sergeant had been fast and thorough. A naturally painstaking man? Or was it because Luttrell was retired military, and those questions might be asked by others? Balthazar persisted. "So you think he must have picked the fruit on Wednesday morning before Green Beach was open?"

"Yeah. Long walk, as I say. Could have been done, though."

"Or maybe Tuesday?"

"No. Don't think so, at least. Biologist says they

wither pretty quick, even in the refrigerator. Tropical fruit, you know." Pulling out a precisely folded handkerchief, he lifted his visored cap and dabbed at his forehead and receding hairline. Without glancing at the detective, he went on. "Another problem. You brush against the *manzanillo* leaves or branches, and your skin'll blister. I asked the doctor to look close at his hands and arms. No signs."

"Careful when he pulled them off? Or he picked them up from the ground?"

"I didn't touch the two we still got. But they don't look bruised. And there's no sand or dust." He put his cap back on, rather unconsciously squaring it.

Outside a black bird with a comically outlined white eye swooped suddenly from an acacia tree and landed near the corpse, pretending disinterest. Balthazar tried to imagine Luttrell, obviously an unathletic man, lumbering down a long sun-soaked, off-limits beach in the noonday sun, carrying four apples in a sweaty hand or in a bag he'd brought for some reason. Obviously a heavy drinker, he might have been thirsty, and was tempted by the juicy fruit. But he didn't eat them there or that's where his body would have been found. He'd have had to put them down as he climbed through a barbed wire fence, then laid them carefully on the broiling seat of the jeep. Yet they were not the least bit shriveled. He'd have had to bring them home, wash them and put them in the refrigerator before leaving for another beach. A man who let other fruit spoil uneaten. A man who couldn't fill an ice-cube tray.

But, as the sergeant said, it could have happened. Balthazar also imagined himself getting up, shrugging his shoulders in dismissal, walking to the front door as if anxious for the hearse, as if wanting to get on with the job he'd been sent to do. He thought Gusto might hesitate and then join him by the door, and in dissatisfied relief, switch the conversation from this sad accident to baseball. Closed case.

Instead, Balthazar stood up and strolled over to stand next to the sergeant. The *chango* tilted its head at the movement from the house and, hopping a little clumsily into the air, settled into a smooth flight over the bright surrounding hills. "Even if he'd washed them," the detective said, "there should be his own partial prints on the apples. He had to handle them to put them in the refrigerator. Of course, he could have dried them on a handy towel and—"

"There weren't any in the kitchen. Not even paper ones. The roller was empty." Gusto volunteered this with a touch of eagerness.

"We'd better send them back to headquarters in San Juan for fingerprinting. If there aren't *any*—we'll have some slight grounds for our suspicions. I suppose it'd be easy enough for someone to leave them by the door for him. Luttrell have any enemies here?"

"No friends." Gusto's wide smile revealed that, although his upper teeth were staggered widely, the bottom ones looked as if a giant hand had shoved them together so that, in several places, they formed two rows. "But I don't know who disliked him that much. If he'd been around longer, probably have a good list. Still, I can bring up the subject, see what people'd say. Everybody'd just think I was passing the time of day."

"Yes. You're right—we'll have to check this out." Balthazar was now himself prowling through the trailer's living area. "Why don't you look through the desk now? See what you can find. I'll see if there's any thrown-away letters in the trash you've spread out. And we'll have to run off the stuff on that machine in the study. It's a Xerox. You know how to use it?"

"No, and it might take some doing to find someone this weekend." Gusto scratched his neck fretfully. "Holidays people here go to San Juan. And," he added irrelevantly, "people in San Juan come here."

"I have a friend here," Balthazar said, liking the sound of those words. "She might know how to operate this one. She's staying at the Kimbles."

"Yes, the Kimbles. They have a phone."

"So I've heard. Has Mrs. Luttrell been told of her husband's death?"

"No." With the edge of his polished black shoe, Gusto began scraping anxiously at a glop of tar embedded in the carpet. "At least I don't think so. Her friend Yung said there was no answer, but he'd keep trying to call her at her

sister's. Otherwise, she'll be here in a few hours. Even if
we weren't going to have to check through this, she
shouldn't have to see this. And where she's going to
stay—"

They both turned at the quiet knock on the front
screen door. The Chinese man standing on the porch was
surrounded by wooden flats filled with square green pots
of ferns and budding flowers. He gestured toward a dented
blue pickup at the bottom of the hill with a wistful white
poodle hanging half out the window. "Do you think,
please," he said, glancing sideways at Gusto, "I could take
out dead ones in garden, put these in? Mildred might not
then know. She have enough bad news when she arrives.
No one answered St. Croix phone." His smooth almond
lids were so lowered that his face looked eyeless, but his
nose was tipped back in pug-dog fashion, destroying any
Oriental impassivity with its cheerful tilt. He was a short,
handsome man with a slim youthful frame, but Balthazar,
staring down at the top of his head, saw a widening bald
spot beneath the black, brushed over hair. He was introduced as How Yung, the owner of the Lotus Garden.

"Well," Gusto began, "the body is still out there on
the patio."

Yung interjected, "I stopped on road by hearse because hood was up, but driver say he could fix it, get here
damn quick."

Gusto flicked his cap back and worried aloud. "The
real problem is where the woman is going to stay when *she*
arrives. Island's pretty full for Memorial Day. You know of
any women she knows well, Yung?"

The Chinese leaned over thoughtfully, nipping a brownish leaf from a golden-throated orchid. "No. And I thought,
too. She very shy, does not talk much to people. I am
friend, but I have only a small room at the back of the
Lotus. I could sleep outside, but Mildred, she would say
no, it wouldn't look right. I am a single man."

The black Cadillac hearse pulled into the driveway, its
sputtering muffler spoiling its stately appearance. The two
attendants got out, looked glumly at the steep, gravelly hill
to the front door before taking out the stretcher in back.

Behind them on the road, there was a quick clopping,

and the palm-weaver, upright on his glistening horse, fronds in panniers behind the saddle, rode into view. Gloria was right, Balthazar decided, you did see everyone on the island twice a day.

"Tell you what I'd better do," Gusto said as the attendants climbed toward the house, "I'll go use your phone, Yung, call around. See what I can find for Mrs. Luttrell. Guess there's no reason you can't go ahead with the garden."

Peacefully stretched out on a webbed nylon lounge chair in the shade, Balthazar watched the Chinese man skillfully tap the plants in neat squares from their containers, and mound them in the new soil he'd heaped on the terraced shelves. His gentleness contrasted with the fury with which he'd yanked out the shrivelled ones. He moved efficiently down the rows held in place by cemented bricks, as if he'd already arranged the placement in his mind, draping a graceful asparagus fern just where it'd trail most effectively against the whitewashed wall, inserting a pink-petaled impatiens where the acacias blocked the sun. And he seemed far more interested in the living greenery than discussing the dead man, repeating the story of finding the body tersely. He didn't seem alarmed at his morning's discovery. "Death does not blow a trumpet," he shrugged.

But he described at some length Mildred Luttrell's kindness to him when he arrived. "I know nobody when I come. She help. She had nice herb garden." He pointed to the tiny pots by his feet. "Dead now, but we start again. Thyme, ginger, rosemary, cilantro—all these. She give fresh ones to me. 'It easier to capture a tiger than to ask favors from people.' Her I not have to ask. When I open the restaurant, she bring flowers. Nice lady."

"You have sort of an isolated location up here. How's business?"

"So far, so good. I leave leaflets with coupons at the hotels, tourists come. Have to see—only in business a few months. Confucius say, 'To open a shop is easy, to keep it open is an art.'"

"Did you have a restaurant somewhere else?"

"No. Other businesses. Not make money. Sometimes I think if I trade in coffins, no one would die."

"Is that another old Chinese saying?"

"No." Yung flashed his sideways grin. "Arabian."

"Luttrell doesn't seem to have been very well liked."

Without replying, Yung watered the soil carefully around a newly placed ladyslipper and brushed dirt off its fat leaves. Then he said slowly, "He not come to my restaurant. I not know him." He reached for another orchid, then added under his breath, "Why he let plants die? Take two minutes to water."

"You must have heard people talk about him," the detective persevered.

"What one knows, it is sometimes useful to forget."

"Confucius?" Balthazar asked drily.

Yung brushed his short nose, chortling. "Old Latin proverb."

"Sometimes, Mr. Yung, you sound very Chinese, and sometimes you don't," Balthazar observed, standing up and reaching for the sliding door.

This time Yung laughed aloud. "I was born in San Francisco, but I grew up north in the redwood country. My mother was born in America, too. Matter of fact, my dad was only half Chinese. I don't know more than three words of the language. But, what the hell, people think you cook better Chinese if you sound it."

8

IT WAS NOT his hand, but a paw, a tawny ocelot's paw with thick shining claws. And the muscles of his arms were encased in that wildcat's fur, dotted and striped in mottled chains. With an exhilarating swipe of that agile paw, he had cracked the neck of the paca and, salivating, had sunk his glittering, prehensile teeth into the fat rodent's hindquarters. But as he tore away the first savory mouthful, he saw, with fascinated repugnance, that it was a human face whose cheek he'd gouged, and his teeth bit through his own lip. The blood and saliva on his chin was partly his victim's, partly his own. It was Doug Blaylock's face, staring up unsurprised. Then he became aware of the dark shape slipping through the jungle trees behind, stalking him. Tensing, swiveling his amazing cat's eyes through the grove, he could just make out the form. He thought it a black jaguar, the most difficult to see because it wore only the camouflage of shadow—no color at all. That made no sense. A jaguar would not hunt the ocelot. Run the smaller cat off to steal its kill, perhaps. But the instinct to flee sizzled through his veins. He knew, for the first time, the prey's liquid fear.

He woke, groggy but breathless, in the bower of sea-grape on the Vieques beach. He gulped oxygen thirstily. Afternoon dreams were, he reminded himself, both extraordinarily vivid and explicit. The subconscious reached up boldly, instead of waiting until the conscious sank unwillingly and completely into the deep sleep the lightless, uninterrupted night allowed. The sun, so low on the horizon that its glare and heat were mellowed, touched the grayish-white bark of the trees surrounding him, flickered on the kidney-shaped leaves, as large as a man's outspread hand. No doubt the slanting light, now beneath the protecting trees, had made him feel exposed, endangered.

As usual, he would be out late this evening, and he needed the midday sleep. With the Solveyos, of course, he'd grown accustomed to napping in the day's hottest times. When out hunting, the Indians at night had huddled their naked bodies close together for the warmth, but even during the day, they slept very near one another. Sitting up, he felt the absence of others with a physical pang.

The memory of Doug's ravaged face rose up, inspiring surprised guilt in him and a too familiar regret. He hadn't expected the grief would be so leaden this second time. He pushed those emotions aside. Although the proverb maintained that loving a thing meant wanting it to live . . . it had had to be done. Even on the long journey here on the freighters, with too much time at night, he had not ever reconsidered. All that he had done, his cleverness in getting the proper papers, his turning his hand to any work, his willingness to take on roles, had been with one single thought. Even if the Solveyos could not have been saved, they must be avenged. The Indians had rescued him and, even if they always regarded him as something exotic, touching his skin, his hair so unlike theirs, he had not felt like an outsider in all those happy years. The men most responsible for their destruction must be annihilated. Personal feelings had to be suppressed.

He summoned up that lurking jaguar figure. His years with the tribe had almost convinced him of the possibility of warning dreams. Commonly, the jaguar—the most powerful of the South American cats—was brownish-yellow with variegated black spots. A black one suggested the unforeseen. A new CIC agent had arrived today. A tall Anglo—yet an agent with the Puerto Rican *Policía*. There'd been no gossip about a replacement for Carillo, and if one were envisioned, it would surely be another older man. Of course, this Anglo had a slight limp. Sent here to recuperate? Difficult to imagine. He could hardly be here long. Perhaps it might be better to postpone Kimble's and Clay's executions. A reassessment of his plans might be in order.

Slowly he stood up, using the graceful cross-ankled rising of the Solveyos, not touching the sand with his hands, and walked toward the ocean. Today he'd indulged himself by coming to Blue Beach, cutting through the edge of the marine camp, to the Caribbean side of the island. The rugged road almost always ensured it would be empty, and swimming here was like diving into a sunlit aquarium. The jewel-like fish swam by undisturbed, and one could stand shoulder-high in the water and see them inspecting ankles and toes, interested but unafraid. Wading out, the deep sand cushiony beneath his feet, he went over tomorrow's program.

The Kimbles were leaving in a few days, and Saturday night was the perfect time. He'd already sent the message, and Clay's would be received the next day. He imagined the two men would confer fearfully, speculating about his presence, but Kimble would not have long to worry. As usual, he and his wife were hiring the boat owned by Vieques Divers for the trip to the Phosphorescent Bay, apparently an annual outing with their friends before returning to the States. And he was quite familiar with that lovely bay. No moon tomorrow. The boat's lights would be turned off at the entrance to the mangrove-surrounded inlet. Everyone on board would slide into the warm water—half fresh, half ocean—to see the dinoflagellates shining along the swimmer's limbs. He himself was a very good swimmer, and with the Indians had often practiced the clean jerk of the legs that caused water to rush forcefully into the nose of an unsuspecting victim. They'd done it as joke, howling with laughter as they'd then pulled their senseless tribesman to the surface.

Kimble was an older man, not robust. Stout seaweed or mangrove roots, looped ahead of time, submerged near the shore until needed, would hold him under. And then, that careless destroyer of one of the clearest Amazon tributaries would drown without a whimper, his arms waving below the dark surface like strands of kelp. A fitting end.

By the time the group reassembled on deck, towelled off, had their drinks poured, it would be too late. They might never miss their host until they'd arrived back at the dock in Esperanza. Flipping over and floating on his back, his shoulders shook with suppressed mirth.

Eventually Kimble would be found, but Clay would not. The arrangements there had taken some time, but they were in place. He only needed the opportunity. It might not come until Monday night, but he had determined that his retribution would be complete by the end of Memorial Day. After that, he could remember his own dead in peace, savor the honey-sweetness of revenge, recover the bones.

The salt water held him like a swaying hammock, lulling him. He had not relaxed for a very long time. When this was over, he could sleep. To change those careful plans would be a mistake. Kimble would be leaving. It would be foolish to upset the symmetry because of a dream. The sun was dipping lower. He rolled over, and swam purposefully back toward the shore.

Blinking as he got out, he reached the sheltering trees and shut his eyes, letting them tear up to wash out the salt. In any case, he mused, the arrival of the CIC agent could not have anything to do with Luttrell's death, unless Gusto Mulero, immediately suspicious, had called the main island right away. That was unimaginable. Quite possibly the San Juan man was there on holiday and had simply been drafted in Carillo's absence. If so, he too would be eager to label it an accidental death. If not, there was no way to connect any individual—let alone himself—with those apples. No fingerprints.

He opened his eyes quickly, wondering if the *absence* of fingerprints would alert the detective. His eyes prickled, and he shook his head quickly. The question would never arise. Even if that man were the hunter, the dream was wrong. He, the quarry, was the invisible one.

A flash of black on his right caused his stomach to lurch. Slowly he turned in that direction. There was not the slightest breeze to dip the leaves, and he studied each branch for a now motionless lizard. But there were only the erect flower clusters of the tree, still in the heavy air, broadcasting their winy fragrance. A bee hidden inside had perhaps dipped one, despite the impression he'd had of something larger. Picking up a towel, he reassured himself. Perhaps those hallucinations served some purpose. Nature could be reminding man that danger was always present. One always had to be careful. But he had been, he knew.

Tonight he'd learn more about the agent. On a quiet island, rumor was transmitted more efficiently without telephone wires. No need to ask questions—everyone spoke freely in his presence. A part of the background, he conformed to their expectations: people saw what they expected to see. Stereotypes were forms of camouflage.

On the whole, he decided, the detective's presence added amusement. Here was a man concentrating his every thought on him and yet the search would be futile.

9

"AN ISLAND of soft amber, I think, is an apt description of Vieques," Lyle Templeton was saying in answer to Balthazar's casual question about how well he'd known Chet Luttrell. Templeton's superbly fitted blond toupee gave a little fullness to a very thin face reminiscent of a British actor typecast as a duke's pleasantly ineffectual younger brother. His pale silk shirt and immaculate pleated trousers accented that impression. Clasping a silvery rum and soda, he was relaxed, discursive, and bore little resemblance to the dogged, balding runner the detective had seen earlier on the road to Isabel Segunda.

Given the widespread knowledge of the poisoning, some Paul Revere on a *paso fino* pony must have spread the news to every outlying farm on the island. Here in Esperanza, the village on the Caribbean side, the very mimosa leaves seemed to whisper the name of the dead man. As soon as the two policemen had walked up to the square bar at Bananas, Templeton had pulled out the stools next to him, greeting Gusto affably and introducing himself to Balthazar. He'd inquired what they'd like to drink and relayed the order urbanely to the owner, who was standing directly in front of them. Templeton had been eager with his questions but had apparently decided a preface was necessary for his response.

"Not," he continued, "that there is any actual amber here. I meant that remark as a metaphor. In prehistoric times, the pine sap flowed and then hardened around whatever was caught in its sticky path—insects, twigs, leaves—fossilizing them forever. And here, the sunlight seems . . . thicker, and people seem to be stopped in their most characteristic stances, transfixed in liquid gold." As if to illustrate, he froze, holding up his almost empty glass as if posing.

Above his head, a sign proclaimed that Bananas was "a genuine sleazy waterfront dive," and, although scrupulously clean, it was. A jutting corrugated tin roof was the only protection for both the bar and the adjoining heavily varnished tables of the small restaurant, now filled with vacationing Americans, the men in polo shirts and canvas shorts, the women in floaty sundresses. A busy narrow road separated the flimsy building from a scrap of a beach and a few small boats, swaying lazily, tethered to a dock. Here, the twilight ocean was an unassuming gray, but farther out it flamed with the sunset's orange-streaked amber. Gusto, who'd predicted they would be popular this evening, was hailed by a couple in their fifties, residents identifiable by their deep tans. Picking up his beer, he excused himself and joined them.

"You have to remember," Templeton strayed even farther from the subject, "that an island is a compressed continent. So each person has to represent every member of his group. Howard Yung is the only Chinese, in fact the only ethnic, really, since the locals are so . . . mixed in their backgrounds. He's a bit of a philosopher when he settles down to talk, a well-educated American. But someone else here already has that role. Yung then becomes the Compleat Chinaman."

"Are you the Well-Educated American?" Balthazar asked, smiling.

"Not at all." One of Templeton's blue eyes was almost precisely a quarter brown. His rueful, answering smile gleamed, except in that dull quadrant. "I'm the Dissipated Person. I do nothing at all useful, except attend an occasional Navy League party. I jog, of course, but that's a modern trend. In the days when Vieques had large sugar plantations, I would have had a peon run for me while I sat on the veranda and fanned myself, sipping a planter's punch." He rattled his ice cubes with regret, then continued. "At one time, profligacy was done with more flair.

One took the royal road to damnation, going the easy and direct route in a carriage. Now that we have superegos instead of consciences, we pursue our vices halfheartedly. I even have mine routinized." He signaled for another round of drinks, although Balthazar was only half finished with a Heineken. The trouble with alcoholics, the detective reflected, was that they were often posing, hiding from themselves. Some bumped downhill quickly, claiming they were Good Old Boys at heart and nothing could be expected of them in a bad new world. Others, not abstaining, tried explaining. Templeton might be a superficial self-analyzer, ostensibly forgiving himself because he understood what he was doing. Or he could be desperately trying to impose order on a boozy chaos with words.

"Wait," he said now, brandishing his refilled glass, "when I think of it, I have another role, too. Since this is such a small island, we have to fill in while another is absent. When Grover Clay is gone, I'm the substitute Expert on Things To Do While Here."

"So you've been here a long time?" Balthazar had thought the man might be a useful source of information, but his digressions seemed to be getting longer. Still, Templeton had obviously shared a lot of drinks with Luttrell, and his own dormitory-bull-session-style conversation might encourage others to be, by turns, as earnest, malicious, and indiscreet as he himself seemed. The detective stretched his stiff knee, settled patiently on the bar stool to listen despite the seductive evening breeze that wandered into the bar, brushing his cheek with light fingers, conjuring up better things to think of on a tropical island. Like Maira.

"I don't know," Templeton at last responded vaguely. "Have I been here a long time.... Well, to begin with, there is no 'here' here. And you might have noticed that doing nothing takes a great deal of time somehow. I barely have a chance to drink my morning juice when I have to be off running. Then I usually rest on the beach too long, have to shower hurriedly and begin my evening rounds. Luckily, I don't have to take Clay's other position—Man With a Mission. He's determined to set a Museum of the Caribbean here, possibly in the fort. He wants to trace the

Indians' start in South America, and their movement up the island chain. Collects all sorts of artifacts. The navy has some stored here, but I believe there's a disagreement between the U.S. and Puerto Rican governments about who owns them. Anyway, Clay's ideally set up for acquiring— since he's a travel writer, he goes everywhere. Busy fellow, amazingly energetic for someone of his girth. He's also the Master of Revels. He suggests ideas for parties, brings interesting people to meet the Island Elite."

"A large group?" The detective picked up one of the two fresh beers in front of him. He was falling behind quickly.

"One couple—Elliott and Virginia Kimble. Even the admiral attends their gatherings. And the Italian count who owns two palatial homes that he never lives in. He doesn't come often to Vieques, although he rents his houses to notables. Did you know that they filmed *Lord of the Flies* here? Appropriate. And a Clint Eastwood movie, too. What were we talking about?"

"The Island Elite. Did Luttrell know them?"

"He wouldn't be invited. Now and then they do ask lesser mortals to make up a group. Afterwards, everyone discusses the food because your ranking on the social scale here depends on which hors d'oeurves were served. Although Virginia Kimble is aways polite, she is exact in her estimate of where to place you. Island food—nothing flown in—indicates a low rank."

Trying to recall what Maira had said about her hosts and how she knew them, the detective asked, "Who's going to assume Luttrell's position?"

Templeton grinned. "Many are called, but few are as well qualified. He was the Island Boor. Both conversation and courtesy were wasted on the man. Even a boil on one's behind served a more useful purpose, since presumably it's draining off some irritant in the body." The owner of Bananas, whose curly beard gave him a piratical air, paused in front of them. Introducing him as Jan van Sant, Templeton appealed to him with a derisive eyebrow, "Even dead, can you think of a good word for Luttrell?"

Van Sant shook his head and gestured with a spread hand, "The trouble with having an outdoor bar is that it's hard to throw someone out." He tapped the bar. "Soup, Lyle?"

"Yes, yes. All around," Templeton agreed. Glancing at the busy ponytailed waitress, van Sant moved toward the kitchen, apparently to get it himself.

"You'll like the black bean soup here," Templeton assured him. "Add a little sour cream, grated raw onion, bit of minced cilantro on top. Always have it at this time myself. And they have wonderful pastrami. But," he lowered his voice, "although the lobster is very good here, too, wait a bit and have it up the road at the Beach and Tennis Club. They sauté big chunks of it quickly, and serve it with *arepas*—little fried corncakes light as air. Besides, Gloria will be singing. Be a good crowd. And," he continued with a touch of the tour guide, "if you have time, you should watch that souvenir-maker setting up temporary shop across the road."

Balthazar glanced over his shoulder to see the side-baskets of palm fronds being unloaded from the elegant horse, now tied to a stunted sea-grape tree. Already, the craftsman had begun his unvarying sales pitch, having arrived at "And something new, a butterfly and a frog." At the moment, his monologue was addressed only to his mount, happily munching the beach's sparse grass. But several of the locals, idling by a shack with a faded sign showing a joyous crab about to be deep-fried, were ambling up. A smattering of tourists, obvious new arrivals whose sunburned noses ranged fom shrimp pink to lobster red, paused curiously.

"Something New's ornaments aren't unusual, but they are extremely well done. He's our Artisan-in-Residence. Clay had hopes of him—showed him a description in Columbus's diary of an Indian animal figurine, asked if he could make cheap palm reproductions to sell in the museum gift shop. But the guy just shook his head, backed away. He finally said he couldn't read. After that, he avoided Clay—probably embarrassed. Pity."

Turning back, Balthazar noted that Templeton's glass was again empty, despite the fact that the man seemed to be only taking an occasional civilized sip. "Something New is his name?"

Templeton shrugged dismissively, then smiled in pleasure at the arrival of the soup, motioning for another round of drinks at the same time. Seeing three bowls, Gusto hurried back. Sliding onto the bar stool, he murmured to Balthazar that he'd been told that Joan Blaylock was staying with a couple named Gifford in Isabel Segunda. Templeton was engrossed in arranging the garnishes on top of the thick black beans. At last satisfied, he handed a bowl to each of the two policemen, and watched anxiously as they took their first taste. Instead of trying his own, he pushed it to one side and sipped his new drink as judiciously as a rum connoisseur.

When Balthazar praised the rich soup, and Gusto raised his spoon in tribute, Templeton beamed. "Another thing I'd recommend is the bouillabaisse at Casa del Frances," he said. "Nice fresh conch, lobster, and shimp, and I believe the chef adds just a bit of Pernod at the end. And their Vieques lime pie made with cream cheese is delicious. Casa del Frances has an interesting history—once a moldering mansion—it's been renovated, turned into a guest house. But it's vine-covered, inward-turning." He spun his ice cubes with a finger, then gulped most of the drink. "You can tell by looking at it that it had an old scandal, definitely sexual in nature. Involving a priest, I think, and a young girl. You get the impression that people are buried somewhere about on the grounds." His *S*'s were slipping sideways off his tongue; his voice slid into a mumbled conclusion. "Grover, of course, knows the story."

He stood up as suddenly as if he'd been ordered to do so and set down his empty glass. Slipping folded bills beneath his untouched bowl of soup, he thanked them gravely for joining him, and stepped out onto the road. Staring down at his feet as if they might do something unexpected, he veered a little too far onto the blacktop. A bicyclist whizzed silently by, and Templeon jerked his head in alarm, nearly losing his balance. He blinked befuddledly a moment, then headed up the hill towards the neon lights of the Trade Winds Bar.

Resignedly, van Sant stacked the two empty bowls and stared at the full one. "I try serving it earlier and earlier, but he never eats his soup. I've never seen him eat anything but a few nuts." Picking up Templeton's bowl, he carried it to a railing on the far side and rapped his knuckles sharply. An almost ghostly white, bony hand reached up and took it. As van Sant returned for the other bowls, he waved in that direction and grumbled, "But old Santo has Lyle's schedule down pat. Templeton comes in after his run, Santo after his nap on the beach. He waits on that bench outside, and every day he complains that the raw onion on the soup gives him heartburn." He shrugged and headed for the kitchen.

Reaching for the shot glass of toothpicks on the bar, Gusto said thoughtfully, "First person we find who says he liked Luttrell, we arrest. The rest of them must be innocent. Mr. Ridder that I was just talking to over there said he'd have had the cook make *manzanillo* applesauce and sent it over if he'd thought of it. Well, *Mrs.* Luttrell was really upset. Last person you'd think would be from the gossip, but she wasn't pretending. Have to fill you in on what happened at the airport." Balthazar had stayed behind taking a careful look at the Luttrell house in the afternoon, leaving Gusto to look after the widow.

A full bottle of Heineken stood midway between the two policemen, and Gusto appropriated it politely and took a swallow before continuing. "Glad that Yung went with me. He handed the poor lady the dog before we told her, not that he had much choice. That poodle was squirming all over once it spotted her. Good idea, giving her the dog, gave her something to hang on to. She was crying, the little dog licking her face and moaning along with her, and she kept saying, 'Party, what are we going to do without him?' That's the dog's name—Party." He flicked imaginary dog hairs off the fresh *guayabera* he was wearing. "And then when she heard she'd be staying at the Kimbles', that didn't help. Well, maybe it did, because she got so worried about that, it gave her something else to think about."

"She doesn't like the Kimbles?"

"Said she'd known them a long time, but they weren't good friends. But that's the only place there was and Mrs. Kimble said they'd be glad to have her. 'Course she would say that, kind of person she is, never know if she means it. Yung kept patting Mrs. Luttrell's hand, and then he said he had to get back to the restaurant. I think he was flustered himself, seeing the tears just running down her face. On the way to the Kimbles', she tried to fix her face a bit, and she hunts around in her purse for a new collar she'd bought for the dog on St. Croix. Pink with seashells on it, and she puts that on saying at least Party would be pretty. She just hung onto that poodle like a drowning person. Good thing your ladyfriend was out on the porch when we got there."

"Maira? Why?"

"Old Kimble's mouth got kinda pursy when he saw the dog, but your friend, she saw how the widow's clutching it. So as soon as she's introduced and they all say how sorry they are, she tells Kimble how much she loves dogs and how she was missing her own dog and how nice to have this one for the weekend. Both the Kimbles seem to like her a lot. Pretty lady. She got a poodle, too?"

"No." Maira didn't have a dog. He picked up his glass and toasted her silently.

"Mmmm. Well, then Mrs. Kimble says she's sure it's well trained, and she puts her arm kind of stifflike around Mildred Luttrell and takes her back to the cabana." With his hand as a shield, Gusto picked assiduously at his crowded bottom teeth.

Balthazar peeled the label off the empy Heineken bottle. "Did you tell Maira I was here?"

"I did." Gusto ran the toothpick hurriedly over his straggly upper teeth and closed his mouth.

"Well, what'd she say?"

"Said she knew how to run that word-processing machine Luttrell's got. Do it for us in the morning if you could pick her up. By the way, I sent the apples off to San Juan for fingerprints, like you said. Told them we needed the results right away. I'm sure sorry you have to spend so much time on this. But Carillo says he'd run out of his gout medicine. That's why he had to run over to Humacao. And his left foot is pretty bad." Gusto stood up, snapped the toothpick in half, and smacked his lips in disapproval. "Don't know who thought these peppermint toothpicks were a smart idea. Flavoring burns the edges of your mouth and your tongue."

"What time am I suppose to pick Maira up?"

"She said just give her a call when you're ready. Anyway, now we'd better go up the road to the Trade Winds, catch the Beach and Tennis Club later. Most of the Anglos who live in Pilon, and who knew Luttrell, hang out down here in Esperanza rather than going to Isabel Segunda at night. We better talk to the rest, don't you think?"

"Did Maira seem to mind? She is on a short vacation and—"

"No, no." Gusto's nut cheeks bunched smilingly. "She acted like there was nothing she'd rather do. Seemed real pleased to help. Said you should be sure to call first thing. Said that twice."

10

A CHILD'S FORT, made of white Lego bricks, Balthazar thought when he saw the sweeping rear of the Kimble residence as he rounded a curve in the sun-dappled lane below. A citadel where none was needed. Jutting from a placid hilltop, the main house, with a crayon-blue sky as backdrop, was a perfectly square two-story structure, its severity softened by the witty crenellations around the top of the flat roof. A giant soup bowl, presumably the pool, with concrete pillars like flying buttresses supporting it, stretched out an amazing distance into the surrounding low trees. The blocks decorating these walls were smoothed into scallops. From what he'd heard of the Island Elite couple, the detective hadn't imagined the Kimbles would employ an architect with a sense of humor.

As the blue-and-white jeep bounced sedately up the almost vertical gravel road, his heart was humming somewhere near the base of his throat. Thinking of Maira, the few pertinent questions he hoped to ask Mildred Luttrell kept slipping away. Instead, he craned to see his left cheek in the rear view mirror since the sixty-watt light in the police dormitory had made shaving inexact, checked the polish on his shoes, glanced complacently at the creamy *guayabera* he'd bought in San Juan and anxiously at a small butter spot on his brown trousers. Again he reviewed the brief phone conversation he'd had the previous night with Maira. She'd assured him that she didn't mind running off the disks on Luttrell's word processor. Brushing aside his apologies for disturbing her weekend, she'd sounded really pleased that she'd be seeing him. Hadn't she?

The entrance was marked by two curved white concrete slabs. From each leered a dragon with erect bat wings, serpentine necks, and lewdly upcurved tongues. Parking in the circular driveway, he saw Maira in white beneath the fernlike foliage of a jacaranda tree. The shadows of the leaves flecked a lace pattern on her soft blouse and skirt; the sun sprinkled gold on her hair. Bending down, she was playfully trying to wrest a stick from a tiny poodle. Nestled in the back of her swooped-up hair were five-petaled, waxy white-and-yellow flowers. He wanted just to stare, to adjust his breathing. Instead, he turned off the jeep's ignition, opened the door, and climbed out.

Looking up, coming towards him, she seemed to be trying to arrange her face but was unsure what the final expression ought to be. She put out her hand, then suddenly stepped closer, and reached up, pulling down his head, pressing his cheek fiercely against hers. As quickly, she stepped back.

"Succumbing to idyllic island atmosphere," he asked with a dry mouth, "or more hopefully, finally surrendering to intense, long-lasting passion?"

Fixing her eyes on the top button on his *guayabera*, she replied, "You have another new shirt."

"Please don't change the subject," he entreated.

The screen door banged gently, and a light, pleasant voice remarked, "So, 'Brave Balthazar is come out of the West.'"

"I believe the poem reads 'young Lochinvar,'" Maira corrected, smiling.

"Ah well, fits the metre. How do you do. I'm Virginia Kimble." A woman in her seventies, he guessed, taking her hand, feeling the fragile bird bones beneath her firm grasp. Virginia Kimble's fluffy hairdo was intended to give softness to a rather long face, and each pale apricot hair was teased and sprayed into doing its duty. Her silk shirtdress was a shade lighter and her earrings a matching coral. Despite the fact that it was only nine in the morning, she had carefully applied makeup that did not quite succeed in concealing the deep lines on the sides of her mouth or the faint, downy hairs on her cheeks.

Her gray eyes studied his face at length, without smiling and without self-consciousness. "Perhaps Maira told you that we did our doctoral work together. Not only do I delight in having a friend who can talk intelligently to me about books, she is the daughter I never had. She's told me about you. You were, I understand, a lieutenant on the New York City force. Does that unusual spelling of Marten indicate Dutch ancestry?"

"My father was Dutch, my mother Irish," he replied, suppressing an almost irresistible impulse to add that he had good teeth and excellent benefits and that homicide detection was an expanding field.

"Yes. I should have guessed. Those Celtic eyes. Wonderful." She turned to Maira. "Herman Melville was Dutch-Irish. I was just reading one of his biographers who pointed out that that particular combination of national groups gave America stable, imaginative citizens."

"On what evidence?" Maira grinned at him. Now sunlight was pouring over her blonde hair and white dress, and reflecting in her shining eyes. To him, the bright background was out of focus so that he could see nothing but her.

"Herman and me," he interjected gravely.

The older woman's eyes returned to her calm assessment of him. "You must come on our outing this evening to the Phosphorescent Bay. And I believe you wanted to talk to Mildred Luttrell. We are letting her sleep, however. We had some difficulty getting her to take the sedative that Dr. Reyes sent last night. Only Maira's gentle persuasion, and her offer to take the dog out, won her over. Perhaps you could talk to her on your return." Obviously Virginia Kimble expected complete agreement down the line.

"My dear." The tall, straight-backed man shut the screen door with some care and came forward. The widow's peak of his thin gray hair emphasized a lengthy, miserly nose, beneath which was a smile of chilly courtesy. He had a great deal of neck and his prominent Adam's apple echoed his pointed hairline. "The caterer is on the phone. That Chinese fellow. Some problem with the fish.

If you want off-island varieties, they'll have to put them in packages of dry ice on an airline seat." He turned to Balthazar and offered a dry, hard hand. "Elliott Kimble." His mouth softened when he turned to Maira. "How very nice. The frangipani in your hair." His fingers rested lightly, but almost possessively, on her arm as he bent his head behind her, with the air of someone who invented the flower and regarded the wearer, too, as part of the display of his work. The miniature poodle, who'd been sitting patiently on his haunches, paws up, stick in mouth, glittering black marble eyes fixed tenaciously on Maira, let go of his prize and growled throatily at Kimble. Balthazar's estimate of the animal's intelligence rose, and he leaned over and treated the dog to a thorough ear-scratch.

For the first time, Virginia smiled. "I'll look forward to seeing you this evening."

"Virginia, my dear. The phone," Kimble reiterated. "Perhaps you'll also put that dog somewhere."

As they drove through the gates, Balthazar nodded at the nearest gargoyle. "Portrait of the owner?" he murmured.

"Elliott makes politeness a put-down," Maira answered, laughter bubbling in her throat, "but, on the plus side, he spends a great deal of time in his study, or doing what seems fifty thousand daily laps in the pool. You'll like Virginia when you know her. Of course, by combining a straightforward personality with a great deal of money, you do come up with an autocrat. But she's also extremely intelligent, thoughtful . . . I love her. Beneath that reserve, she's warmhearted. She really felt sorry for poor Mildred Luttrell, who is a gentle soul. Last night, I was passing her guest house on the way to mine, and I heard her weeping, saying so heartbrokenly, 'Bones, Bones, Chet's dead. What'll we do?' I knocked and we talked until it was quite late. Finally I persuaded her to take the sleeping pill."

"'Bones'? I thought the dog's name was Party."

"Bonaparte."

"Is a short dog."

"Mildred was thinking of his extraordinary cleverness, she said. He is a great consolation to her now. But after hearing about her husband from the Kimbles, I think I'd turn the wake into a celebration."

"Talking to people last night, I became convinced that quite a few would have been willing to send Luttrell a basket of that particular fruit," Balthazar agreed. Because of her presence, he found that his automatic driving skills deserted him. He had to remind himself to shift, to check rearview and side mirrors, to steer around the ruts.

Along the side roads of the Pilon area, the wired-together fence posts had sprouted into willowy trees that arched above them, creating a haven of green. The jasmine scent of the frangipani mingled with the morning's freshness. One of the flowers slid out of her hair, drifted over her breasts, and plopped softly in her lap. "Mildred probably married him because she was afraid, and wouldn't leave him for the same reason. Her sky is always falling. She pre-worries."

"I have an English professor friend in San Juan," Balthazar said meditatively, eyes on the road, "who diagnoses pneumonia every time her five-year-old nephew sneezes."

"My grandmother was given to whipping up mustard plasters because of a family tendency to weak chests," she retorted. "At the drop of a sniffle, my mother smeared Vicks VapoRub from my nose to my waist and pinned a flannel cloth to my pajamas. I am alive today. They knew pneumonia is rampant."

"In Puerto Rico?"

She launched the flower at his ear. "Speaking of that, if Luttrell's death was an accident, why are you so interested in knowing what's on his machine? Besides, you're not here because of his death. I gathered from the sergeant yesterday that you were with a daring young man in a flying machine when they found his body."

"I was on my way to interview Joan Blaylock. She's staying on Vieques, although I am told that today she's on St. Thomas, shopping."

"Douglas Blaylock's widow? I met her a few times at university functions. He taught an occasional class there, you know."

"What did you think of her?"

Maira slid forward in the bucket seat, looking at him

with narrowed, speculative eyes. "When Lady Macbeth hears that the witches have prophesied that her husband will be king, she begins to plot to kill the current one."

He nodded solemnly. "I finally understand. A chemical found only in Vieques water. It causes intense maundering, inability to answer a question directly."

Rubbing her hands together broodingly, Maira continued, "But she thinks about Macbeth and says, 'Yet do I fear thy nature;/It is too full o' th' milk of human kindness/ To catch the nearest way.' At best, Doug Blaylock had skim milk in his veins." She leaned back, staring at the car roof. "Macbeth says of his wife that 'she should have died hereafter.' Joan should have been *born* hereafter. In the fifties, women didn't go in for MBA's. She'd have made an ideal CEO for a large corporation. But all she had was a poet to manage."

"His books were successful, I thought." They were now on the main road nearing the turnoff to the trailer, and his foot was reluctant on the accelerator.

"Book. He only wrote one. *The Sepia Mirror.* It's marvelous. Reading it, you feel as if you're in the Amazonian jungle. Your arms itch from the fly bites. You're getting whiplash from trying to see out of both sides of your head because you're not sure which vine is a snake, which rustle a predator's approach. But then nothing more—for years. Maybe nothing ever again inspired him like that fearful beauty. He did publish an occasional piece in poetry journals. A few months before he died, I read one of his poems in a Caribbean magazine—it was embarrassingly bad."

"It did make them rich, didn't it? The book?"

"It won awards, perhaps a Pulitzer, I don't remember, but publishers make more from books on toilet training than they do from best-selling poetry. At the university, everyone always assumed it was *her* money."

He slowed down even more, then asked, "Was he faithful to her?"

She responded promptly. "By inclination."

"What does that mean?"

"Report from the Psychology Department. There I have a friend, Leila. Sexiest woman alive. She said that

when she talked to the handsome poet, her signals just
bounced back. Dead air."

"Was he discreetly gay?"

"No rumors at all—and there are few secrets in my
shop at the university. 'All literature is gossip,' a writer
said, and we try to keep up."

After setting the emergency brake on the steep grade
of the Luttrell driveway, he stared at the steering wheel.

She brushed faint yellow pollen off her white skirt.
"Are you detecting?" she asked.

"I was thinking," he looked at her seriously, "that I
need to talk to Leila, the sexy psychologist."

"Not a chance," she replied firmly, stepping out of the
jeep.

The pastoral landscape, the surrounding beds of pansies
and geraniums, the high trees in back, hid the double-wide
trailer origins of the house, suggesting a cottage instead.
The air was warm and still. He preceded her through the
screen door with apologies. "Pretty much of a mess inside.
But the processor is in the back bedroom and it's okay.
After we're finished, Gusto said he could get someone
to—" He turned and saw her dismay at the sadness of the
disorder. Despite the open windows, the smell prickled the
eyes, caused the throat to close. "I shouldn't have brought
you," he said regretfully, putting his arm around her
shoulder, rubbing her upper arm.

"Gulp," she said, her transparent eyes now on his.
"But this is only . . . messy. There's a Latin phrase, *lachrimae
rerum*—'the tears of things.' A pain inbuilt in the universe.
Then, to see little cherished belongings strewn around
every which way . . . and they exist and the person who
owned them doesn't. I'm not being very clear. I'm feeling
vulnerable. Yesterday on the dock waiting for the ferry—"
Vexed, surprised at her quick turning to the shield of his
embrace, even when the danger was past, Maira stopped.
After all, she lectured herself, she had not really been
endangered yesterday, and all that was in this trailer was a
reminder of death.

Aiming at a matter-of-fact tone, she commented, "I'm
just glad that Mildred won't have to see it." She stooped
down before the heaped contents of the kitchen container.

"Zar, why are all her things in the garbage? Surely she wanted these pictures of Party. And look at this wonderful framed butterfly. Blue as an electric spark."

Footsteps scrunched on the gravel outside. An airy tap on the screen door was immediately followed by the light-footed entrance of a plump, middle-aged, beaming man. Silvery hair rose from his pudgy forehead, lifted to a crest, and swept back into a wave over his outsized head. From there, each segment of his body grew increasingly rounder before subsiding somewhere near his hips. His stuffed cheeks gave way to the spread of complacent jowls. A hot-pink tent of a shirt was stretched across naturally padded shoulders, a sausage-roll chest, and several concentric paunches that lay loosely on the vast inner tube of his waist. The outsized white pants of expensive cheesecloth covered the tops of canvas boat shoes in a surprisingly small size.

"I'm Grover Clay, a friend of the Kimbles." The rather delicate hand he extended to Balthazar was suede-smooth and laden with enormous Indian turquoise rings. "And the lovely professor Knight." He pecked Maira's cheek, patting her hand as he did so. "Always a pleasure to see you." His voice had a margarine texture. Then his narrow, active eyes under the fat eyelids darted around them, surveyed the jumble of the trash container in the entryway and went on to the littered living room. His nose wrinkled. "Heavens! Look at this! It *was* wise to whip poor Mildred immediately to Elliott and Virginia. I just stopped in there myself to see her."

"How is she this morning?" Maira asked concernedly, picking dried egg-white off the butterfly's Lucite case.

"Frankly, I thought a little . . . incoherent. I couldn't tell when she was talking to me and when she was addressing the dog on her lap. But Virginia had breakfast served by the pool, and prevailed on her to take a Valium with her pineapple juice. A relaxed day will no doubt help a great deal." His busy eyes swiveled to Balthazar. "You're here in the role of a friend? Surely old Chet's demise is not a police matter?"

"Accidental deaths are a CIC responsibility," Balthazar responded noncommittally. "You were an old friend?"

"Not to say that," Grover's quick glances were everywhere, as if he suspected the answer was spray-painted on the walls. "No, not at all. We had an occasional drink together, of course. Small island." Despite the placidity of his enormous body, his fidgety eyes gave him a nervous air.

"My goodness." He moved nearer to Maira to peer at the startling blue of the butterfly and then looked down again at the trash container's contents. "Were the Luttrells thinking of moving? Why throw away these mementos?" With one white shoe, he nudged the delicate palm frog. "Something New's handiwork, I can tell. One sees so many of those, but his are very good. The local craftsmen usually aspire only to clunky belts of small gourds. And that butterfly you're holding is a rare Brazilian one. The Morpho. Morpho means beautiful. And those huge wings give them a soaring flight." His hand moved gauzily aloft. "At one point, you know, they were endangered because those wings were used extensively in jewelry and butterfly-wing pictures. The blue is structural—doesn't fade. Happily, I think, that is no longer the custom."

"I've seen another, though," Balthazar responded, thinking that to repay Maira he'd buy her something in that breathtaking blue.

"I shall have to get one for the museum room that will recreate the surroundings of the Caribes' starting place in the Amazon. In the past years, I've collected some wonderful artifacts for that room. The South Americans are not yet ready to protect the Indians' past. My museum will have some of the few remaining examples of their culture. Posterity will be grateful. Perhaps I can talk Mildred out of this butterfly." Clay picked his way into the living room, and stared through the glass door at the vigorous new plants blooming outside. Nodding approval, he pirouetted back to Maira, fussing with the heavy ring on his index finger.

"Do you know that Mildred seemed quite upset at the idea that you were involved in this? Murmured about something . . . sordid. Whatever did she mean? Some past misdeed?"

"We haven't gotten that far," Balthazar interjected.

Maira put the butterfly aside. "I did think I'd look

around and see if there was anything Mildred might want. Did she mention anything?"

"Yes, yes." He lightly clicked his fingers, rings bobbling. "Glad that you brought that up. A bag of dry dog food under the sink and a yellow housecoat. She said to tell you it had daisies on it."

Maira crossed to the farthest bedroom, and rather hurriedly Grover stepped back to the detective and lowered his voice. "No doubt you don't want to say anything worrying in front of a lady, but you are sure that this was just an accident?"

"Do you know anything that would make you think otherwise?"

The fat man's oily smile appeared instantaneously. "Too eager for a little gossip, a little titillation in this dull place, I suppose." As Maira came back with the sack of Puppy Chow and a sprigged housecoat, he remarked to her, "But you'll agree, my dear, that Vieques will become livelier once my museum opens. We'll get stimulating visitors, as well as many more of the ordinary sort of sun-soakers. And, the poor locals will be able to find work."

"Everyone here appreciates your efforts on his or her behalf, Grover," Maira returned, with a sweeping bow of the arm holding the dog food. "In fact, 'Earth from afar has heard thy fame,/And worms have learnt to lisp thy name.'"

"Well, too kind of you." Clay's nod was pleased, but he blinked uncertainly. "Yes. You'll have to come up with an appropriate quotation for the museum inscription. I'll relieve you now of those articles. By the way, Virginia hopes that you can return for lunch. She thinks you have a very soothing effect on poor Mildred." He waved and stepped nimbly out the door.

"Worms lisp his name?" Balthazar raised an eyebrow at Maira.

She tucked her lips mischievously between her teeth, then replied. "People think if you quote poetry at them it's bound to be complimentary. And those lines are too bad to be forgotten. That man deserves even worse. Virginia Kimble spends her summers in the Yale library, and her articles on Melville appear in scholarly journals. Still,

Grover always twinkles at her and asks how her little monographs are going. He inquires about my teaching as if it were an amusing hobby. Where's the word processor?"

It was in a nook rather than a bedroom, a denlike opening off the living room apparently not often used by Luttrell, given its neatness. Balthazar pulled up the white plastic blinds and cranked the windows. Sunlight through the acacias fingered the hanging macramé baskets that held a deeply dispirited, but not dead, Boston fern and a spider plant that had clearly given up the ghost. One of Something New's dark green parrots, suspended in a bamboo ring, twitched its palm tail in the breeze over a long white Formica desk containing a sleek, humming, ivory-and-black Xerox Memorywriter against a side wall. Behind a few of the rows of neat gray squares above its keyboard, red lights glowed. Its high-tech efficiency seemed out of place in the cheerful room. A white couch splashed with flamboyant tropical colors took up another wall, and a wide bookcase layered with outsize gardening books, rows of cookbooks, and china figurines the third.

As she moved toward the machine, Maira was considering that if they found a house with a den like this, she could move her desk out of her bedroom, which she'd have to do if Zar—. It was only at this point that she realized how her desire had sidled past the intellect's sentry. Averting her face, insisting on a change of mental subject, she made a steeple of her fingers. "Is it okay if I slather my fingerprints everywhere?"

"No point in dusting the whole house." His answer was matter-of-fact. "Anyone who delivered the apples personally and stayed for a drink was obviously a friend whose prints could have been left at any time. I've gone through everything except the bookshelves and the disks, but I didn't turn off the machine because I didn't know how to do it without erasing."

"Just as well," she replied, blessing the solidity and neutrality of machinery. "This is a computerized typewriter with a memory rather than a word processor, but unless it's instructed to store, it probably wouldn't. This has a good-sized storage. Ideal machine for the tropics because it doesn't get sulky without air-conditioning." Flipping through the plastic container of unlabeled, new-looking black squares, she commented, "Most of these disks look unused. Is this the only box?"

"All I could find." He began stacking one shelf of books on the couch. A thin volume stuck moistly onto a fat tome entitled *Healthy Eating* slithered to the floor. It was a copy of *The Sepia Mirror*. Retrieving it, he riffled the pages, then laid the book on the desk, pointing to Douglas Blaylock's flowing signature on the title page. "Look at this. Indicate at least an acquaintance with the author?"

"Not really." She nibbled her lip. "Enterprising authors ask if they can sign all the copies in a bookstore's stock because some publishers won't take them back then. And, in any case, this might have been a gift."

"Likely explanation," he agreed, flipping again through the pages. "I didn't see any other books of poems." Recalling Joan Blaylock's sour expression at the dedication, he tapped that page. "Is this different from the usual wording?"

"'Poetry is King. *Vive la poésie, vive le roi*. The first is the last.'" She read it aloud musingly. "Well, usually a person is mentioned, but authors are capricious. One dedicated a book to a brand of underwear that didn't bind when one was seated at the typewriter. This does strike me as a little . . . repetitive." She flipped back to the account of the author's life beneath the photograph on the jacket. "But he was pretty young when he wrote this. I hope that his idealistic belief in the supremacy of poetry didn't fade as he grew older."

Balthazar put the book on the couch arm and picked up another. Inserting the paper, she peered over her shoulder. "You're going through the cookbooks?"

"Basic Detection 101 teaches thoroughness."

His left eyebrow was permanently lifted by a curving white scar which, she decided, added that air of skepticism to what he said, as well as what he heard. He'd inherited the long Irish skull and angular jaw. A sensual mouth, she was thinking, but what she said was, "But Holmes, you're starting with the gardening books. Even if Mildred knew of the peculiar properties of the Fatal Apple, that woman— No. You haven't met her yet."

"She would have had to have a little help from a

friend. It was fresh fruit. Gusto can't believe she could have whipped back and out, unobserved. But the total of those government insurance policies in the desk drawer is impressive. She won't be a bag lady."

Slipping into the chrome-armed leatherette chair before the desk, she remarked, "Last night she was regretting the fact that they'd had his retirement all planned, house paid for, and he didn't live to enjoy it."

"Their lifestyle was pretty comfortable for retirement pay. Mildred might have been frugal all these years, but since he's arrived on the island, Luttrell certainly hasn't been. Even when Mildred was here, he didn't sit at home nursing a bottle of cheap rum. Paid cash for a brand-new jeep. And frequenting bars, eating lobster, doesn't come cheap even on Vieques. I was wondering how they could manage without extra income."

"Mildred mentioned something about his writing, but that seemed to summon up more tears, and I changed the subject. She said twice that she wanted me to know that she'd always bought the food from his *military* income. I don't know what she meant. Makes me curious about these disks. If her husband's work is really terrible, I shall gently suggest the immortal dedication by Julia Moore, the Sweet Singer of Michigan. 'And now, kind friends; what I have wrote,/I hope you will pass o'er,/And not criticise as some have done/Hitherto herebefore.' If you find any good recipes, let me know."

As she pushed several gray squares, the machine clattered obediently and briskly. Her voice rose above it. "This is a list of titles, and the user makes up whatever abbreviation he thinks will help him remember the contents. First one is called 'acct'; the second 'newwork'; the third 'tech.' I'll recall the first title. Okay, and, not surprisingly, it's a letter to his accountant, regarding capital gains on the sale of their house in New Jersey. You'll want that address. Quality printer on these machines—looks professional. Whoo, houses there have gone up considerably in price since I grew up in New York. You could get several beachfront condos for that in San Juan. They had acreage with the house. Difference between what they bought it for and sold it for wasn't that much, though. His writing must have paid a bundle."

Laying a copy of that letter on the couch, she pressed two more squares. Suddenly, she let out a strangled gurgle, and her shoulders twitched. Dropping his copy of *Plants and Flowers of Puerto Rico*, he jumped toward the desk. "What's the matter? Please don't cry, Maira. I'm sorry. I should never have—"

Both hands covering her face, she leaned back in the swivel chair, which rocked with her shaking. "Please, Maira, don't." He pulled her up, and as her hands dropped, he could see that she was overcome with giggles. She pointed helplessly at the machine, moving energetically across the page: "The tall, broad-shouldered man bsrked at her, 'You fitch! On your stomach! Crawl to me!' He lay naked on the bed to watch her. Her breasts were like oranges, with stems. She creeped, forward on the bearskin rug with desire for him, her niggles erect. With writhing buttocks, the rug came as well, jerking across the floor. She begged, 'Let's fock! Or I will die!' "

He blinked, reread, watched the machine sedately typing: "Sucking, sucking hard, she cried out, 'Look at the size of this cuck! I am so wet so wet—' "

Sinking back down on the couch, he groaned. "Porn."

Wiping smeared mascara from under each eye carefully, Maira slipped back in the desk chair. She glanced at the typewriter, turned and said quietly, "His pesticles are big, too. Size of plums." The printer stopped and *Insert Paper* flashed greenly. "Zar, I'm thinking of assigning this page to my beginning composition class, asking them to correct all errors of spelling, grammar, and punctuation. Everyone would do their homework."

"Could he make money from this? Is it . . . saleable?"

"I'm not up on the smut market, what readers want. But in the preface of *Delta of Venus*, Anaïs Nin explained why she turned to writing erotica. Kid needed glasses, telephone bill wasn't paid. But she said that she started inventing glorious sexual fantasies and every time the publisher kept saying, 'Leave out the poetry.' No matter how clinical she got, every time the guy said the same thing. 'No flowery stuff.' At that time, right after the depression, she was getting a dollar a page. It probably doesn't pay a whole lot better today. Crowded field—a number of people whose spirits are willing, even if their imaginations are weak."

Picking up the first plant book on the pile next to him, he flipped the pages quickly and turned to the index. "I'll bypass Mildred on that question, take it up with the accountant. If you'll show me the right buttons, I'll print the rest of it out."

"I consider this research," she returned resolutely, twirling a new sheet into the carriage, "and I will sacrifice myself."

A moment later, he complained, "Your whoops and snickers are distracting me from this very interesting cholesterol-free diet book."

"No one but an English professor could possibly benefit from this. It's all dominance and phallus-worship. A decent person could not find it sexually stimulating." She sailed another completed page over her head at the couch.

He read a few lines, and then carefully arranged a large book on orchids over his lap. "You're right. Disgusting, absolutely disgusting. But this bit about putting the champagne 'bobbles'—"

"Wait," she interrupted seriously, stopping the Memorywriter. "Come here and read this line."

Carrying the orchid book over, he leaned behind her and saw, "She screaded with pleasure. 'If only Braylots could make me feel like this! But he has only a' she wivvled her little finger to show..."

He went over it again. "Are we reading Braylots for Blaylock because we were just discussing him? Is that what you're thinking?"

Putting both elbows on the sides of the machine, she studied the screen gravely. "Well, if he does have a writer in mind for that name, Luttrell would have been drummed out of the Porn Manufacturers of America on the grounds of intentional use of his inventive powers."

"Something to check on. I don't think it would have occurred to me to ask Mildred Luttrell about the Blaylocks."

"You know, Zar, I can see why they assign detectives

in pairs. Feeding into each other's ideas. You're probably missing Sixto."

"Not at all," he said truthfully, picking a petal off her shoulder. "*He* doesn't know a thing about the smut market."

11

"I was just dialing you, *Baltasar,* when the lab technician handed me this report." The popcorn crackle in the long-distance connection emphasized the animation in Sixto Cardenas' voice. "He said you wanted a rush check for fingerprints on the *manzanillos.*"

"Not exactly. Here on Vieques, we don't use the words 'rush,' 'fast,' or 'pronto.' Breathing and sweating take up all available energy," Balthazar replied, as he draped a sodden handkerchief over the metal desk corner. The creeks of perspiration were at least trickling coolly down his back now. Only minutes before he'd panted into the refuge of the air-conditioned Vieques police station as a survival measure. He hadn't really expected the report from San Juan yet.

"The apples," his partner continued, "seemed not to have been touched by human hands. Is this good news?"

"Cuts seriously into my Atlantic swim time." Balthazar reached across the dusty desktop for a pencil, abstractedly bouncing it on its eraser. "But it's what I expected. Makes accidental poisoning questionable in the death here of an ex-chopper pilot. But the guy was not the type to wash fruit painstakingly and stick it into the refrigerator with a pair of tongs."

"You miss the excitement of San Juan already? You have to go looking for work to keep awake? What made you suspicious of clean apples?" Sixto sounded as if he were anchored to the ground only by the phone cord, a

118

Introducing the first and only complete hardcover collection of Agatha Christie's mysteries

Now you can enjoy the
greatest mysteries ever written
in a magnificent
Home Library Edition.

Discover Agatha Christie's world of mystery, adventure and intrigue

Agatha Christie's timeless tales of mystery and suspense offer something for every reader—mystery fan or not—young and old alike. And now, you can build a complete hardcover library of her world-famous mysteries by subscribing to The Agatha Christie Mystery Collection.

This exciting Collection is your passport to a world where mystery reigns supreme. Volume after volume, you and your family will enjoy mystery reading at its very best.

You'll meet Agatha Christie's world-famous detectives like Hercule Poirot, Jane Marple, and the likeable Tommy and Tuppence Beresford.

In your readings, you'll visit Egypt, Paris, England and other exciting destinations where murder is always on the itinerary. And wherever you travel, you'll become deeply involved in some of the most ingenious and diabolical plots ever invented... "cliff-hangers" that only Dame Agatha could create!

It all adds up to mystery reading that's so good...it's almost criminal. And it's yours every month with The Agatha Christie Mystery Collection.

Solve the greatest mysteries of all time. The Collection contains all of Agatha Christie's classic works including *Murder on the Orient Express, Death on the Nile, And Then There Were None, The ABC Murders* and her ever-popular whodunit, *The Murder of Roger Ackroyd.*

Each handsome hardcover volume is Smythe sewn and printed on high quality acid-free paper so it can withstand even the most murderous treatment. Bound in Sussex-blue simulated leather with gold titling, The Agatha Christie Mystery Collection will make a tasteful addition to your living room, or den.

Ride the Orient Express for 10 days without obligation.
To introduce you to the Collection, we're inviting you to examine the classic mystery, *Murder on the Orient Express*, without risk or obligation. If you're not completely satisfied, just return it within 10 days and owe nothing.

However, if you're like the millions of other readers who love Agatha Christie's thrilling tales of mystery and suspense, keep *Murder on the Orient Express* and pay just $9.95 plus postage and handling.

You will then automatically receive future volumes once a month as they are published on a fully returnable, 10-day free-examination basis. No minimum purchase is required, and you may cancel your subscription at any time.

This unique collection is not sold in stores. It's available only through this special offer. So don't miss out, begin your subscription now. Just mail this card today.

☐ Yes! Please send me *Murder on the Orient Express* for a 10-day free-examination and enter my subscription to <u>The Agatha Christie Mystery Collection</u>. If I keep *Murder on the Orient Express*, I will pay just $9.95 plus postage and handling and receive one additional volume each month on a fully returnable 10-day free-examination basis. There is no minimum number of volumes to buy, and I may cancel my subscription at any time.   70110

Name_____

Address_____

City_____State_____Zip_____

QB123
Send No Money...
But Act Today!

NO POSTAGE
NECESSARY
IF MAILED
IN THE
UNITED STATES

BUSINESS REPLY MAIL

FIRST CLASS   PERMIT NO. 2154   HICKSVILLE, N.Y.

Postage will be paid by addressee:

The Agatha Christie
Mystery Collection
Bantam Books
P.O. Box 956
Hicksville, N.Y. 11802

condition brought on, Balthazar was sure, by the anticipated two days with the delightful Dr. Silva Casas.

"Let me tell you," the New Yorker groaned, starting to sketch a butterfly on his notebook cover. "Carillo, the CIC agent here, is in Humacao with gout. So when I . . ."

At the end of his account, he heard only silence. Even the static had disappeared. "Sixto, are you there? What'd you think?"

"That," his partner responded thoughtfully, "if you had not arrived, it *would* have been an accidental poisoning. But it was not, I agree."

"Gusto Mulero is a good man, though, no mistake. It's just that he has to look down the U.S. Navy's big guns every day, and he wants to keep low. He lives here. Imagine asking the military for background information on a retired officer when your suspicions regarding his death are based on the man's untidy personal habits."

"Yet *you* plan to do this?" Sixto was obviously relishing the idea.

"Come Tuesday morning." Balthazar grinned. "*I* live on the next island over. The look on some commander's face will be worth the price of admission. But what I'm really curious about is the possible tie to the Blaylock case, flimsy as it is."

"Perhaps, *Baltasar*, Mrs. Blaylock, on her return to Vieques, will have some information on the Luttrells."

"If so, it'll probably take the Heimlich maneuver to get it out of her," Balthazar grunted.

"Anyone there who can tell you anything useful?"

Balthazar drew quizzical antennas on the small head above the outspread wings. "You ask these people a question, they break into song, and the accompanying dance is spectacular. What's more, I get the feeling everybody's playing musical chairs behind my back. Yet when I turn around, they're chatting to each other, hands folded in their laps, feet stuck to the floor. But . . . you said you were calling me for something?"

"To give you my phone number for Sunday and Monday since Inez and I will be in the mountains here. Together. In the Monte Guilarte forest. It is very cool.

And faraway. Many miles from San Juan." He read off the number.

Jotting it down, Balthazar blinked. "Sixto. That's the number here at the Vieques police station."

"I know," the young man responded happily. "But I gave this one to my mother. For emergencies. And when, *Baltasar,* has my mother gotten through two days without an emergency?" The widowed Señora Cardenas had dissolved in worried tears when her only son joined the Puerto Rican *Policía.* But she'd become reconciled when she saw the advantage of having Sixto at the end of a car radio, easily locatable. His colleagues cheerfully fielded messages, even stopping by if they were in the neighborhood, to reassure the anxious woman. Señora Cardenas's coffee was excellent and her kitchen was always well stocked. "By the way," Sixto concluded, "Mama says you must come to dinner soon and she will make us *pasteles.*"

Thinking of a plateful of this delicious version of the Mexican tamale with lean pork enfolded in a green banana paste wrapped in a plaintain leaf, Balthazar said graciously, "I'd be happy to take calls for you while you have unfortunately just stepped out of the Vieques station. Is there a phone where you *can* be reached?"

"No, no. Inez would give it out to her answering service, and even though another dentist is covering for her, she feels deep interest in every twinge in a patient's tooth. I have left directions to this highly desirable mountain cabin here at headquarters. You may want to rent it yourself. But . . . one more thing."

The pause was so long that Balthazar had just started to reach for the button, assuming they'd been cut off, when Sixto blurted, "I need to think of something . . . nice to say to Inez."

"Like what?"

"Exactly," Sixto replied gloomily. "What? One is holding her hand, and one wishes to say a sweet something. And, you know, in the soap operas, the movies, those Latin lovers all seem to be . . . you know?"

"Silver-tongued devils?" Balthazar offered. "I see your point. Hollywood was irresponsible there. Hard to live up to the stereotype."

"One cannot," Sixto pointed out, with a touch of despair, "just keep saying, 'You are truly lovely,' even if this is what one is sincerely thinking."

"Nothing wrong with mentioning it a time or two, of course." Balthazar was now trying to sketch a pair of delicate lips, only to find that the outline more closely resembled a seagull above a scooped wave. He felt any advice he could come up with would be equally inadequate. He stared uneasily down into this gap in his own experience.

"Of course—" Sixto seemed to be considering cheerful alternatives. "I am—all Puerto Ricans, that is—are good kissers."

"Must be perfect, considering the continual practice I see in cars all over San Juan. And that's always good. But what do you admire about Inez personally?"

"She is so gentle . . . kind. Sometimes I arrive at her waiting room early and I listen to her talking to her patients. I can imagine this frightened person, clutching very hard the arms of the chair. Her voice is so soothing. Even in the other room, I can hear the patient's jaw muscles unclenching. But that is not . . . *romantic*."

"But she'll like that," Balthazar said, smiling in relief. "Trust me."

12

"**. . .** **Y**OU'RE EATING cooked shrimp shit," Howard Yung was explaining to Balthazar in a low voice. "That's why I shell and devein them *before* I boil them. It makes them fluff out, too."

The Chinese restauranteur was presiding over a long folding table covered with hors d'oeuvres and orchids, set on the wooden dock by the Beach and Tennis Club. Cold Caribbean shrimp, the size of small drumsticks, were curled between slices of moist pink smoked salmon and the bright red shells of cracked crab. Golden papaya-and-pineapple salad was heaped on crinkly lettuce. The grape leaves of Greek dolmades ("had to use pork instead of lamb," Yung had confided) glistened next to moist goat cheese and black olives. The wine-dark slices of Chinese drunken chicken were surrounded by rice balls and fingerling barbecued ribs. Scooped-out watermelon shells held green honeydew melon and peach-colored mango chunks, as well as bite-size strawberries. Scattered everywhere were intricately carved radishes and cherry tomatoes, fan-shaped carrot sticks, marinated snow peas, and julienned peppers.

The detective had also just spotted a bowl of octopus salad and was wondering if there was room on his heaped plate. "International cuisine tonight," he said, before biting into the sweet, solid flesh of a shrimp, thus opening up a small corner of the plate.

Nodding, Yung flipped a crisp, delicate scallion pancake over on the sizzling frying pan perched on a portable gas grill. "The problem was that she said keep the food pretty light because some people would want to take a dip in the bay later, but not too salady because there'd be naval officers coming. Last party of the year for the Kimbles, but the Lotus will be busy tonight, too. Had to get the souvenir guy to do the veg. Thought he'd be pretty good with his hands." He flipped his thumb toward Something New, who was now attaching his woven angelfish around the metal frame of the canvas roof of the boat's midsection. The floating fish, filaments of palm strings waving in the soft evening breeze, gave the Vieques Divers craft, rented for the occasion, the appearance of a gaily fringed surrey. As he worked, the artisan murmured, "Han'made souvenirs, han'made souvenirs," listing his wares musically, not forgetting to make the word grasshopper jump or to sound the bass on the frog.

"Do you know," Yung lowered his voice, although there was no possibility that the craftsman could overhear him, "that he keeps up that singsong even when he's chopping peppers? Chants like a Buddhist monk. He gets right on with things, though. No chitchat. And when I gave him lunch, he took it outside to eat by himself. Heard him giggle a bit at his fortune cookie. Pleasant enough—not one of your morose-type loners. Maybe his lip muscles just get too tired in his regular line of work for him to bother with gossip."

"Or," Balthazar suggested gravely, "he may be aware of the Spanish proverb: 'Many a man's tongue has broken his nose.'"

"Hm. I've never heard that one. It'll work right into my Charlie Chan routine."

Ice clattered noisily as bags were unloaded into plastic-lined paint buckets. The boat owner and his mate, doubling as bartenders, then added a liter of rum to the golden mixture of juice and fruit on another flower-bedecked table at the end of the wooden pier. Balthazar noted that the placard with the Vieques Divers slogan, "Come Down with VD," had been removed from the deck of the boat.

"Here, eat this. I do these perfectly." Yung wrapped the edge of the steaming pancake in a napkin and handed it to the detective. "Watch it—it's hot!"

"Old family recipe passed down from father to son?" Balthazar asked, the oniony fragrance making his mouth water.

"My father was a good cook," Yung responded, "but he usually fixed—" He stopped himself, inspected new rounds of bubbling batter. "Well, he was only half Chinese. By the way, I told Mrs. Kimble I'd take Mildred up some of this food when you all leave on the boat, sit with her for a bit. Got a nice bit of Peking duck that the maid can heat up for her too. Mildred always likes that with plum sauce. I guess she's not eating, but if I look upset and hint that she doesn't like what I fixed, she'll make herself swallow something. Maid has to stay later because I'm coming by." His eyes slanted upwards in amused half-moons, and he happily smoothed a starched white jacket. "Makes me feel dashing—as if Mildred thinks that without a chaperone, she'd immediately yield to my middle-aged Oriental charm."

Although the dying sun had slipped behind the island's western hills, it had bequeathed all its colors to the placid Caribbean which then gracefully lent a citrine glow to the southern cove. Balthazar turned to the land's end of the dock, watching Maira, who stood beside the Kimbles, talking to another couple. She wore a pale yellow ankle-length T-shirt over her bathing suit. A bandeau of satiny orange circled her waist. The wind was already loosening the prim bun of her hair, bound with a matching ribbon. The golden air shimmered around her. His knee twinged a reminder that he'd not had time to stretch it in a swim, and his whole body ached with pleasure at the thought of diving with her into the dark water.

As more guests arrived behind them, the first couple detached themselves from the Kimbles. Although he looked in his early forties, the man's red hair had not dulled, or else the fading sun was adding copper. He advanced with an outstretched hand, his narrow face collielike. He had a friendly-dog glint in eyes that were set a little too closely above the nose. "Stewart Connell. Call me Stew." His beige-caftaned wife, who had an Afghan's hauteur, lingered before the buffet as if she would be called on later to list the items.

"You like try shrimp? I make pancake?" Yung asked her, his hands clutched over his forearms as if hidden in kimono sleeves.

"Navy?" Stew inquired after carefully repeating Balthazar's name.

"No. I'm here on business. Are you in the service?"

"A commander—stationed at Roosevelt Roads," Connell replied with a complacent modesty. "Ah, Vieques is paradise. Partly cloudy here, of course, but then most places are now."

Balthazar's puzzled expression stopped him, and he jerked his head first toward the black mate on the boat, then at Something New. "And you know," Stew continued, "the Puerto Ricans just don't have any eye for that. Intermarry, don't seem to care about color. Funniest thing." He took a gulp of his drink, and leaned his head nearer to the detective's. "One other little problem here: they don't push the bilingual hard enough. Some of the locals can't get restaurant jobs because their English isn't good enough. Too bad."

"I've noticed," Balthazar said in a clipped tone, "that bilingualism seems to mean that both Anglos and Hispanics speak only English."

"Only way," Stew said seriously. Gesturing expansively, he commented, "Kimble's parties are always a treat. Pleasant man. And this is the only time I ever seem to get to the bioluminescent bay. We—the navy, I mean—have made sure that's been preserved. You have to keep the balance between fresh and salt water so the dinoflagellates won't die. Little organisms—they're what makes the shining when any movement disturbs them. Only a few of the island residents truly understand what we've done for this place. I could detail—" At this point he interrupted himself, looked carefully at the group of new arrivals, and waved himself off.

As if they'd synchronized watches, these guests appeared together. In a cluster they surrounded the drinks table, then lined up in formation before Yung's sumptuous repast. Maira laid butterfly fingers on Balthazar's arm, "And did you inspect the food as Virginia ordered?"

"I had three of everything. Without me, Yung would

have had glorious leftovers for tomorrow's fried rice. What can I get you?"

"In a minute I will descend, teeth gleaming, on those shrimp. But I think I'll abstain from the rum punch until the way back. I've been to this season's-end party before and the bay swim is the best part."

"Have you met most of these people before?"

"I don't know. Last year, a retired stockbroker told me that going to the beach ate up the day, so he'd had to cancel his *Wall Street Journal* subscription. Five minutes ago, someone else made the exact same remark, but I don't think it was the same person. There's always the navy, and the St. Thomas crowd."

Balthazar tilted his head toward Lyle Templeton, who stood at the bar, refreshing a clear drink. "Does he look familiar?"

"No. And I don't think I've ever seen a better toupee. When Virginia introduced him, she mentioned that he'd only arrived a few months ago."

Suddenly, overriding the high chatter and scattered laughter on the dock, Santo's voice resounded from the shore. "It is fit that we gather for vespers to praise the Lord who has made all this possible. He made the sun and the sea. The sea, which has an enormous thirst, is salt and it contains the scaly little fishes. Their tender flesh, after appropriate degutting and skin removal, sustains us."

At the intrusion, Elliott Kimble's protruding Adam's apple bobbed in anger. Glaring at the ectomorphic white-clad figure, he then swiveled and caught sight of Balthazar, and apparently decided he was the appropriate man to deal with a nuisance. Charging over, he'd almost reached the policeman, when Templeton stopped him.

"Elliott, old man," he said conversationally, "from past experience, I'd say the best way to close down Santo there is to give him a nice plate of food. No fuss, no pack drill that way."

Kimble's face relaxed into a minimalist's smile. He inclined his long neck toward Templeton. "Perhaps you'd see to that."

"Glad to. And something too for Something New?" He gestured amusedly toward the palm-weaver behind

Santo like a dark shadow, packing up his baskets. Elliott bent his head in fretful assent, then turned toward the largest group, assembled near the drinks table.

". . . and although we mourn the sun, we must remember that stars are not seen by sunshine," Santo's voice still reverberated, but the guests resumed their conversations as Kimble moved through the crowd, making dry jokes about the uninvited "chaplain."

"No," Yung was saying as Templeton reached for the dolmades. "Not for Santo. And no peppers. Bothers his stomach. Not sure about those spicy pea pods. Rice balls'd be good. Give the other guy a lot of fish—he's probably sick of veg." The two of them went down the long table, consulting together. As Templeton approached with the laden plates, Santo speeded toward an amen. Something New finished packing and squatted expectantly down on the sand.

Collecting glasses of punch for the two men, Maira started to follow Templeton. Balthazar intercepted her, held out his hands for the drinks, pointing out that the platter of shrimp was being rapidly depleted. Templeton's blond hairpiece bobbed ahead of him, heading for the shore.

When Santo saw the detective's tall figure approaching, he put down the plate he'd just been handed and scrambled up from his lotus position on the beach. In meek irritation, he reached around his back, jerked up his cotton shift, and drew out something apparently tucked beneath the elastic band of his underwear. He first relieved Balthazar of one of the plastic glasses and then, with a flourish, handed the detective a square folded in Saran Wrap. His hazel eyes, sunk into a skeleton's deep sockets, had a triumphant gleam as if his prompt production of the paper were sure to discomfit the policeman. As he sank down and rearranged his heavily callused feet and hairless knobby legs, he intoned, "Render unto Caesar."

Plucking the other glass from Balthazar's hand, Templeton put it into the outstretched fingers raised diffidently by the palm-weaver. Something New settled his drink securely into a sand hollow, and throwing covert glances at the detective, began vaguely patting his jeans pockets as if wondering where he'd left his wallet. Templeton hovered over Balthazar as he untangled the clinging synthetic.

Santo finished chewing a chunk of lobster, swallowed, and remarked with satisfaction, "Just as the lilies of the field, which neither toil nor spin, are dressed by the Lord God, He also feeds his servants." He picked up a fat crab leg, and waved its tip at the parchment Balthazar had opened up. "Praise to Him who also provides the proper documents."

The discolored gold lettering, arched across the top, spelled out in ornate calligraphy, "Pentecostal Assembly of the Holy Testifiers." Although the once-stiff paper was quite worn at the folds, the typed name "Richard León Reyes of Los Angeles, California" was easily legible on the black line above the paragraph which certified this person as a minister. Several paragraphs followed, detailing the rights and duties of said minister. A metallic starburst decorated the bottom.

"Mail order?" Templeton asked Santo brightly, after a quick perusal.

"Correspondence classes," Santo retorted stiffly, his pallid face expressionless. "A great deal of Bible study was required."

"Los Angeles. You are a long way from home, Mr. Reyes," Balthazar remarked, gazing down at preacher's head again bent over his plate. Only the faintest touch of salmon pink distinguished the flesh from the thin white hair. A Chicano albino? Balthazar wondered.

The evangelist jerked his face upward, glaring. "My name is now *Santo*. The very name Reyes speaks of worldly monarchs, of all that I have renounced. And I have not returned to California for years. During the...even when I was a young man," he amended, "God was preparing me for my life's work. I dreamed one night; when I awoke I knew I was to go to Mexico to discover my true origins."

"During the Vietnam war? Is that what you were going to say?" Lyle Templeton inserted with interest. "Do you mean you were avoiding the draft?"

"God appeared to me in the desert in Baja! He told me that I must live to save others," Santo shrilled. "I have been to all the world's holy places, seeking enlightenment. I visited the shrines of the Mayans and the Aztecs. I have studied in Tibet. I am a sanctified man, dedicated to God." The bony fingers holding a papaya slice trembled.

Handing back the creased parchment, Balthazar said calmingly, "You are not required to show me any identification." He was reflecting that, in offering that particular document, Santo had not done so in any case. In apparent relief, Something New stopped his pocket-patting, and picked up a barbecued rib with both hands.

Still indignant, Santo thrust his certificate in front of the artisan's nose, demanding that it be read aloud. Something New's eyes darted over the paper in alarm, then focused on the red sauce on his fingertips. Licking two brown fingers apologetically, he shook his head.

"See here, see here," Santo insisted, tapping a paragraph at the bottom. "Tell them what it says! They will not believe me. Read it to these doubting Thomases."

Without getting up, Something New edged away, sliding on his shanks across the sand, his plate in one hand, drink in the other. His eyes were stricken as he muttered, "Can't read."

Holding his certificate at arm's length, Santo squinted. "As noted here," he began, then stopped and leaned his head back as far as he could, peering at it again. Finally, in frustration he waved the paper over his head, shouting, "It says that I am entitled to spread the word of God, that I may instruct and teach! Everywhere."

"Zar!" The detective turned to see Maira standing by the boat, beckoning to him. The drink table had been transferred on board by the two Vieques divers and, lemminglike, most of the guests were following. The Kimbles were rounding up stragglers. Yung and an agile teenager were rapidly loading boxes of food in the blue pickup.

Taking anxious note of the disappearing food, Santo picked up his half-empty plate and scurried toward the truck, throwing an incensed scowl over his shoulder. Something New, clutching his own plate, scuttled after him without a backward glance.

"I see it now," Lyle Templeton said musingly as they walked down the pier. "Santo's condition is a combination of sun-fried brains and sun-dried Mexican mushrooms. Peyote, of course. Causes hallucinations, I'm told. It could bring on paranoiac behavior, too."

When the detective made no reply. Templeton added darkly, "I never thought of it before, but the man might bear watching. Santo could be just a harmless crank, but religious fanatics sometimes get the idea they're God's vigilantes. The next step is cleansing the world of evil men. And they can be sneaky. No one pays Santo any attention—he just drifts around the island, could be up to anything." He shuddered. "Once your brain has been zapped by a powerful drug, who knows? Best thing is to stick to good old alcohol. Then you know where you are."

13

SQUEEZING NEXT TO BALTHAZAR in the space-and-a-half he'd managed to preempt on the built-in seats in the boat's stern, Maira gently patted her stomach. "Wonderful food—I'm replete. Nothing could disturb my good cheer. Or, as the poet put it so notably: 'Irks care the crop-full bird? Frets doubt the maw-crammed beast?'"

"Another melodious line from the Sweet Singer of Michigan?" Balthazar asked, slipping an arm behind her to make more room.

"Actually, that's Robert Browning—on an off day, of course."

"I should have put Sixto on hold this afternoon and called *you* for a soulfully romantic quote to give him." As the more raucous party-goers shouted around them, he told her about the afternoon's conversation.

She laughed in delight. "How sweet of Sixto—to plan a compliment! But he could probably get away with whispering baseball scores. He has those warm, speaking eyes—his heart shines through."

"He is handsome, isn't he?" Balthazar sounded more than a little crestfallen.

"Oh yes—but *young*. Your response couldn't have been better, Zar." Maira quickly changed the focus of the conversation. "She'll feel Sixto is thinking about her, and not her beautiful eyes. While we women long to have men sing of our perfections on lutes of amber, we're always afraid that your love will fade when we catch a drippy cold."

"Colds are not a problem. I am not so sure about the mustard plasters on the chest."

The boat rocked as the mate cast off the thick rope, and drinks sloshed in overfull glasses as the standing guests giggled and grabbed for handholds. The motor roared, and general conversation stopped abruptly. People turned to stare at the technicolor ocean. The light left in the sky was now only the day's memory.

Balthazar leaned back, and let the wind lift his hair. The water's cool spray filmed his cheeks. Then he felt Maira's warm breath on his ear. "You had a long talk with Mildred—did she know Blaylock?"

"No." He put his own lips next to her ear, thinking it an ideal way to communicate. "Never heard the name. Didn't know a damned thing about her husband's business affairs. Says he was a helicopter pilot in Brazil for an American company before Vietnam, then joined the military. That's where she met Chet."

"Doug might have met him since they were both—"

With the tips of his fingers, he turned her chin closer. "I can't hear you," he lied.

"I said they might have known each other there. Says on the book jacket that Blaylock served in Peru in the Peace Corps."

"Hardly a hop, skip, and jump apart."

"You," she smiled accusingly, "are aspirating your *h*'s with unnecessary vehemence. I'm curious. Were there any apples that Luttrell didn't eat?"

"Two."

"Did you send them for fingerprinting?"

"Yes."

"And?"

"No."

"There weren't any fingerprints? When did you find that out?"

"This afternoon."

"Zar, why are you speaking in such short sentences?"

"Elementary. So you'll keep blowing in my ear."

*   *   *

The wife of the naval commander also had her husband's ear. "You didn't circulate enough, Stew. This is the only party of the Kimbles we've been invited to this year. You didn't say two words to *her*. You completely ignored Captain Vandier, and you know how much he likes to have someone standing by to fetch drinks for him. And *he's* such a close friend of Rear Admiral Jeffries." Her snarl was smooth and sustained.

"But, honey, I—"

"After all this time, your social skills are on the level of a warrant officer's. There was no point in bothering with that good-looking blonde. She was here last year, but her jewelry's all silver. And why were you talking with the help?"

"Who?"

"That attractive man in the back that the blonde is nuzzling. I heard he was a policeman. Probably only here for security. He could even be Puerto Rican, even though he's tall. He's got dark hair. And there you stand for five valuable minutes—"

"I've got a secret," he interrupted, desperate for a distraction. "But you can't tell anybody. The admiral's moved up the date of his visit."

"So?"

"Well, he's getting here Monday instead of Wednesday. We'd planned a big show for later in the week, after the island cleared out. Night bombardment over here. Show him what we can do. But Jeffries and Vandier got to talking in the club about what to do to commemorate the war dead for Memorial Day. Guess what I came up with?"

"What?"

"I said why not make the bombardment a real tribute to the fallen navy heroes? We take the admiral out for what he thinks is just a routine shelling, and then whammo! Battle stations, all guns blazing. Tracer bullets, magnesium flares. It'll light up the sky Monday night. It'll be a welcome to the admiral and a real nice observance of the holiday. *But*, no one's going to be told until the last minute so the surprise won't leak out. Promise you won't breathe a word?"

*   *   *

Virginia Kimble was staring at the dark ocean sliced cleanly by the boat's prow, curls of white water like wood shavings beneath the running lights. "Elliott, I think this is the first end-of-the-year party that Grover's ever missed. And he invited a guest—then didn't come himself."

"Who?" Kimble cranked his head peevishly to look at the assemblage, but it was already becoming difficult to distinguish faces.

"That Templeton man. At least I didn't send him an invitation. Did you ask him to come along?"

"No. Only know him to nod at when I see him in a bar. Pleasant enough fellow, though. Bit of a compulsive talker, but asks questions, knows good business sense when he hears it. Probably does know Grover. Is he all right, do you think? Grover, I mean."

"He *should* lose a great deal of weight, of course. Traveling does make dieting difficult, and he naturally has to sample the food for his articles. But this afternoon he looked . . . pasty, like an underdone muffin. Still he didn't say he was ill, just tired—thought he'd stay at home, which is odd because he'll have to fix his own food. No cook. George has gone to visit relatives for the weekend."

Kimble smoothed his wind-ruffled hair. "I was thinking about his mental well-being. This afternoon he was quite agitated about Luttrell's death. Says he's sure it wasn't an accident, and that Marten shares that idea."

"Why should that bother old Grover? Does he think there's some mad fruit-pusher here? He can't have had any connection himself with Luttrell surely?"

Her husband's compressed lips made Virginia lift her eyebrows in surprise. "They had some minor business dealings in the past," he finally answered reluctantly. "And after talking to Mildred this morning, he's concerned that she knows of that . . . affair."

"Heavens! That's absurd. She's not the sort to take an interest in business matters, become an active partner. It would bore her as much as it does me. But when Grover gets going, he does gallop off in all directions, doesn't he? Now whenever he utters the word 'museum,' I briskly insert a comment on the weather. On this island that definitely taxes one's ingenuity."

*   *   *

At the mangrove-shrouded entrance to the inland bay, the boat's engine was cut to a hum. The arching foliage and erratic up-and-down growth of the stilt roots obscured the evening sky, whose last clutch on light made the stars aloof. The covered lights of the prow picked out only the upward grasping branches of an occasional overwhelmed tree that had ventured out too far. The night's surrounding blackness had the density and sound absorbance of velvet pile. Dramatically, the captain flicked off the lights and stilled the engine entirely. None of the guests let out a whisper. The silent swoopings of the bats were felt rather than seen. The deck swayed gently in the swish and suck of the inrushing salt water on one side and the outgoing thrust of the fresh on the other.

Then the boat's two front lights came on, and Virginia Kimble called out gaily, "Swimmers, prepare to dip." Shouts, laughter, and noisy scramblings to kick off sandals and pull off shirts filled the quiet bay. Elliott Kimble was the first to dive in and, as he did so, the water burst into fire. He surfaced directly and waved encouragingly.

"Wait for me, Zar." Maira's muffled appeal came as she struggled to pull the long cotton gown over her head. "You'll love this!" She joined him poised on the railing, and he caught only a glimpse of white suit on white skin as she flashed into the bay. Plunging after her, he was startled at the warmth of the water. Its buoyancy almost thrust him back to the surface. When he came up, he saw Maira's arms and legs dazzlingly outlined in diamonds. As she floated on her back, each loose curl and tendril sparkled. She was a creature of light. Reaching an arm toward her, he found that it was coated in a sleeve of gleaming, weightless mail.

A child's pink rubber ball, dashed with glitter, surfaced beside him. It was Lyle Templeton's head, his hairpiece apparently safely stowed on board. "Why do these creatures glow?" He ran pianist's fingers over a phosphorescent piano before swimming away.

"To attract males to females," Balthazar said, lunging for Maira's leg.

"I don't think so." She avoided his grasp by nimbly flipping toward him. "That's what fireflies do, but without us, these little guys would just be groping in the dark."

"I wish we were," he said grumpily, noticing that the swimmers' surface movements were clearly visible to those on deck. "I thought there'd be just a little glow, instead of fluorescent lights. We could, of course, hide out under those trees near the shore."

"There are probably all kinds of crawly things round there. And, if he'd been born in the tropics, Edgar Allan Poe would have lined all his ghoul-haunted weirs with mangroves. Those dangling brown fruits like dead fingers, waiting to catch hold. That's how they propagate, you know, advancing farther and farther from the shore. If they can find something to hold on to, their roots can live in air. Now that I think of it, those trees seem to be creeping nearer when we're not looking."

"Best to stay very close to me," he advised, circling her waist with his arm.

Some of the women lay gracefully back, making water angels with their arms, or stretching out hands that looked gem-bedizened. The men were ducking and diving like noisy porpoises in the gilded water. Finally, they tired of fish-play and, by twos and threes, climbed exuberantly back on board. Towel-snappings and the clink of ice cubes echoed through the enclosed inlet. Maira and Balthazar floated, shoulders touching, gazing upwards at stars lit with even greater phosphoresence in a night sky untainted by artificial light. "I feel," she sighed contentedly, "like a happy amoeba in the warm beginning-of-the-world soup."

Glancing over, he thought she was all evolution could ever hope to accomplish.

At last they, too, headed regretfully back toward the boat. As she pulled herself up, Maira wiggled her foot, as if shedding a jeweled ankle bracelet.

"It wasn't easy saving dry towels for you two and Elliott, but I am the perfect hostess." Virginia smilingly handed them each one. "Get yourself drinks and there are platters of lobster salad sandwiches about. I ordered this perfect starry night so we can take a spin about the Caribbean. Now if I can just locate my husband—" She scanned the now dark water towards the shore. "Must be on the other side of the boat." She disappeared through the crowd. But before Balthazar had done more than dry his face and towel his hair, she was back with a puckered forehead and a trembling lip. "I can't find Elliott. He's not on board and you can see he's not in the water. Elliott!"

The plea, the quiver in her voice stopped conversation. The boat owner, a squat, heavy-shouldered man with overlong arms, spun from behind a makeshift bar and abruptly flipped on overhead lights that yellowed the surprised faces of the party-goers. The suspended palm fish, which had seemed to be swimming lightly in the dark air, now jumped jerkily in the brightness. Each person stared first at his neighbor, then uneasily over the side, as if their host were lurking below in an incongruous game of hide-and-seek.

"Any chance he could have gotten tangled in those roots near shore?" Balthazar asked the worried captain.

"Only place he could be. You could sure see him if he were out in the open. Even if he'd taken a cramp, he'd bob right up in this water. Wait, I got a couple of underwater lights." He rummaged in a side storage compartment along the hull. "Took most of the scuba gear out to make room, but there's these." He clicked one on with trembling fingers, slipped it onto his forehead like a snorkeler's mask, and handed the other to the detective.

Balthazar adjusted the black rubber strap on his head, raised his voice. "We'll need six or seven strong swimmers. Fan out like the spokes on a wheel. Swim directly to the shore. Keep checking on the man next to you. When you get to the trees, move slowly clockwise. You," he pointed to the captain, "go off the prow, I'll take the stern. Three men on each side."

This time, the undressing was quiet and very quick. Templeton, and a few other men, grimaced shamefacedly at their drinks, as if to say the amount they'd consumed would make them victims themselves. "Virginia," the detective turned to the hostess, whose fingers were clamped on Maira's arm, "you assign a watcher for every swimmer. That person doesn't take their eyes off the man they're assigned." Still holding the younger woman's arm, she moved quickly to obey. Those who had been hesitant to take to the water volunteered for this duty with relief.

He clambered up on the stern, swiftly checked on all the poised men, and dived back in. The beam on his forehead tunneled the water, sending a few tiny tadpoles scurrying to escape it. When he came up for air, it swung crazily through the drooping leaves like a frantic beacon searching for a lost plane. Even with its aid, below the bright surface the water was murky, and its salt stung his straining eyes. The only objects he could easily pick out were the floating foot-long mangrove fruits, brushing against the body in tentative hope of anchorage. He saw no fish, then realized that the mix of salt and fresh water was not hospitable to species who preferred one or the other.

As he neared the shoreline, the glossy underwater branches undulated like giant plastic aquarium plants. At a glance they looked impenetrable, and he could see the enormity of the task. The men without lights, dependent only on the water's eerie glow, would really be hampered. But would Kimble have been so foolish as to swim far beneath the mangroves? Surely the best strategy would be to first execute a quick semicircle through his half of the bay, letting his beam hit the outer layers. Or was he telling himself that because he had no desire to push through that algae-covered tangle that seemed to be reaching out for him?

Surfacing, snatching a quick breath, he battled down again, marveling at the water's upward urge, pushing the nearest branches roughly aside, swimming on, rising back up and gulping air. As he redived, the need for hurry began to press on him like the desire for air. He brusquely swept a thick knot of roots and sprang back as a flotilla of fat frogs darted out. Their white underbellies flashed before his light, their panicked legs scraping at his chest, his back, his own legs as they scrambled and zoomed around him. One unblinking amphibian eye stared into his before streaking past. Instinctively he threw out his arms to thrust them from his face and caught his elbow in a coil of foliage. As he pulled back, it tightened on his forearm. Trying to yank free only trapped his wrist. He compelled himself to move forward instead, then clawed at the entangling whorl until it snapped. He burst upward, missilelike, gasping.

Forcing himself back down, he almost swam right by Elliott Kimble. The older man's sticklike arms were floating upward among the aspiring branches near the surface, his white head surrounded by dark leaf clusters. Squeezing through the mat, Balthazar wrapped both arms around the thin chest and tugged. But the man's legs and feet were held as if tied. Balthazar gave one more futile yank and resurfaced. As he panted, his bobbling beam caught Stew Connell treading water not too far off, wiping his eyes. At his shout, the officer flung himself forward.

"It's him—we have to free his legs." Plunging back, the detective focused the light on the nooselike coils and the two men rapidly freed the unresisting legs. Slipping Kimble's long foot through a loop, it occurred to Balthazar that the mangrove trap could not have been more effective if it'd been hand-shaped. Rapidly heading for the boat, each one holding an arm, the swimmers pulled the limp body forward.

14

THE DOG WOULD BE A PROBLEM and would have to be killed first, he'd decided. Its barking might alert her, cause her to lock herself safely in her guest house. But once in his grasp, it could easily be dealt with. It was very small, and he could clamp his left hand over its jaws and strangle it with his right. Neat and noiseless.

The dog was also a plus. She would surely let it out before going to bed, quite probably accompanying it herself. Seeing the dog yapping at a bush would frighten her. But there was no need to squat waiting in the shrubbery. With everyone else away, he could sit comfortably in the nearby guest house, leaving the screen door slightly ajar. When the dog snuffled in to investigate, probably expecting a friendly welcome, he would dispose of it. When she came looking for the dog, he would dispose of her. Slip a cord around her neck and pull. Equally neat.

It was only by a lucky chance that he'd become aware of what she knew. A heart-stopping discovery. It amazed him that Luttrell had told her, but drunks were given to loose talk, babblings. The shock of her husband's death had obviously caused her to do the same thing. Her disjointed references to bones made it clear that the subject was uppermost in her mind. Who could tell what action she might take on reflection? There was too much at stake to let her live. So this would have to be done, and tonight if possible.

He'd been waiting now for some time. Although the maid had left over an hour ago, the widow was not yet

ready for sleep. He'd heard her shower, and could catch a
few of her comments to the dog when she stood near a
window. A tea kettle had whistled recently. In this cabana
also, there was a carefully fitted kitchen unit behind
slatted closet doors, with a bar refrigerator, a small sink,
and two-burner stove. A soothing cup might be part of her
nightly ritual, the last thing before bedtime. Undoubtedly
he would soon hear her unlatch her screen to walk the dog.
But he had plenty of time. The Kimbles would be quite
late.

Gently pressing her camomile tea bag with a spoon against
the side of a china cup, Mildred was trying to convince
herself that this would make her sleepy enough to forego
one of the pills. The doctor had said she should take it, it
would be good for her. But there was a problem. Party was
such a good dog and had never made a mistake inside, but
she'd slept very late this morning. And, because of the pill,
she hadn't even heard that nice Maira Knight come and get
him. Last night she'd felt safe enough leaving the door
unlocked with Maira right next door, but being alone until
they all came back worried her. At home alone, she always
locked up securely. But then in the morning, she might not
waken and Maira wouldn't be able to let him out. Or
Maira might herself sleep late and not think of Party. He
might yip and awaken Mr. Kimble, who had so kindly
offered his hospitality. And she was afraid he would mention the noise at breakfast. He was definitely the kind of
man who made Remarks. Only this morning he'd offered
to drive her to the beauty parlor.

If only she'd listened to her sister and had her hair
done on St. Croix! But all of Helen's friends went to that
shop and they looked at her, probably thinking how different she was from her sister. Helen had always been
good-looking. And once before when she went there, the
hairdresser wouldn't do the front right to hide her high
forehead and tried to talk her into coloring it, getting a
new hairstyle. But if she'd known she was going to have to
stay at the Kimbles! If only she'd asked Helen the name of
the friends on St. John that she was going to visit! Helen

didn't even know yet about poor Chet! Tears of grief and self-reproach pooled in her throat, filled her eyes. She covered her mouth with both hands. Here she was fretting about her hair and her husband was dead.

The poodle, who'd been lying a few feet from her at the foot of the bed, watching her with anxious eyes, padded over hurriedly, nuzzled her arm up, and crept into her lap. "Bones, Bones," she cried out, "all we've got—" she buried her face in the little dog's soft white curls, ending up in a whisper, "is each other." He licked her throat, which was as high as he could reach, and whimpered softly. "I suppose I was just too young when we got married. Had silly ideas about what it was going to be like. And I must have made him act so irritable, the way I do things. I'd try, but I get started thinking about one thing and forget what else I'm supposed to do. Maybe if we could have had kiddies, he'd have been different. He never got to enjoy his retirement at all. Maybe he would have started writing about other kinds of things when he got older... when he was over all *that*. I can't complain about him, Bones, I really can't. I always had a nice house and a lovely garden. And Chet *was* gone a lot."

Blotting her eyes with a tissue from the bedside table, she dabbed at his coat, fluffing it. He hopped from one foot to another on her lap, making comforting dog noises. "Poor Party. Well now, I'll try to cheer up." She stroked his head, swallowed some tea. "I'll bet Howard Yung gave you a few bites of that duck when I wasn't looking, didn't he? He spoils you. I know that people here Talk because we're friends, Howard and me. And I know what my mother would have thought if she saw a man and woman who went around together, saying they were just friends. But we are, aren't we, Party dog? Isn't it fun to go with him to market, pick out the produce, check over the new plants? And he's so pleased when I give him my cuttings, start new ones for him. 'Mildred,' he says, ' "God the first garden made, and the first city Cain." ' He came here without knowing anyone, and look what a good job he's done in only three months."

The tea tasted better somehow from such a delicate cup, and she sipped it, wishing she were sleepier. Usually, after a day's gardening, she'd be dozing over her catalogs by nine o'clock. Then it occurred to her that she might just wait up for Maira and hear about the trip to the Phosphorescent Bay. She'd never been there herself, and although Mrs. Kimble had invited her tonight, she wouldn't have dreamt of going out so soon after . . . But she hadn't even had a chance to tell Maira how nice her policeman friend was. He'd even apologized for having to ask all those questions now, said it was routine, and he'd listened so to everything she'd had to say. Thank goodness, he hadn't said one word about Chet's writing. And he wouldn't have mentioned it to Maira. That kind of writing would have shocked the poor girl.

Yes, Mildred decided, she'd wait until Maira came back to take Party out unless he showed an inclination. The Kimbles had metal lamps all around the edges of the pool, and she and Maira could sit outside, look at the stars, and she'd make them both some tea. Maira was the kind of person who said things that made you feel better. "Remember, Party, last night she was sitting right there, and she said, 'Mildred, you have beautiful gray eyes. In medieval times, they thought true beauty was pale hair like yours and gray eyes.' Helen once said my eyes would be fine if I'd just put on some eyeliner. But, of course, I have this big nose so what's the use? Howard says things, too, that you can repeat to yourself later and they make you feel good. One day I told him that Helen said my problem was I just didn't have enough gumption. He smiled, and said 'gumption' two or three times. Then he said, 'A diamond with a flaw is worth more than a pebble without imperfections.' That made me happy." She held up the little dog's paws, admiring the seashells embedded on his new pink collar.

Since the tea had become a little cold, she drank the rest quickly. Depositing the bag in the plastic-lined wastebasket, she peered under the sink for detergent, then opened the cupboard above. At last she squeezed a drop of liquid hand soap in the cup, added hot water, swished it about, and poured that over the saucer. She rinsed them and dried both with the bedside tissues. Running a finger over the roses with gold leaves on the cup, she inspected it by the light of the marble bedside lamp, pleased at its fragile translucence. Then she set it down gingerly on the shelf. "Mrs. Kimble does have nice things," she remarked, looking at the bleached wood of the furniture and door, the wildflower blue walls and blue-striped sheets, letting her fingers drift over the cool stone of the iris-bulb-shaped lamp. "Helen would like this, say it was tasteful. But it is awfully *plain*, isn't it? Only one picture. I suppose those are sailboats, and that blue squiggle the sea. Of course, maybe she normally keeps plants in here, but she's moved them because they're getting ready to leave. Maira told me her cabana was like this but all done in lemon yellow. That'd be more cheerful. But then there's that really lovely blue butterfly in the bathroom. I'd better look at it again; maybe I can order one like that. Lucite," she added, crossing the room, with the little dog at her heels, "is perfect for bathrooms—the moisture doesn't cloud it up." Against the wall's matte gray finish, the blue of the butterfly was magnetic. Gently she lifted it off the wall, tilted the case back and forth to admire the shimmer of the wings.

It was the suddenness of the noise—a heart-rattling bang—that made her drop it, let it smash face down on the darker gray tiles of the floor. Party yelped, shot to the front door, and stood there, ears back, letting out sharp staccato threats. She herself was frozen, her breath stopped, but her thoughts scuttling. There was no further sound, except for the flapping of the window's half shutters.

Then it came to her. It was the wind. Probably Maira hadn't quite latched her door and one of the quicksilver tropical breezes had caught it. She ran a blue-veined hand over her thin chest as if to calm her thudding heart from the outside. But, picking up the butterfly, turning it over, she had a worse shock. A long, lightning-bolt crack slashed across the clear plastic. As she laid it on the counter, she wondered agonizedly what she was ever going to say to Mrs. Kimble.

He, too, had been robbed of his breath by the screen door slamming open. If he crept out quickly, pulled it to its previous position, just open enough for the poodle, the wind might send it crashing back again. Not realizing it was the wind, she might quail inside her own cabana—not come out at all. Or she might come briskly out alone, close this door tightly before the dog could get in. Still, it would be best to stay with his original plan. Crouching, he stooped across the floor and with the tips of his fingers, edged the door back. The dog kept up its high-pitched yapping.

Although he had wiped the bulb on the overhead light carefully after loosening it, he was aware that he'd left his fingerprints splayed on the tile floor as he'd made his way over, as well as on the door itself. The police would undoubtedly assume that Mildred had heard a chance intruder next door, taking advantage of the Kimbles' absence, and that the burglar had panicked, killing her and the dog. So they would dust the room for prints. But it would hardly matter when they found his on the door. He grinned with satisfaction.

It would be all right, she told herself. She would just have to take the butterfly to Mrs. Kimble when she was alone, explain what had happened, and offer to replace it. But supposing it was rare. Although she knew there was a shop in Old San Juan that sold butterflies in cases, their ads in the catalogs only showed red, orange, and yellow ones. Still, the insect itself was unharmed. It was only the case. She would just put the butterfly in the bedside table so the maid wouldn't find it and show it to Mrs. Kimble before she herself could explain. She wouldn't want her hostess to think that she wasn't going to pay for it.

Now the thing to do was to take Party out for a little stroll around the swimming pool. It would make them both calmer. After all, *he* might want to sleep, even if she didn't. As she walked to the door, the little dog's rump wiggled in anticipation. She slid the damaged case in the drawer and then unlatched the screen.

He heard the dog's toenails purposefully clittering on the smooth concrete of the pool's deck, headed straight for the open door. Everything was going according to plan. As soon as it entered, he would grab it, step back behind the room's wooden door, and wring its neck. He'd killed chickens that way as a young man. One of the advantages of a rural upbringing was that it did away with squeamishness. Then he'd wait until she got well inside, slip behind her. She was short, and snapping the cord would take little strength.

"Good dog, Party. You remembered Maira's door. We'll just shut that tight and take a nice walkie around the pool. You do remember the bush I showed you this afternoon, don't you? Oh no, wait, Party. Come here! Don't go in Maira's place. She isn't home. Party!" But it was too late. The dog was inside and already sniffing around the bottom of the door.

Perhaps it was his silence that made the poodle apprehensive. It didn't bark, but let out a low, questioning growl. "Here boy," he breathed, bending down. Just outside the door, its owner commanded, "Party, come!" The animal turned its head, but then danced a little nearer to the man. Finally it sniffed his sandal. He seized its body, got one hand over the jaws before the dog let out more than a surprised yip. But one of its teeth, sharp as the point of a manicure scissors, pierced the ball of his ring finger. It almost made him lose his grip. He pincered the neck and the thin shells on the wide collar cracked under the pressure, digging into the tender skin between his thumb and index finger.

"Bad dog, Party! What will Maira think of our rummaging through her room!" He heard her hesitant step on the threshhold. With two fingers, he squeezed the dog's neck hard, and the animal sagged. He laid it down quietly, wrapped the nylon length around each hand, tugged it taut. With one eye around the door, he could see her outlined in the discreet lighting from the pool. She fumbled at the light switch, and he expected her to go directly to the bedside lamp near him, which he'd unplugged. But instead she hiked up the skirt of her robe and flopped down by the end of the bed, sliding beneath it to her shoulders.

"Party," she cajoled. "We can play this game at our house. Please come out. Now!"

Horrified, he heard the unexpected squeal of fast sliding tires on the gravel in front. How could they be back so soon? A car door slammed. "Oh dear," Mildred groaned. "They're back and whatever will they think—" She edged out, stood up, frantically brushing at the front of her housecoat. As she turned toward the door, he grabbed for the marble lamp. Unaware, her hand pushed at the screen, and he swung its base at her head. It slammed into the bone behind her ear. As he stepped forward to hit her again, the dog's needle teeth sank silently into his bare ankle. He raised the lamp to club it, but without relaxing its grip, it whirled its rump between his legs. Another car door clunked shut. He jerked his leg free, sending the dog flying against a wall, swabbed his prints hastily from the lamp, threw it on the bed, stepped over the woman's still form, and fled.

15

"THANK HEAVENS, thank heavens, I did bring a set of keys."
Virginia Kimble's thin quivering fingers dug into her
small straw bag. "Thank heavens—period. And you." She
looked at Balthazar, blinking rapidly as she disentangled
the key chain from a wadded Kleenex. Maira gently took
the keys as the three approached the front door.

The older woman quavered on compulsively. "If those
mangrove roots hadn't been quite so stretchy, he wouldn't
have been bobbing occasionally up to the air. And how
lucky to have men experienced in CPR right on board!
Now if his heart will just hold up. I'm sure it will. He's
almost seventy, you know, but he's always been careful
about his diet, good about exercise. Dr. Reyes said it was
just that his blood pressure was so extremely low. Maira,
wasn't he pale, lying there in the emergency room? He
looked just like that albino preacher."

Unlocking the door, Maira encircled her shoulders,
hugging her as they entered. The detective followed them
into a spacious foyer. The quiet of her own home seemed
to recall Virginia's patrician self-control, and the need to
settle small matters to calm her. Slipping on a pair of
half-glasses handy on a rosy marble-topped hall table, she
slid open a small drawer and took out a pad and pen.
"Maira, I'll just write down the name of the hospital in San
Juan where we'll be. Elliott will be in intensive care, of
course. Oh dear, I don't know the address—you'll have to
find that out so that people can send flowers and messages.
I did reach his brother in Connecticut already. My sister-

in-law will take care of notifying family and close friends."
As she repeated plans already discussed, her voice stead-
ied. "You won't forget to try Grover again tomorrow and
tell him to contact me at the hospital? With his man gone
for the weekend, he's probably unplugged the phone. And
if Mildred ever gets in touch with her sister, you must
invite her to stay here, too. It might be best if you checked
on her now, she might still be awake. Do tell her that you'll
be staying with her, assure her that she must not cut short
her visit."

Laying down the glasses, she took a deep breath.
"Now, I'll just change and pack a few things that we'll
need. I won't be long, Zar, and then you can take me to
the helicopter at Camp Garcia. By then, Elliott should
be aboard. It's a comfort that Dr. Reyes will be accompanying us. And I so appreciate your help." She tried
for a bright smile. Turning toward the staircase, her
foot almost missed the bottom step.

"I'll come with you," Balthazar said, taking her
arm. "Carry down the bags."

"Yes, please," she said, leaning on him. "And there
is something I want to ask you."

Opening the door to the kitchen, Maira called
back, "I'll knock on Mildred's door if there's a light."

When they reached the master bedroom, Virginia
sank down on the bed's light ecru satin coverlet and
gestured toward a wall of closets. "Would you get the
two small tapestry bags on top on the far left?" He
brought them over, set them near her, zipped them
open. Each suitcase had built-in plastic compartments
containing jars and tubes—shaving supplies and toiletries
in one, cosmetics and lotions in the other. Straightening
her back, she stood up and began opening drawers, taking
out packaged shirts, folded underwear.

The room itself was as well ordered, almost to the
point of severity. The wood trim was natural beech, the
brown and beige tones of walls and bedspread carried
only a suggestion of yellow in their mix. Even the
scattered Haitian paintings lacked the usual prismatic
colors. The sprays of gold-tinged orchids, in bowls and
vases on dressers and tables, drew the eye, the rest of

the room perhaps designed for that effect. Without facing him, she began, with an unusually tentative tone, "When I was alone for a moment with Elliott, he clung to my hand desperately, begged me to have a guard posted at the hospital in San Juan. He believes that someone tried to kill him there in the bay. Could this just be the aftermath of shock? It's so unlike him to have . . . imaginings."

"Did he tell you why *he* thought so?"

"Only that he was sure he felt hands on his ankles before he became unconscious." She retrieved two pairs of shoes, two pairs of trousers from her husband's closet, and put them in his case.

"Getting his feet tangled in the roots might have given him that impression. Panic could set in. Do you know of any other reason for such a suspicion?"

As she wrapped one of her own silk blouses in tissue paper, a corner of her mouth twitched. He could see she wanted this problem glossed over, wanted his permission to do this. And he felt it was not an unwillingness on her part to give information. She was simply not used to having Kimble privacy impinged on. "He stressed that I must tell Grover what he thinks. I don't know why. Earlier he'd told me that Grover and Chet Luttrell were once business partners. I hadn't known that. Perhaps he's making some unreasonable connection."

"He himself had no business dealings with the two?"

"With Grover, yes. They were always conferring in Elliott's study, poring over stock reports. But I know nothing of my husband's investments. I have money of my own, and I handle that. We file separate tax returns."

"Have you ever heard him mention the name of Douglas Blaylock?"

She was checking the contents of the packed cases now, and seemed distracted. "The poet? No. Elliott picks up an occasional espionage novel, but not books of poetry."

"I'll see your husband when I get back to San Juan. In the meantime, if it'd comfort him, why not get a guard? There are a number of private companies in San Juan."

"You're right, of course. If it calms him, the expense is worth it. There, that's all ready. If you'll just put those in the car, I'll slip on a dress and be right down."

Halfway down the stairs, he heard the kitchen door slam, looked down to see Maira's alarmed white face and her frantic beckoning. She kept her voice low. "Quick, quick, Mildred's hurt. She's lying on the floor in my cabana."

He dropped the bags, and as they raced out the back door and along the poolside, Maira added breathlessly, "She has a pulse, but I couldn't see what was the matter. The light won't work. She didn't answer her door. And the dog didn't make any noise. I thought they were walking around the grounds, so I looked around a bit. Then I saw my door swinging open."

He knelt by the unconscious woman, sprawled on her side, felt the arrhythmic throb of her wrist. Maira was fumbling near the head of the bed. "Zar, the bedside lamp is gone. No—it's on the bed!"

"Don't touch it. Let's take her to her room."

As he lifted the woman's slight body, he saw Party staggering forward from a corner. "Get the dog. It's not in good shape either."

When Mildred was laid on her bed, they could see the broken skin below her right ear, the blood-splotched fair hair surrounding a lump that seemed to be swelling as they stared. The poodle squirmed in Maira's arms, his mouth moving in a vain attempt to bark.

Balthazar squeezed her shoulder. "You'll have to take Virginia to the helipad. I'll take Mildred to the hospital in the Kimbles' jeep—faster than an ambulance. But I'll have to check outside first, call Gusto Mulero. I'll be right back."

Clutching the dog, Maira inhaled, leaned against the door frame. Party craned to look into her face, twisting his neck with an odd stiffness, the white hairs above his eyes raised as if in anxious alarm. "I know how you feel, old boy," she said out loud. "In my mother's portmanteau word, I am myself limpsy, really limpsy. But," she whispered reassuringly in the dog's ear, "I can vouch for Zar. A good man. Solid. Don't worry."

As she set the wriggling poodle beside Mildred, he began frantically licking her cheek, nosing her chin, and she moaned. "An ice pack—that can't hurt," Maira murmured, swung open the bar-sized refrigerator, and started dumping cubes in the sink. She wrapped them in the plastic liner of the small wastebasket, then hurried into the bathroom for a clean towel to pad it.

When she returned, Mildred's eyes were open but unfocused. "My head, there's something wrong with my head," she sighed.

"Lie still," Maira said soothingly. "You've got a bad bump. I'm just going to put an ice pack on it."

Mildred felt the dog's caress and buried her fingers in the silken coat, then sucked in her breath at the touch of the pack. "Maira, I'm so sorry. Must have fainted . . . doing everything wrong tonight."

"Don't talk now," Maira urged her. "We are going to have that head looked at at the hospital. Zar'll carry you to the car."

The widow squinched her eyes against the lamplight. "This room is blue. I'm in my room. Whatever could have come over me? I didn't mean to pry in your room, really. Party got in. And Maira, I broke Mrs. Kimble's butterfly." She gestured feebly toward the table, tugged open the drawer, then half rose and wailed. "And now I'm going to be sick!" Maira scrambled for the empty wastebasket.

When Balthazar returned, tightening already grim lips, Mildred was again resting, with one hand futilely working at the buckle of Party's shattered collar. As he bent to pick her up, she fluttered her eyes open. "We have to take this off. Shells like broken glass. Can we bring him? He'll be so afraid. And Maira, please, please tell Mrs. Kimble how sorry I am about the butterfly!"

*   *   *

"Really good coffee," Gusto reiterated appreciatively, yawning as he put his cup on the white plastic poolside table.

"I think what's really good about it," Balthazar said wearily, staring at the stars' withdrawal into pinpricks at the first flush of dawn, "is that Maira poured a lot of the Kimbles' best cognac in it before she went to bed." Since Mildred had been stiff with fear on their return from the hospital, they'd moved one of the pool's padded loungers into her cabana, and Maira had gratefully slipped into exhausted sleep on it next to Mildred and the dog, both deep in pain-killer oblivion.

"It's Sunday. We'll have a tough time rousing the island no-goods to make them account for their time last night." Gusto brought his shoulders to his neck and twisted, trying to relieve the tension. "But I'll get a couple of men started on that soon. All the locals would know about the Kimbles' party. They do it every year. Anyway, the Vieques Divers always have a sign-up sheet on the tree outside their place for tourists who want to take the bay trip. No sheet out—that means the boat's rented. So, somebody here, or a relative from the main island, might just have meant to toss the guest houses for small stuff. You can see the big house is wired. Mrs. Luttrell hears a noise, goes in, guy panics, hits her." He tilted back in the nylon corded chair. "I suppose. But it's a funny thing. She'd have had to walk in as soon as he got there. No drawers opened, nothing touched. And there's the outline of somebody's rump on the spread. Guy unscrews the lightbulb, unplugs one of the lamps, and sits down to rest?"

"I noticed. Still, I don't think she'd have gone in if she was suspicious. But if the door was open, the dog could have and she went to get it, thinking it was just the wind. The dog did get a piece of the guy. The paramedic at the hospital said that a couple of its teeth are loose." He was brooding over whether Party could adjust to a new, much larger friend, like a Doberman.

"We'll look at everybody's hands and ankles. Even their toes. Dog's pretty little."

"The paramedic said he'd bet it's going to be hoarse for a few days. That wide collar saved its neck. And maybe the dog saved Mildred's." He remembered her hand working at the collar clasp. Crinkled knuckles, sunburned from gardening, small vulnerable unpolished nails. What could be done to protect the world's Mildreds? Get them to meditate five minutes a day on the nature of evil, followed by a remedial course in Steps To Take?

Gusto fished for a used toothpick in his pocket, apparently decided it'd do, and chewed it studiously. "Trouble is that we got a lot of excitement here all at once. Not natural. We got a born beefeater picking fruit, a good swimmer almost drowning, and a scaredy woman going all alone into a dark room. Next thing you know it'll be snowing on the beach. Come to think of it, I'd like that. Never have seen snow. Once in Barranquitas I was almost cold—got down to fifty degrees."

"We also have too damned many butterflies."

Gusto unintentionally bit the sodden toothpick in half, as he turned toward Balthazar. "Did you say 'butterflies'?"

"You saw that big one in the Luttrell's trash. Well, Mildred says she never had one. It must have come in the mail after she left, and Chet pitched it, thinking it was another of her knicknacks. There's one in the Kimbles' guest house, but Virginia said her husband picked it up at their post office box. They thought it was some thank-you gift from a visitor whose note didn't get included in the package. Told the maid to put it in the cabana. And Doug Blaylock had one in his study. But Grover Clay says they're rare. I'll be interested in where the Blaylocks got theirs."

Gusto was holding the toothpick halves and couldn't find an ashtray. He unhappily returned them to his pocket. "That's another funny thing. After asking two dozen people, we find somebody who knows how to get ahold of the people she's with on St. Thomas. I just leave a vague message saying to call in connection with the Luttrell case. And I get a message back she's returning today. Sunday. Why's she doing that? Maybe she wants to tell us something."

"That's unnatural, too."

"Well," Gusto said wearily, "it's normal for Carillo

to have a gout attack near a holiday. He does have gout, though. Big toe swells all up, and I guess that's real painful. But we could use him now. My men are spread pretty thin this weekend, watching the tourists don't hurt themselves."

"This afternoon," Balthazar glanced at his watch, "well, yesterday afternoon I talked to San Juan, checked in with the detective on the Blaylock case. I wanted to know if any of their friends mentioned Luttrell's name. We'd better have him come over."

"Your partner?" Gusto inquired.

"No." Balthazar winced at the hint of morning in the sky. "No, Negrón'd never describe himself that way. That would happen the day after the Vieques blizzard."

16

ALL THE ESTABLISHED MEMBERS of the Vieques Welcoming Committee were gathered at the terminal, Balthazar noticed as he parked the police jeep in the cul-de-sac and crossed the pavement cracked by exuberant weeds. Fanning themselves stoically, the usual spectators occupied the front-row benches. As Something New bent his head over his work, the spirals of his hair gleamed blackly in the sun. Tourists, mesmerized by both the repetitive Veg-a-matic spiel and the twisty skill of the smudged-knuckled fingers, waited with dollars ready. Santo was gathering inspiration from the asphalt; a rare noon breeze plastered his thin garment against his skin, outlining the Jockey briefs. Although he did not raise his eyes, he scrabbled over at the detective's approach, blocking the path. Steepling his fingers below his gaunt chin, he pronounced: "I have trespassed. The Lord Jesus saith in the Sermon on the Mount: 'Agree with thine adversary quickly, whiles thou art in the way with him; lest at any time the adversary deliver thee to the judge, and the judge deliver thee to the officer, and thou be cast into prison.' Matthew 5:25."

"As far as I know, disagreements—or for that matter—preaching in front of airport terminals and on public beaches," Balthazar said patiently, getting ready to execute a quick step around him, "will not get you cast anywhere." On the other hand, he reflected that the municipal jail, centrally located in downtown Isabel Segunda, would not only be comfortable but would provide a convenient open-air pulpit. A chain-link fence surrounded a small yard, and

behind that was a cool, one-room retreat. Food was provided at the public expense. Perhaps Santo wanted to be
arrested and, unable to con the seasoned Gusto, thought
he'd have more success with a newly arrived agent. He
continued more brusquely, "Furthermore, the law against
being a public nuisance usually—"

"No. My sin was even worse than failing to follow
each admonition of the Christ. It was Pride!" Head down,
with only his white, baby-sparse hair visible, Santo shuf-
fled farther to the right to maintain his blockade. The
audience paused in midfan as Santo loudly continued. "For
my lack of humility, I must acknowledge my sin and atone
for it. Yesterday evening, like a tongue of fire, anger licked
my bowels. Because of that, I raised myself up, proclaiming
that God needed my paltry powers." Carefully lifting his
shift, exposing soup-bone-size knees, he sank down. One
knee landed in a surface crevice occupied by a hill swarming
with red ants.

"Santo, you're kneel—"

Pincerlike, a claw hand clenched a piece of Balthazar's
trousers and Santo, throwing his head back, boomed out,
"Prideful, I boasted of my mission. I insisted that you use
my chosen name. I reject my given name of Richard
because it means 'he who rules.' God alone has dominion.
Therefore, only a proud man would set himself up before
other men as a ruler. But in the night it came to me: is not
insisting that others call one Santo—'holy'—also setting
oneself up? I have prayed to find an answer."

Raising his own eyes heavenward, Balthazar caught
Something New's hunted glance. The craftsman, intimi-
dated, shifted his eyes so quickly and fearfully that Balthazar
felt like a hard-eyed, potbellied Southern sheriff. Perhaps,
he considered, the man thought a license was needed for
street vendors here.

Just as Balthazar was about to disengage Santo's clutch
on his pants, the evangelist hooted in pain, hopped up,
brushing madly at his leg. At this unusual development,
several of the bench-warmers actually stood up to see what
was happening.

Thankful that the preacher's knees were not as hardened as the soles of his feet, the detective hurried inside.

The Air Link plane was already offhandedly jouncing down the runway. He was there to pick up Angel Negrón.

Because the two of them would be sharing the investigation and the police dormitory, he'd made a resolution not to respond to the man's habitual offensiveness. It stemmed from a built-in resentment, which was merely a half-assed anger. Some of the other deadly sins were lively, understandable. Lust, now. Gluttony. Sloth had a real appeal in the heat of the Vieques sun. But it was difficult to sympathize with someone suffering from chronic umbrage. *Why*, Balthazar muttered testily, *am I supposed to apologize because Negrón's sergeant in the Marine Corps years ago had refused to pronounce An-hell properly?* And it was not a matter of Negrón's failing in earlier cases, but rather that Puerto Rican *Policía* had succeeded with the loud publicity going to Sixto and himself. They were colleagues, not competitors— there was too much of the schoolyard in all of this for his taste. He himself planned to ignore all signs of the man's hostility, say nothing, do nothing.

Negrón was the first passenger out, having been accorded the copilot's seat. As Balthazar recalled he'd also done two days before, the Sanjuanero took a deep breath. Then Negrón frowned in surprise at the sun and went to the rear of the plane where the luggage was being unloaded. Crossing the tarmac, he had, Balthazar noticed, a cowboy's stride. His weight settled on his heels rather than the balls of his feet, thrusting his powerful shoulders backward. Although half a head shorter, Negrón was a good twenty pounds heavier than the waiting detective. Once inside, his eyes hidden by reflecting lenses, he took in the terminal. Without a greeting, he dropped his bag by the New Yorker's feet, and disappeared in the direction of the bathroom. There was a slight greenish tinge around the lips framed by trimmed beard and mustache. His scar seemed sunken, rather than puffy. He was gone rather a long time.

". . . and we are here on an isle full of sounds and sweet airs that give delight. Let us praise God. Amen." A group of South Americans in Hawaiian shirts had paused in front of the preacher but were now drifting toward Something New. Santo briskly made way for Gloria, who

culminated her fingers' approval of the state of her orange
Afro into a friendly wave at Balthazar. She began a hymn,
and the plangent hunger and thirsting in her voice as she
begged to be in the number of the elect stopped even
Negrón in his forward motion to the jeep. In her refrain,
one could hear absolute certitude in the happy thunder of
the march of the saints. At the end, one of her upflung
arms swung down dramatically, the other motioned a
potential customer to her Monte Carlo.

Heading for the jeep, his feet in harmony with the
song. Balthazar reflected that the isle *was* full of sounds
and sweet airs. Then he realized that he was familiar with
that line. Santo was quoting somebody. Shakespeare? He'd
have to ask Maira. He hummed into the driver's seat.
Negrón lagged behind, on the edge of the flowered shirts
surrounding the souvenir maker. As he got in the jeep, he
silently reached into his *guayabera* pocket for his thin
cigars.

Backing out, Balthazar asked neutrally, "Been here
before?"

"No." Negrón took out a dark cigarillo and clicked his
lighter. "Why am I here now?"

"I think there's a possible connection between the
Blaylock case and the death of this Luttrell." He went over
his and Gusto's conclusions, mentioned Kimble's near-
drowning, and finished with an account of the attack on
Mildred Luttrell the previous evening. "Heavy lamp, if it
hadn't caught her on the bone, she'd be dead. Mildred
shouldn't be hit on the head," he added inconsequentially
but firmly.

Negrón produced that contemptuous lip-blow that
Balthazar had thought only the French could manage, and
snapped, "Burglar."

The New Yorker stoically slid his eyes over the shrubs
of red hibiscus silhouetted against the turquoise Atlantic
on his left, took a deep breath, and replied, "Maybe. It
was a ham-handed assault, and the first two murders
showed considerable finesse."

"*Two* murders? No prints on the fruit and you con-
clude homicide? He could have been an apple polisher."

Balthazar swung out slightly to pass Lyle Templeton

on his determined island marathon and persevered himself.
He noted Kimble's suspicions and fear. "Kimble and a man
named Grover Clay were in business together. Clay and
Luttrell were also. Blaylock's money is hard to account for.
They all could have had a deal somewhere in the past,
possibly in South America. Clay's spent a great deal of
time there, so did Blaylock and Luttrell."

"Probably ran into each other all the time." Facing the
window, Negrón's sardonic words blew away, but the
weight of his massive disinterest remained.

Almost standing on the accelerator, despite the twingy
pain in his knee, Balthazar gritted out, "I smell something
wrong. These people could be in danger. We can't take a
chance. Clay must know something, but he doesn't answer
his phone; the officer sent to check his house says it seems
empty and there's no sign of his Mercedes. He could have
heard about Kimble and taken off for the hospital in San
Juan, but no one has yet reported seeing him leave."

Negrón's only comment was a deep inhalation of
tobacco. The smoke with its acrid-cherry odor drifted
across and curled out the driver's side.

Balthazar's fingers were strained as tightly around the
wheel as they would be on gymnastic rings holding his
entire weight. Maira had once described his hands as
capable. He himself has always thought them disproportion-
ately large and their size, with his more than ordinary
length of arm, made him feel rather apelike when he
dressed before a mirror. But that reach—and his height—
had made the police coach enthusiastic. The instructor had
followed him around for days, pleading that, with a little
fattening, he could be entered in the department's light
heavyweight ranks. But he'd never been interested in the
sport. In fact, he'd never hit a man with his closed fist.
When anger flash-flooded his veins, the desire to lunge out
was almost overwhelming. But when that had occurred,
it'd been the wrong place. Like now. And when, in the
past, he'd arrived at another place, his anger had subsided.

At the moment, he contained it behind an embank-
ment of words, saying in a flat, report tone. "Joan Blaylock
arrived this morning. She should be able to help. If her
husband's killer is also involved here, he would have been

off-island on March twenty-eighth. Gusto is making a list of residents who were gone then, as well as people who've arrived in the last couple of months. But he's got to check on people here with a record of breaking and entering because of Mrs. Luttrell. He says that's very uncommon. One more thing. Mrs. Blaylock said her husband received a threat, but that doesn't mean it has to have been a letter." Keeping his eyes on the road, he described the Morpho butterflies. "But, Clay doesn't seem to have received one. And neither Kimble nor Luttrell paid any attention to them. We can ask Joan Blaylock where hers came from."

Negrón tossed his cigar out and said flatly, "I'm not talking to that gringo bitch."

They slid into the parking lot before the police station in silence. As Balthazar pulled up to the front, Negrón adjusted his sunglasses and turned their blankness toward him. Then, without a word, he shoved open the jeep door, stepped out, and set the bag down. He slammed the car door viciously, and spat out, "The connection between Blaylock and these happenings here—for which the San Juan CIC is in no way responsible—is a misspelled mention in a porno piece and a blue butterfly?"

Balthazar glared back, gripping the steering wheel so sharply that he heard the tires slip and dig into the gravel. Then he yanked the wheel, reversed quickly. There was a crunch as one of the tires ran over Negrón's canvas bag. He didn't look back, but he mentally replayed that satisfying sound. He was actually some distance away before he began to wonder if it was an accident.

17

BOUGAINVILLEA IN APRICOT, white, and fuchsia bowered over the wooden lattice archway before the entrance to the Esperanza Beach and Tennis Club. Immature palms stretched alongside the massive old sugar mill which now housed the lobby and convention center of the resort. Despite the solidity of the Spanish-built structure, the handsomely exposed red brick walls, it seemed to float in Vieques' substantial air. Behind it, the new chalet guest buildings, grouped around flower-lined sidewalks that meandered to the lapping Caribbean, shared this after-noon dream quality. The deep white sand at adjoining Sun Bay had looked as if it could be plumped like a featherbed. Going in to meet Joan Blaylock in the lobby, Balthazar decided that his perceptions were colored by an intense desire for a Sunday nap.

Inside the former factory, the high raised ceiling was lowered with floating panels of blue, yellow, and green canvas swayed by breezes from the walls' open arches. Wicker high-backed chairs and tables were scattered through-out the expansive room, and he paused before the recep-tion desk to look for her. Just as he'd decided she might, after all, be waiting in the beachfront bar, she leaned around a chairback in a secluded corner at the far end. Right, he thought, an inclination for privacy had led to her choice of meeting place, but she'd not considered that it was important to find her to meet.

As he shook hands, then sat across from her, she didn't smile nor let her back rest against the chair.

Her dress of bleached raw silk might have looked casual on someone else, or with other shoes than matching bone pumps. Decorous pearls encircled her throat. A Joan Crawford outfit—that was it—how could he have forgotten Joan Crawford? And her namesake had the same hard eyes, the sensual soft mouth that denied the eyes.

She began abruptly, "Did you come to Vieques to talk to me?"

He nodded, went over the evidence of the dart in the tire that confirmed her surmise. "But," he added, "that doesn't provide any leads to the killer's identity. I'm going to need your help."

"This man Luttrell. Was he also murdered?"

Right. Another question and question interview. He explained, ending with the information that Luttrell's widow had also been attacked last night, without elaboration. "Do you think your husband knew Chet Luttrell?"

"Possibly. When we were first married, he repeatedly called out the name in his sleep."

"Since then?"

"I don't know. We soon stopped sharing a room. He felt his troubled dreams would disturb me."

It was two o'clock in the afternoon. He could imagine them drinking tea at sunset, carrying on primly. "Was your husband a homosexual?"

Her eyes were dark topaz rocks. "It *was* one of them that killed him, wasn't it? I knew it!"

"Then you know a great deal more than I do," he replied exasperatedly. "Did he have lovers, Mrs. Blaylock?"

The pliant lips were infinitely regretful, but her tone was clipped. "He never admitted it. Now they do. But *we* didn't. He'd disappear to other islands, come back without a word about where he'd been. I checked his passport. That's why I gave it to you, so that you could trace the murderer. It took me a long time to figure it out. And then I couldn't confront him for fear he'd leave. But I was sure one of them *must* have killed him. And I wasn't going to let him get away with it." Her whole face was now an enamel mask of anger. "But that wasn't the worst."

He could see beyond the spare Picasso lines of her sketchy account. The worst was not that he'd had male sex partners, but that he'd loved one. Her husband had once remarked bitterly he had not known he loved until it was too late—she'd thought that romantic. Believing she was competing with a dead woman, she was determined to outshine her memory, be a newer, brighter muse. The apprehension that it was a man he was idealizing, idolizing was swallowed acid.

"Who was he?"

"I don't know. I don't *want* to know. Someone he knew in the early days of the Peace Corps. You remember *The Sepia Mirror*'s dedication page? 'Poetry is King. *Vive la poésie, vive le roi.* The first is the last.' Once I remarked that in the new edition, we should correct the typo on that page, pointing out that 'King' shouldn't be capitalized. He insisted that it should be left unchanged because it was a play on words."

She rolled one of the hard pearls between her fingers, stroking its smoothness. Lowering her voice, she bit out, "There is a Peace Corps base named Camp King— they name them after dead volunteers. So, in a sense, Doug's first love was his last. He meant, no doubt, that he never loved anyone more than King . . . . But this can't matter. It could hardly have been *him*."

"Is your income based on the proceeds of *The Sepia Mirror*?"

Even the responsive mouth tightened. "What has that to do with his murder?" she shot back. He sat in rigid, stony silence. Finally, she answered reluctantly, "A few months ago, I would have said, 'Yes, certainly.' Even when I talked to you in Barranquitas. Neither of our families have any money. The book had been published several years before I met Doug, and he said that he'd invested the proceeds. So I was terrified that I might have to give a lot back. But the executor says that my future is assured because Doug had very large insurance policies. At least he did that for me."

"What do you mean 'you'd have to give it back'?"

"How could I know what your investigation would turn up? You looked unnervingly competent. Not what I expected. It was difficult enough imagining there might be newspaper accounts, telling the world about his . . . problem. I had to face that because I was not going to let some misbegotten lowlife get away with killing him!"

"Mrs. Blaylock," he put his hands flat on the glass table and held her eyes, "this killer is going to enjoy a peaceful life and die of old age. Believe me."

"My concern has nothing to do with his murder! If I tell you this, it is only to keep you from wasting time. In any case, I have no proof. I am not an expert—I never even finished my master's degree in literature. I will not repeat this in court, you understand?"

"No, because I have no idea of what you're talking about."

She pushed the words out as if they scorched her tongue. "I don't think my husband wrote *The Sepia Mirror.*"

"Why do you think so?"

"His later work wasn't . . . anything like those poems. In the beginning, every night he'd read his new work to me. He was very pleased with these pieces. At first, I thought they just needed . . . polishing. When I said that, he was furious. But I think that eventually he showed them to a colleague or two. They must have agreed. He came to rely on my judgment, never showed anything of his to anyone else. I let him publish a poem or two. They were accepted on the strength of his name. He himself *still* believed in his 'gift,' but his dependence on me increased my fears."

Leaning forward, her voice was low and hard. "I thought that this other man, this King, might have sent some of the poems in *The Sepia Mirror* in letters to relatives. They might not have been people who read much, but once the connection was made, Doug could have been sued. He'd lose his reputation—and all our money. But after I met you, I checked with the Peace Corps. King's mother died before he joined. He listed no relatives. And it had to be him—someone who saw that river, that jungle. And someone who could never accuse Doug of plagiarism."

She stood up, both hands gripping a matching purse, her nails whiter than its bone color. Now her mouth was unyielding. "I will deny ever having said this. Douglas Blaylock will be remembered as one of our finest poets. I can at least save his name."

18

ELLIOTT KIMBLE lay whitely still on the narrow bed in San Juan's De Diego Hospital's intensive care section, his chest, arm, and nose attached by umbilical cords to machines whose vivacious blinkings, jiggly lines, and pert beeps made them seem more alive than he. They took up half the bare room. In the interests of absolute sterility, there were no windows, pictures, clocks—not even a bedside table for personal belongings. But patients spent little time in these anterooms. They either lived—showing steady signs of improvement and then assigned more pleasant rooms—or they didn't.

The mother machine was right outside in the hall, scrutinized by a robotic nurse who kept glancing from the monitor to Balthazar. He was sure that he'd be ejected at the slightest ping. Kimble at last opened his eyes, above the nose that was all bone, and he wore the flinty expression of a man massively imposed upon. But he seemed willing to talk to the detective, if he could stay awake long enough to do so.

His voice was as drawly as a record played at too slow a speed. "The Brazilian government has the stated policy of protecting Indian land. In exchange for waiving their own rules, we agreed to only a lifetime interest in the operation. We financed the mining and the shipping of the ore to an aluminum processing plant downstream."

"Who's 'we'?" Balthazar almost whispered to placate the nurse.

"Four partners. Clay, Luttrell, Blaylock, and I. When

one of us died, the interest in the company went to the surviving partners, rather than to anyone's family. When the last one of us dies, it reverts to the Brazilians. They, of course, will use the proceeds to help the Indians adjust to modern life." The noise that issued from his nonexistent lips might have been a doubtful wheeze.

"Where did those three get that kind of money?"

"At the time I didn't ask. I knew Clay had proceeds from the sale of his parents' farm. He met the other two because they were trying to dispose of some Indian artifacts. Later I heard they'd been lucky enough to discover some sizeable gems along with these. They also brought information to the partnership. Blaylock suspected the existence of the bauxite; Luttrell had pinpointed its probable location." The record ceased to revolve.

Balthazar touched his shoulder. "You believe that there's a connection between their deaths and your near-drowning?"

Kimble's nostrils took in air so indignantly that the taped-on oxygen tube fluttered, too. "The attempt on my life! Yes. Now I do. Blaylock wrote to Clay, saying he believed that the other Peace Corps volunteer had survived and had returned, furious at the despoiling of Indian land. I thought it a farrago of nonsense. There had been some equipment sabotage which was beyond the Indians' capability at the site, but it was possible the supervisor had himself sold the bulldozers, pocketed the profits, and needed them replaced. The Peace Corps was satisfied that the boy was dead." Papery eyelids slid down, then up. "But then Clay learned they were basing their belief on what Luttrell and Blaylock had told them. Blaylock's accident seemed straightforward, but Luttrell's was much more questionable. Clay became panicky. After Saturday night, I believe he had a right to be."

"We can't find Clay. We had men checking his house all day Sunday. Do you know where he might be?"

"Is today Monday already?" Kimble tried vainly to lift an arm anchored with needles to gesture in vexation. "I don't even know what time it is." He closed his eyes pettishly, but to Balthazar's relief he continued talking. "As for Clay, both Virginia and I are surprised he didn't come here on hearing the news. But," Kimble's voice was now a sigh, "perhaps he doesn't know. He may be hiding somewhere in fear. He travels . . . knows a lot of places." Kimble was fast reverting to his former state of suspended animation.

"What were these artifacts?" Balthazar asked urgently. There was no response, and the nurse stood up, her uniform crinkling.

"Bones," Kimble said dreamily. "Clay still has them in a warehouse. For the museum."

Since this was now his third flight, Balthazar climbed into the copilot's seat of the Jonas Islander with a Lindberghian nonchalance. He approved of this pilot's brisk clicking on of switches, calm replies to the control tower, and immediate lapse into silence. If time-consuming, the trip to San Juan had been fruitful in one respect. Elliott Kimble had unwittingly provided Grover Clay with a stunning motive to eliminate his partners. While his income seemed quite sufficient for a comfortable life, Clay's resources might not stretch to the establishment of an expensive museum. But by disposing of Blaylock, Luttrell, and Kimble, he could quadruple his profits from the aluminum mining. And it was Clay, quoting Blaylock, who'd reported this resurrection of the former Peace Corps volunteer, who was possibly named King.

At the hospital, Virginia Kimble, with all flags flying bravely—unwrinkled blue silk dress, matching sapphire jewelry, precisely applied makeup—was able to tell him quite a bit about the travel writer. Glad of the distraction from her own worries, and thinking that the detective's interest in Clay stemmed from his concern over his whereabouts, she filled in the man's background and habits. On Vieques he spent most afternoons at the beach with his friends and was a moderately good swimmer. She couldn't recall his evincing any interest in other sports, even sedentary ones like target shooting. But he was given to momentary enthusiasms; he'd become proficient at something and then lose interest.

His work took him to many countries, and he often left on a moment's notice. But Clay did research new places thoroughly before leaving, in the interests of his articles' accuracy and his own comfort. Smiling, she'd quoted his comment that he was an armchair traveler in the sense that he knew where the easy ones were everywhere in the world. Since he was a gourmand, he also checked restaurants ahead of time. An observant man with a sly sense of humor, his work sold well to the opulent magazines that catered to older people who wanted a plush change of scenery rather than adventure.

Closing his eyes against the glorious distraction of the Caribbean vistas below, Balthazar reviewed the tidy hypothesis for Clay's guilt. Blaylock's murder required a knowledge of the man's habits, some patience, and good marksmanship. Nothing he knew ruled Clay out there. Luttrell's poisoning suggested a cagey efficiency that fit what he'd been told about the man. And certainly Clay had been anxious to know if murder was suspected in that case. The attack on Mildred might have been laid on too quickly—he simply hadn't had time to plan. His motive there was that her husband had been too talkative, although at the moment he couldn't imagine what she might have said that gave him that impression. Luttrell and Clay had a joint past that the writer had made every effort to conceal when he'd stopped by the trailer. The attempt to liquidate—appropriate word—Kimble in that fashion seemed unduly arduous, but that alone might misdirect suspicion if it weren't regarded as an accident. Very neat.

On the other hand, postulating a return from the jungle of a vengeful early environmentalist was a fanciful writer's notion. Clay's own perhaps. He sent the butterfly to Blaylock, for whom it had a frightening meaning. In order to be able to hint later that this was some sort of retribution announcement—thus buttressing belief in the reappearance of the Peace Corps volunteer—he sent them to Luttrell and Kimble also.

The only flaw there was that the perfect time for Clay to get all broody about the butterfly was when he examined it at Luttrell's. Instead, he'd only shown a mild interest in the insect's rarity and beauty. Perhaps the blue Morpho signified something else. He could check with the Vieques biologist. When he talked to Maira on the phone, she could only suggest the tradition that any butterfly was

a symbol of the soul. Rebirth into glory from caterpillardom.
Dead butterfly—dead soul?

He'd spent two persistent hours on the phone at
headquarters in San Juan that morning, trying to find
anyone at home who worked at the Peace Corps base in
Arecibo. But not only was it a holiday, the few he'd
reached could only suggest calling the Records Department in Washington. While the Corps always tried to hire
former volunteers in administrative capacities after their
tours, the policy was that they would only stay five years.
Fresh people, new ideas. Anyone from the sixties era
would be long gone.

If a live King were not a figment of Clay's imagination, he'd have to be middle-aged, somewhere between
forty-five and fifty. Since the Peace Corps had then recruited
from prestigious college campuses, he would be well-
educated. If he were the true poet of Joan Blaylock's
nightmares, he'd be facile with words. He would have had
to be in Barranquitas on March 28, the day of Blaylock's
death. Assuming that he'd come after that to Vieques, he'd
be a recent arrival. Balthazar stopped, amended that. King
could have established himself earlier, but he'd have had to
have been off-island on that date. But until federal offices
opened tomorrow, no one on Vieques knew damn-all about
what he looked like.

Baggageless, the detective was the first arriving passenger
and cut quickly through the late afternoon Memorial Day
departures encircling the weighing-in scale. Peeling noses
and shoulders abounded, and plastic bags overflowing with
sand buckets and sun hats gave those leaving the appearance of exiles who'd had to pack too hastily. In front, there
was only one *publico* driver, slouching thoughtfully in the
driver's seat of his six-passenger van. Although Gusto had
been advised of the detective's flight time, the forecourt
was empty of salesmen, preachers, and police jeeps. In the
distance, however, he could hear a horn hooting a repeated
phrase, and soon the yellow Monte Carlo spun around the
turn, with Gloria gaily belting "Hello Dolly" over the car's
klaxon.

The rear seat of her car, if one did not count a San Diego Freeway of miniature cars and a month's supply of squashed juice cans, was also empty. In a festive mood, her effervescence was shaken cola. Her right hand, whose nails were newly varnished in a scintillating henna, semaphored an upcoming explanation of the absence of the children, but she said, "You'll have to come over more often, stay longer. Popping in and out isn't restful. And you'll have to bring your friend occasionally, the one born with sunglasses on. You know, Big Beard."

"You talked to Negrón?"

"Not me. But he spent yesterday and today interviewing the island layabouts. After a short talk with him, my second ex-husband confessed to a murder in Miami."

"Really?"

"You bet. And the man's never even been there." Her grin lit up the inside of the Monte Carlo. "After he left the police station, Carlos came over to my house sweating so fast I won't need to mop the floor for a week, gave me two of his back child-support payments, and offered to take all the kids horseback riding. See, Carlos is supposed to exercise the Ridders' horses all the months they're gone, but usually from May to November he only exercises his index finger—he goes by and counts the ponies. They just left Saturday, but after his brush with the Beard, he decided to get to work today! I dropped them all off up there, went home, washed my hair, did my nails, and took a nap. Maternal sabbatical."

"Santo holidaying, too?"

Thinking about this, she came close to getting under the speed limit. "Don't know where he is. With the island so crowded, everyone's been ticking over and now they're winding down at home or at the beach. Haven't seen a single jogger. Something New hasn't been around since noon. And Yung even closed his restaurant after lunch. That man needed Scotch tape to keep his eyes open. Well, reliable help's hard to get. I suppose chopping veg is boring." Meditating on that, she resumed her pursuit of Mach One.

"Did Negrón or Gusto locate Grover Clay?"

"Now that you mention it, I haven't seen him myself.

I suppose I thought he was visiting Mr. Kimble in the hospital. But I did think it was funny when I saw his Mercedes in the Ridders' garage."

Balthazar jolted upright. "What was it doing there?"

"That's just what I said! He has a perfectly good garage of his own. I thought he'd put it there because his man George was off-island and he was leaving himself. But then I thought he must have known the Ridders were gone, too, so if he was worried about it being safe, what was the point? No kids would take that car out joyriding. Cops'd stop them two feet onto the main road. Everybody knows his car. Besides, Mr. Clay doesn't do walking. And even if the Ridders don't live all that far, he'd have had to—"

"I'm sorry to interrupt, but was Negrón at the police station?"

"Sure was. I went by there to see how many other sinners he'd converted and that's when Gusto sent me to—"

"Gloria, I think we should hurry there."

She looked at him admiringly. "You know, you're the first person who ever said that to me."

19

SKELETONS HAD terrified him as a child. They came after him in dreams, where he was unable to run, so that their slow, implacable jerks toward him brought them nearer and nearer. Soundlessly, he howled in his sleep as they approached, groping with ineffectually twitching castanet fingers that would finally grasp him in an unbreakable hold. Their malicious, eyeless grins were far more fearful than any grimace. Being told once that all Carmelite nuns in a nearby cloistered convent slept with skulls by their beds had made him think them the bravest of women. The printed word made him shudder—skeleton. He was already a teenager before it occurred to him that he was one.

The Solveyo children, he assumed, had no such nightmares. Although they watched with interest as their elders ceremonially unearthed the bones of a recently dead tribesman from a shallow grave, their keen senses did not even seem offended by the putrefying smell. For years, on every occasion, its foulness would prickle his eyes, inflame his nose, sandpaper his skin. His throat would lump as with someone else's vomit. Even the shaman's rattle and conversational chant, telling the deceased of the wonders of the days of feasting that had occurred while the body was decomposing, scraped his ears. Then, bored, the children wandered off to their games while the adults took manioc leaves and wiped and wiped the glistening skeleton. The older ones would be recalled when the ornamentation of the separate bones began.

It was a time-consuming task. Having been scrubbed

with sand, rinsed at the river, scrubbed again, all but the tiniest bone would be embroidered with birds' feathers. The tame parrots and toucans that fluttered under the thatched roofs would be denuded of their most brilliant scarlets, golds, and emeralds. Flamingos were deprived of their amazing pink pinions, egrets of snow-soft white ones, rare tropical varieties of purple and black plumes. The feathers were sewn on scapula, ribs, pelvis, tibia, fibula, radius and ulna, delicately overlapping as on the live avians, but no one bird ever displayed such wondrous variety of color. The skull glowed with hummingbirds' iridescent down. Even the eye of the beholder could feel the velvet. Last, the sockets were provided with bright pebbles or chunks of translucent crystal, polished by the river's churning. When he and Doug had first arrived and stumbled on the Lagoon of the Dead, they'd found two skulls with huge, glittering diamonds for eyes. But each piece of the body was in itself now a work of art, a transformation of the individual into something rich and strange, resplendent rather than frightening.

After arranging the beautiful bones in a straw basket, the shaman would place it in his canoe. All of the other canoes were filled with flowers. A cortege of the entire tribe would paddle slowly to the lagoon. The swaying basket would be attached to a high crosslike mast which was deeply planted by the young men in the subsoil under water. Although the Indians came here on ritual occasions, as well as for funerals, they never again looked at their handiwork, knowing the dead were appeased, that they would therefore protect the tribe. That was what mattered. If Doug and Chet Luttrell had only taken the contents and not the baskets themselves, the Solveyos would perhaps never have known of the theft.

Still mulling over this, he rose silently from his observation post across the road and slipped through the late Monday afternoon quiet to Clay's back bedroom window. Set in a lowland glen, this house was one of the few surrounded by willow trees. Their water-loving roots must have found an underground stream. By shinnying up a thickish trunk and clinging koalalike, he had been able to see through two twisted slats near the top of the closed plastic blinds. As if under siege, the man had confined himself since late Saturday night to this secluded room, even bringing his food here.

Easily clambering up the trunk once again, he peered in. Clay was sprawled across the mattress. Pressing his own body against the bark, he stayed lizard-still, listening to the silence.

Initially, certain that this retreat was inspired by the terror of seeing the ominous butterfly in Saturday's mail, he'd gloated. Clay had not attended the Kimble party, and as soon as he himself had finished, he had come directly here. Tired as he was, he intended to spend the night observing, in case the panicked man decided to flee. In that event, Clay—or rather his body—would not be available for the Memorial Day rites so elaborately planned to honor the Solveyos. True, it was an unregarded holiday— there were no significant Western rituals to honor those who were gone, as if the living were shrugging the idea aside with the New Testament's indifferent "Let the dead bury the dead." But it was appropriate.

On Saturday night, when he'd arrived here, he'd at first feared he was already too late, that the man was gone. The house huddled dark and empty-looking under slippery, sighing branches. But he'd decided to wait, thinking perhaps he'd just retired early. To his amazement, Clay had come on foot and entered his own house with burglar stealth. He'd turned on no lights, although he'd showered, fumbled about in the bathroom for a long time before going to bed. In the early light of dawn, peering in, he could see the lumpish shoulders covered by a sheet to his chin, the mouth obscenely agape like an enormous fledgling waiting to have food crammed down its craw. Gobbling and snorting, Clay slept soundly. The snaky nylon phone cord was tossed some distance from the instrument by the bedside.

It had made no sense. A frightened man would not turn off the phone, be without a car. Even odder, he had never answered the doorbell on the several occasions that uniformed patrolmen had stopped by. He'd theorized that Clay was using extreme caution. Since he could not know what the threatener looked like, he could not even trust the police. But two different officers had come, one very young, so he could only assume that Clay was hiding from everyone, creating the impression that he was gone, having even hidden his car. By midmorning Sunday, as Clay brought in a breakfast tray laden with eggs, ham, muffins and a pot of coffee to his bedroom, he could see that there were no plans for departure and therefore had hurried away himself.

When he had returned Sunday night, he'd risked a quick peek. Leaning against the headboard, the fat man was petulantly tossing a heel of French bread at the wastebasket. But he'd decided to wait for full darkness. The ground was soft and he'd settled comfortably against a smooth willow tree, flexing his bare toes pleasurably. All those shoeless years had coarsened the pads of his feet, yet left them amazingly sensitive. He could feel the tiniest twig and lift lightly over it before it snapped.

That thought catapulted him into the past. And the willows' cool and somber shade had recalled the jungle's perpetually faded light. Even the almost clean-swept earth beneath these trees had reminded him of the jungle's tidy ground. Before he'd gone to the Amazon, he assumed one had to wade through foliage, cutting away with a machete before taking a step. But the insects' constant struggle for food assured that it was as spruce as a good housekeeper's floor. The Indians never bothered to choose one spot in which to defecate. In a few hours, there was no trace.

With an effort, he'd wrenched his thoughts to the present task, forcing himself to concentrate. Once again, on Sunday, Clay had not turned on the lights, despite the setting sun. There was no burglar alarm that he'd been able to spot, probably because Clay's servant lived in year-round. There was a loose screen on the other side of the house. If all went well, he'd planned on killing him that night, as soon as he'd extracted the information he needed. Pulling a pencil-thin knife from a sheath on his curved leg, he had imagined pressing its point lightly under Clay's doughy chins. He knew the man would surely tell him where the bones were.

The bones. He'd again moved into the past. Brooding over the last twenty-five years, he could see that the

Solveyos had never recovered from their initial loss, despite all his efforts. Because he'd awed the chief with his tool-making skills, his hunting abilities, he'd been listened to, and he'd kept the tribe on the move after that. Normally, they'd ranged widely because the soil, even for the meager crops, was so quickly exhausted. He'd hoped by the time they returned to the area surrounding the lagoon, carrying the bones of those who'd died in the meantime, the stark, empty masts could be re-hung with these new baskets, that they would be reassured.

A professor of his had quoted a proverb, "To the brave man, every land is a native country," adding that was equally true of the anthropologist. But although he could comprehend the fears the Indians suffered without the protection of their grateful dead, he did not feel these in the sinews as they did. During the first years, he was a little alarmed at how few births there were, at how many baskets of bones they'd accumulated as they travelled. But he'd attributed it to the unsettledness of their lives, the rigors of the much longer migrations.

Finally, the chief said they must return. Docilely, they'd then taken all the new baskets to the lagoon, and as usual they recounted the stories of their journeys to the dead, caught them up on tribal gossip. He tried to persuade himself that all would be as before. This time, he made sure their village was extraordinarily well-hidden, even though their river was only a minor tributary of the Amazon and never frequented by the white man.

The first boat he spied contained only four men, two of them guides. He'd convinced himself and the Solveyos they were explorers and would not stay. And they hadn't. But in a few months, a larger craft came. Observing them, he heard English for the first time in fifteen years. Although he did not tell the chief what this probably meant, the old man knew when they left on their wanderings that this time they could not come back to their ancient home. Although his oldest living son was barely out of adolescence, the chief had taken to his hammock at their first long stopping place and announced that with the next sun's arrival, he would be dead. And he was.

For a time, the young chief was also amenable to his

direction. But he felt none of his father's admiring respect for this exotic newcomer. If his new ways had pleased them, they'd have modified their own, but they could see no point in numbers at all. Arrogantly, the young leader insisted they go back, install his father's bones in the lagoon.

It was a dreadful sight. Tilted crazily, only two of the masts, neither with baskets, remained. The clear water of the inlet was now red sludge. The wading herons and cranes had disappeared. In the silence, without any of the tropical birds' rusty screeches, their fingernail-on-chalkboard cries, they could hear the flap of a buzzard's wing overhead. And that was all.

Later, he could reconstruct what had happened. They were mining bauxite upstream, damming the river to wash the ore, and then, by opening gates, emptying the stained and thickened water with a roar. Let loose, the river had surged into the quiet backwater where it had never come before, knocking over the thin bark-stripped poles, taking away their precious ornaments, and leaving the residue of tainted mud.

That night, he'd thought the young chief wise to distribute the cassava wine prepared for his father's rites. It was unprecedented, but plans could not be made until morning. Usually they whirled in joy as they drank, but all had only sipped solemnly. He himself had drunk too much. When he'd awakened, they were gone.

Now as he slowly peeled a willow twig and sucked on its woody sweetness, he remembered his agony. It'd been like a child's worst nightmare, to return alone from school, find smoking ruins, a leveled house, no trace of family. He'd dug his fingers into the fine dirt, soft on the surface, unyielding beneath, and wept for hours. Only extreme thirst had finally driven him upright to a stream. As he bathed his face, he jumped back, sure from his eyes' smarting that this water was frothing from chemicals. But it was his body's own excess of salt tears that had burned them.

He was a Solveyo. Revenge was their response to any death. All his tribe would die now because the earth beneath their feet had been taken away for the sake of the ore, because their souls would wither without their ancestors' bones. Imagining the Indians, drifting through the jungle naked and vulnerable, appalled without any protection from their own capricious gods, he'd determined to retrieve what he could. After all, what Blaylock and Luttrell had wanted were the diamonds, not the bones. But their very beauty meant they still existed somewhere. He would find them, return them to any straggling survivors in pitiful recompense. For the moment, he would go back to the white man's world.

Working in the open-pit bauxite mine with other Indians, none of them Solveyos, he heard them tittering about the puffy man who came occasionally. They called him 'the bone buyer' because he was always asking them these silly questions. They'd never heard of feathered skeletons. They were from Manaus, and sophisticated enough to laugh also about the other man with whom he had come—he wanted 'pretty rocks.' They *did* know about diamonds and emeralds. Squatting beneath the trees, their shovels at their feet as they waited for the next explosive charge to jar the dirt loose, they told him these stories.

One day, two years ago, Clay and Luttrell had arrived at the site. With his head covered, red earth clinging to his sweaty face, he had no fear that the helicopter pilot would remember him. The foreman was complaining of the shortage of earth-moving equipment, asking them to tell Elliott Kimble what he needed to remove what he called the overburden—the trees, the plants, the rocks, the soil above the bauxite. During the conversation, Clay had mentioned Vieques. The next night he'd planted the dynamite sticks in the bulldozers, set it to explode at midnight. Then he'd gotten on a rusty tramp steamer en route, eventually, to Belém and the Atlantic Ocean.

On a sunny Sunday in San Juan, pausing to get money to continue his journey to the small neighboring island, he'd wandered into a bookstore. Running his eyes with disinterest over volumes of poetry that had once entranced him, he picked up a copy of one entitled *The Sepia Mirror.* The author was Douglas Blaylock, a lecturer at the University of Puerto Rico. The book-jacket picture was an old one, and in it he saw the past reflected. Then, flipping through the pages, he'd stopped, squinting, sure there'd been a mistake. But no. Holding the book at arm's length, he saw his own words creeping, black-flylike, across the page. He'd felt as if each pore of his skin was attacked by those fierce insects. To his surprise, his lungs continued to fill with air. He inhaled and exhaled as if he were still alive.

Now, his long toes gripping the wood, he climbed quietly down the tree, picked up a willow branch, and erased the sets of parentheses left by his feet. Padding through the scrubby grass to the side of the house, occasionally whisking away his traces, he reviewed all that still needed doing. There wasn't a lot of time because of the gently fading light. It was already after six.

It was not interruptions that concerned him. Clay had done him a favor by hiding his car. Casual visitors would assume he was not at home. Gossip had it that the Kimbles were concerned about their friend; no doubt that was the reason the police were stopping by. But since the servant was due to return tomorrow, the authorities would certainly wait until then before checking the house.

The lagoon where he intended to hang Clay was deep within the restricted area. Consequently, his body would never be discovered, but the birds would clean it and he himself would know of its existence. When he found the remaining Solveyos, he would tell them. A lasting commemorative exhibit. Smiling sardonically, he considered that Grover Clay's plans would not be realized quite in the way the museum designer had envisioned.

He'd already borrowed transportation. That had been easy—with so many absentee owners, no one would be out counting the number of horses in the pastures.

There was only one problem. To reach the lagoon, one had to cross the shelled area. He would need enough light to see any danger from projectiles in the ground. The timing was tricky because that meant he would be visible crossing the main road. He intended to cut through the trees in back of Clay's house to reach the highway, but the field next to the road was open. Because of the holiday, there might be rather more traffic. He'd have to be quick.

Exercising care was still important. He needed to save himself because he had to return the bones to the tribe. Although it would be possible to catch a flight tomorrow, it'd be better to leave things in good order. Perhaps, he paused to consider, he was inventing excuses for a longer stay because it was fun to watch Balthazar Marten prowl fruitlessly. At each of their meetings, he knew he'd hoodwinked him. His disguise was impenetrable, really, because it was transparent. Having those alert cat's eyes hadn't helped the detective.

Satisfied, he nodded and smiled, threw the branch aside, pleased that he was undisturbed by any tricks from the corners of his eyes. His plans were solid, workable, rational. He headed off to gather all that he needed. The light in his eyes was perhaps not quite rational.

20

SNICK ... SNICK ... Negrón spun his thumb abrasively over the top of his cigarette lighter. He was not smoking. He was, quite impatiently, waiting for Balthazar. In the holiday peace of the Vieques police station, the Sanjuanero's irritable pacing across the gray-green linoleum was the equivalent of the drumbeat of testy fingernails on a polished surface. Once again, as he reached the heavy plate-glass front door, he flicked his lighter, checked his watch. It was 6:05 P.M. He jiggled the coins in his pocket like the dried seeds in *maracas*, turned, and strode back across the room.

Negrón had liked the case against Clay, if his imperceptible nod and thumb jerk toward the parking lot could be so interpreted. An immediate visit to the suspect's house was clearly next, in his view. Appropriating keys to one of the new white Isuzu jeeps, he'd hurried out to the parking lot, climbed into the vehicle and started it. When Balthazar didn't follow, he'd gunned the motor. When sharp punches on the jeep's horn still did not bring the New Yorker out, he'd slammed back into the station.

But even as he was outlining the evidence against Grover Clay to Negrón and Gusto, Balthazar had liked it less. Monopolized as the pudgy journalist might be by his dream of a museum—no doubt with eye-level plaques memorializing him displayed by each exhibit—he lacked the cool obsession these crimes showed, at least the attacks on the men. Not dilettantish, custardy Clay. And Clay certainly didn't send those blue Morphos.

183

It was only ten minutes after six. A little time to
revise, construct other theories was called for, Balthazar
decided.

Heads together in the square backroom behind the
police dispatcher's desk, he and Gusto were now going
over the list that the sergeant and his men had painstakingly
compiled regarding people's whereabouts at relevant times
and the dates they'd arrived on Vieques. These names
narrowed down to only a few who'd met the right criteria
of age and education.

Some of the information surprised the detective. He'd
imagined Santo (a/k/a Richard León Reyes) was an island
institution, but the evangelist had only materialized in early
April, or so Gusto recalled. Santo himself shrugged off the
concept of time as meaningless. By Sunday, he was unable
to recall how he'd spent the hours after the boat had left
for the Phosphorescent Bay, let alone account for the last
twenty years. "Missionary work," he'd told the frustrated
sergeant, arcing his arm to encompass half the globe.
Central America, South America, Asia—wherever the Holy
Spirit moved him, he'd said. Although he'd insisted he was
highly educated, he also said he hadn't enrolled formally at
the several colleges he'd attended. "Says he was a college
drop-in at two California universities, another in Michigan, one in Massachusetts," Gusto reported. Balthazar
mused that the preacher's mixture of philosophies, fond-
ness for sonorous words, and elliptical style could indicate
the joyous undiscipline of the self-taught. Or a drug-
addled brain. Or a clever impersonation.

Howard Yung was not legally Howard Yung. The
affable restauranteur had been christened Le Quy Van, as
the passport he'd shown to Gusto confirmed. His father,
who'd died while only in his twenties, was Vietnamese.
The Chinese mother had taken her small son to her own
family in northern California, and he'd used their name.

Tapping the paper with a fresh toothpick, Gusto
noted that Le was a last name and a fairly common one in
Vietnam, according to Howard. "Come to that, he says his
first name isn't Howard, either. He just translates it that
way."

"Hmm. A Chinese name that means Howard?"

"Well, maybe," Gusto considered, rotating his toothpick, "he said 'How.' Can't always tell when he's joking."

Howard Yung, Balthazar reflected, was good-humored, a fine cook, a very likeable man. And he also had qualities that put him on the list of very likely suspects. He was Luttrell's neighbor and knew the victim's routine. Although he had visited Mildred the night of the Kimble party, he'd not stayed long and he'd not returned to his restaurant. Sipping a Chinese beer, sitting in his truck and staring at the ocean, he'd said. Old enough to have been a Peace Corps volunteer in the sixties, Yung had also arrived in Vieques only a few months ago. He'd told Gusto that he'd attended an Ivy League college, but had not graduated.

"Who's Roy?" Balthazar asked, running his finger down the list.

Gusto frowned. "Not sure I got that right, but he told Yung he goes by that. The souvenir guy—'Something New.' Yung said either Royal or Leroy, but he never mentioned his last name. But see, we couldn't ask him because we couldn't find him today. Airport's pretty dead because it's the holiday and people won't really leave until tomorrow. Might be taking it easy somewhere—wasn't at his house."

Pausing at the door, Negrón glared into the room. Gusto, his forehead still creased, continued with his explanation. "It isn't *his* house, really. He sleeps there when he isn't out selling his stuff. What happened is Elias Bermudez just was finishing a little two-room place in Esperanza and, before he got the utilities hooked up, his wife died. Terrible thing—she fell out of the car. Right-side door just popped open when her husband was going pretty fast. Anyway, Elias went to Boston to stay with his sister, and Something New came then and just sort of moved in. Wasn't doing any harm. No lights, but there's an outhouse in back. Horse keeps the weeds down in the yard."

Negrón had listened in angry disbelief to the sergeant's elaboration. Balthazar was aware of the agent's impatience twanging across the small room, but an idea, half formed, clutched even more strongly at his attention. An idea with a double meaning—he snapped his fingers excitedly—you could only see it one way at a time. It was like the black-and-white drawing of two people in profile, with the white space between them forming a goblet. If you saw the ornate wineglass, you couldn't see the people. He stopped. In discovering how to think about it, he realized he'd lost the idea. Gusto looked at him inquiringly, but he could only shrug.

Flicking the bottom of the thin box, Negrón slid out a cigarillo, removed the cellophane wrapper, crinkling it noisily. As he snapped his lighter, the uniformed dispatcher politely pointed to the outdoor waiting area. If it had been possible to slam the felt-lined outer door, Negrón would have done so, as he exploded through it.

"Anyway," Gusto went on unperturbably, "when I go back to Yung's to see if maybe Something New is helping him chop stuff, the Golden Lotus was closed. Not serving tonight. Nobody there."

Something New's muteness, his shrinking away, as if from a raised police fist, nettled Balthazar. But, growing up in the 1950's, an illiterate and inarticulate black might have reason to react in that manner, he had to admit. On the other hand, if he were playing that part, it was wise to keep the lines to a minimum.

Of course, if one typecast the role, Carlyle Leclaire Templeton would be the only choice. The stereotypical poet, writing in English, was slim, blond, and dissipated. Certainly not black, Hispanic, or Oriental. And Templeton was a Harvard graduate, he'd told Gusto. He was a walking, talking exemplar of the purloined letter. He looked like what he seemed, and that could be the shrewdest disguise.

An unlikely group of suspects. In reverse order, an athletic alcoholic, a timid artisan, a Chinese pretending to be a Chinese, and a loony evangelist. And one of them had lied, or at least, Balthazar amended his thinking, had gone considerably out of his way to give the detective a false impression.

Standing up, he clapped Gusto on the back and headed for the parking lot. It was almost six-thirty, but he was too keyed-up to be either hungry or tired. He felt the tension in his very bones. "Bones." He stopped halfway to the jeep. Had that word been connected to the elusive two-way image? Kimble had said Clay had a prized exhibit of Indian bones. But someone else had said the word, and then it referred to . . . What? What else could "bones" refer to?

Climbing into the passenger seat next to Negrón, he said abstractedly, "We'd better hurry on out to Clay's."

21

GROVER CLAY's house was set at the end of a meandering private lane which had apparently last been graded during the sugar cane boom of the 1920's. Glaring at the baseball-size rocks that littered the surface, rather than at Negrón, Balthazar thought sourly that even a delighted Nigerian, driving his first car in America—usually a New York cab—would have gone more cautiously on a road like this. But, despite the jolting that prevented any attempt at arranging his ideas, the New Yorker was himself almost shoving on the dash to push the jeep forward faster. He glanced at his watch; it was almost six-thirty.

Yet he told himself again that there was every reason to believe the house would be empty. Patrolmen had stopped by the writer's residence throughout the day; Maira had called persistently on Virginia Kimble's behalf. No response. Whether Clay was the murderer as Negrón was convinced, or a possible victim as he himself increasingly believed, it was unlikely they could discover anything tonight. Tomorrow the servant could let them in, tell them if his employer had packed suitcases, left a note. Tomorrow, too, the Washington Peace Corps office would be open; it would be possible to get some information on King, find out at least if that was his name. It was not knowing enough, he decided, that made him so restless, edgy, with adrenaline even in his perspiration. And he could feel Negrón's craving for action, any action.

"If Clay's our man, why would he take off?" Balthazar

frowned at the slow settling twilight. Here the living fence
of thin trees made the road even darker.

"Heard that his try at Kimble didn't work. Afraid he
was seen. Hid his car, took the first ferry." Negrón swore
as the jeep was almost swallowed by a pothole.

"Nobody saw him," the New Yorker replied.

"Nobody *noticed* him," Negrón corrected flatly.

"Why put the car in somebody else's garage?"

"It worked. Everyone thought he was around. And, I
tell you this." As Negrón spoke, he jabbed his forefinger at
Balthazar. "None of these island *pendejos* broke into the
Kimbles' Saturday night! Nor did they tell a visiting
relative about the Kimbles or their money or their party or
their guest houses."

Everything he said had the obstinate fixity of a tiny
corn under one's third toe. No qualifications. That he
himself agreed with the statement made Balthazar testier.
If Negrón had sniffed a lie, he'd have nailed the offender
by his tongue to the door of the police station, or so they'd
all believed. No, Mildred Luttrell hadn't been struck by a
jittery island burglar.

"But leaving suggests guilt," Balthazar persisted. "Clay
would have no reason to think we suspected him, let alone
had any evidence. As it is, we're barking up every tree."
Balthazar clamped his lips together. That was it—the
figure between the profiles in the optical illusion! The
poodle. Mildred sometimes called her dog "Bones." But
Grover Clay, panicked at the idea of losing his marvelous
exhibit—no doubt smuggled out of Brazil—could only
imagine that she'd meant the Indian bones. "Clay did it!"
he burst out, his head rasping on the Isuzu's roof.

"Of course he did," Negrón enunciated acidly. "If you
could just have figured that out a little sooner, we could
have been spared that idiot sergeant's drivel about the
Chinese restaurant owner," he whacked the steering wheel
for emphasis, "and the preacher," whack, "and—"

"But Clay only attacked Mildred Luttrell. He planned
to murder, even if he didn't pull it off. Still, I don't see him
blowing Blaylock's tire out or picking poisonous apples.
He didn't threaten his partners—he didn't send those
Morphos. And can you imagine that fat bastard swimming—"

"Not one more word about those fucking butterflies!" Negrón spit the words out furiously.

If he weren't driving, Balthazar thought, scrunching one balled fist inside his open palm. If he weren't driving *and* wearing his sunglasses. He wanted to hit the sonofabitch right in the eye.

Abruptly, Negrón jerked the jeep to the left, and they spun down to a graveled circle before a sprawling, white ranch-style house. The early evening sky held enough light to silhouette the drooping willows above it.

Shielded from the noon's blaze, the long low structure in the wooded glen would have seemed a cool retreat. Now its unlit desertion was gloomy. As Negrón flicked on the headlights, the beams bounced off the picture windows, with closed drapes behind them. The only signs of previous habitation were the tops of scattered chairs on the rooftop patio, and the silvery glitter of an aluminum gum wrapper under the trailing juniper groundcover near the front door. A dove's slight, mournful coo underlined the silence.

Negrón headed for a doorbell set in wrought-iron curlicues, and Balthazar reached in the glove compartment for a long-handled flashlight before joining him. He slapped the head of the light against his palm while they waited, frowning at the unresponsive house. Negrón landed a thick fist on the screen door frame, then opened the unlocked screen, pounded on the solid wooden inner door, jerked at the unmoving knob. He let the screen slam and marched off to the left around the house.

Drapes or blinds were tightly shut before every window. The purple-backed leaves of a spiral of wandering Jew snaked through behind a curtain at one. Negrón jiggled its ill-fitted screen. Balthazar mused that if he were with Sixto, he'd be wondering out loud why a man leaving in a hurry would bother to pull all the window coverings, but he only clicked on the flashlight in the shadows of the trees, sending its beam ahead of Negrón's feet. Brushing the trailing branches aside as he went forward, Negrón let them slap back.

Single file, the fallen willow leaves slightly slippery beneath their tread, they strode around the back. Balthazar let the beam play over the rather steep stone staircase to the roof. Negrón crossed the flagstone apron, climbed halfway up, put his sunglasses in his pocket, glanced around, came back without even a headshake. But the New Yorker had caught a niggle of doubt in his unguarded eyes. Although Negrón tended to act instinctively and always wanted to move fast, he was an experienced detective. He may have thought the idea of an avenging poet absurd, but his confidence in Clay as multiple killer was waning. And Negrón hated being unsure.

But Balthazar was himself very uncertain. Did King exist? Who was he? All he knew was that one man had not apparently told the truth.

Aggravated by the house's stillness, wondering if someone were crouching mutely inside, Balthazar flashed the edges of a back bedroom window. The light hung on two bent slats near the top. Turning, he saw the whitish bark of a willow, a trunk thicker than a flagpole but almost as smooth, bare for the first eight feet. Sixto'd be up that in a minute, he thought.

He set down the flashlight, reached up, but the first heavy branch was too high. His knee was not going to support Negrón's heavy frame if he gave him a handhold and, in any case, being taller, he himself would find it easier to get the nearest handhold. Without his dark glasses, Negrón's eyes looked too small for his face. Little tiny stubborn pig's eyes, Balthazar thought, saying aloud, "How about a boost?" Negrón started to push past him, then whirled and cupped his hands.

Although the New Yorker tried to leap upward, grabbing for the branch, as soon as he put his foot's weight on the Puerto Rican's hands, he heard a grunted curse. Scrabbling around the trunk with his knees, he pulled himself up. He clenched his own teeth around his right knee's sharp complaint. With one arm looped over the branch, he reached down for the flashlight.

All he could see were the tousled pillows and part of a littered built-on bedside table with an unplugged phone, a silver coffee pot, and a stack of dishes. He slithered down the trunk, a knothole rasping his lower chest as it snagged his tan *guayabera*. The flashlight's beam swung upward, startling nesting birds. Brushing off his pants with his free hand, he remarked, "Had breakfast in bed, but that could have been Saturday or Sunday. What did he do on Saturday night when he got back from the Kimbles?" Balthazar tapped the tree with the heel of his hand, studied the scrubby grass around the edges of the patio, as he thought out loud. "He leaves the car at the Ridders', comes back, maybe sneaks into his own house because he's going to lay low. Why? He's flustered, nervous—he doesn't know if he really succeeded in silencing Mildred?"

Slouching sullenly by the stucco back wall of the adjoining garage, his hands on his hips, Negrón did not reply.

"Not a man at all used to physical—" This time Balthazar gave the tree trunk a triumphant high five. "He's got dog bites! He has to hide out until they heal!"

"Dog bites," Negrón mimicked. "It isn't dog bites he's going to die of! Where the fuck is he *now*, asshole?" Wheeling around, he almost stamped around the side of the garage on his way to the front of the house.

Biting down hard on his lower teeth, Balthazar felt one of his filling's crack. His mouth was flooded with the faint savor of cloves and the bitter harshness of metal. A taste of guilt and the acrid bite of anger. He dropped the flashlight. Anticipating the solid smash of his fist against Negrón's face, he launched himself after him. But just as he clawed for the shoulder, he found himself grasping empty air. Negrón had stumbled, slid forward, just catching himself on his outstretched palms. Unable to stop, Balthazar landed with a thump on Negrón's back. They both went down. As the New Yorker rolled to the side, Negrón flipped over and got to his knees. Grabbing Balthazar's hair, he aimed a fist. But Balthazar was halfway up, shoving his longer arm right at Negrón's thick, bearded neck and protruding Adam's apple. The Puerto Rican's head snapped back sharply, and he slammed to the ground onto his left shoulder. Balthazar, levering with his left elbow, scrambled upright. Negrón, braced on a hand flat on the ground, was himself springing up, when he fell back down again heavily, croaking out, "Horseshit!" He was staring at his smeared palm.

Balthazar realized his own elbow was warm, wet, and smelly. Shaking his arm in disgust, he snapped, "Couldn't be." Trying to catch his breath, feeling foolish, ashamed of lashing out in anger, he muttered, "They keep the horses fenced in. A wandering cow."

Stabbing his finger at the pile of horse manure that he'd skidded in as he'd rounded the corner, Negrón hissed, "I know horseshit when I see it!"

Quickly Balthazar picked up the light, shone it along the ground near the driveway's gravel. Two sets of horses' hooves led past him, then under the willows' low weeping branches for as far as he could see. Negrón wiped his hand furiously on a clump of grass, staring after the light.

"Nobody goes for a pleasure ride under those trees. He's cutting through to the main road." As he spoke, Balthazar sent the beam in small arcs over the sparse grass. A gleam that had looked like a gum wrapper on the first pass caused him to stoop over. It was a man's silver ring, a fat chunk of turquoise in a massive setting. "Clay's," he said, as he held it out to Negrón. "I saw him wear it. Could have slid off as he was being thrown over the horse. He either was unconscious or—" He found himself speaking to Negrón's back. The Puerto Rican was already heading for the jeep.

"Wait!" Spotting the outline of bare footprints between two tufts of grass, Balthazar motioned him back. The toemarks were six inches apart, the heelprints almost a foot. "Look at this."

"For Christ's sake!" Negrón snarled after a glance. "You couldn't get a plaster cast from those. You crazy? Move, move. That manure was fresh. We can get this guy at the highway." He turned and raced toward the Isuzu.

He was already throwing the jeep into reverse before Balthazar managed to struggle in. As the New Yorker picked up the radio, Negrón barked. "Tell those fucking uniforms to get their asses out here and make sure he doesn't double back. While they're at it, they can take a good look back there."

22

As THEY BURST out onto the asphalt, the jeep's rear tires skittered sideways. A sharp whiplash pain snaked along the side of Balthazar's neck. Grabbing for the padded handle with his right hand, he massaged it with his left.

"If we'd left the station when *I* said," Negrón spat, by way of apology, "we'd have gotten the *cabrón* at the house."

"Turn on the goddamned brights," Balthazar retorted, as a stray ambling black-and-white cow loomed up on the right. The same uncomfortable thought was troubling him. Negrón rocked the vehicle wide so abruptly that, even seat-belted, the New Yorker's shoulder slammed the driver's. "And slow down—we're going to have to keep an eye out here for where he'd come out."

"For all you know, gringo, he's dillydallying under the willow trees, killing, digging in that nice soft dirt, burying, riding off into the sunset." Negrón floored the accelerator. "And the way they do things on this island, that fool Gusto and his men will put off the search until morning when the light is good!"

"Pastures all around in back of the trees, so people would be poking back there looking for stray calves. Not a good place for a grave." Although Balthazar's hand still wanted to curl into a fist, his knuckles feeling deprived, his anger was damped down by the cool satisfaction of their discovery. Now they knew exactly who the killer was: the man was just what he'd seemed. They knew King's name—

194

first and last. As Blaylock hinted, they were the same.
And he was within reach. That Negrón seemed unwilling
to discuss the subject was petty, Balthazar considered, but
he himself was not going to be accused of boasting by
bringing it up.

A whole herd of cows, determinedly jogging along the
roadside toward Isabel Segunda as if for a night on the
town, were just ahead. "Stop!" Balthazar yelled.

Negrón zoomed past them. "This sudden obsession
with the safety of cows. You have become Hindu?"

"It might mean a fence is down."

Negrón threw the jeep and them into blazing reverse.
Curling through the sprawling above-ground roots of a
ceibu tree, a barbed-wire length caught the headlights. Just
ahead and across the road, near a stand of sunflower-tall
hibiscus, there was another downed fence. As Negrón
scrambled across the road, yanking out the thin perforated
metal pole to make room for the car, Balthazar glanced at
the stone bread-loaf kilometer marking ahead, and clicked
on the radio. The young police dispatcher paused, then
crackled back the information that they were entering the
buffer zone of the Naval Reservation. After approximately
a kilometer, they would be in the restricted shelling area
and must stop, he emphasized through the static, because
of the danger of unexploded ordnance.

Concentrating on guiding the jeep through the poles
and avoiding some jutting rocks, Negrón only jerked his
head sideways when Balthazar relayed that. The remaining
light was deceptive, not sufficient to enable them to pick
out the hoofprints, even in the few areas away from the
occasional stands of trees. Negrón kept on the brights and
Balthazar thought, as he leaned out the window tracking
them, that full darkness might have made the task easier.
Above the sky glowed grayly with a few scattered sooty
clouds in goose formation.

As the jeep waggled over the bumpy terrain, the
slowness of the pursuit irritated him as much as the
speed had before. He hoped that the buffer zone was
very wide, well marked on the perimeter, or that Negrón
was keeping a careful eye on the mileage. The ground
cover was meager, but the earth was hard, and the

horses' marks sometimes disappeared. Even so, a few yards of clearer ones showed what he thought were longer strides, as if they were now hurrying. Negrón's muttered obscenities became louder as the jeep strained up a steep rocky slope and he was forced to dodge the outcroppings. Just before the top, the headlights angled skyward like beacons.

Then, on a narrow ridge half a mile ahead, an upright rider and a second burdened horse being led were imprinted on the horizon. Negrón cut the lights, but not before they'd both seen the dangling wire of the fence at the bottom. Just as suddenly their quarry dropped from sight behind a clump of trees.

Negrón let the jeep slide downhill to the opening in the wire. "On foot, even I can't catch him," he remarked sourly. "You would be useless."

Half aware that Negrón was trying to goad him into action, Balthazar only replied, "Clay could be alive. They're not that far ahead." But their decision, he knew, was already made. Neither of them wanted to stop now, the rush of hunter blood tingling even in their mouths.

"But we need the lights. He won't have a rifle." Negrón almost pulled off the knob, goosing the jeep forward as he yanked on the full beams. "Just my luck to get my Puerto Rican ass blown off by an American dud. If their brains weren't in their star-spangled butts, they'd let the Germans make them."

Clawing at the slippery dash in a vain effort to steady his vision, Balthazar made the split second decision not to let go and strangle him. He kept his own eyes straining on the ground for ammunition. Probably they could see a live one, he hoped desperately. In World War Two movies, they looked big—as if they might have five-inch-diameter heads. But here they'd be buried in the ground surely. How about just an unexploded piece of one? Some things were best not dwelt on.

Fat boulders littered the hilly field, and the jeep jolted and rolled as they zagged furiously around these. There was not a sign of the rider.

"Fuck, fuck, fuck!" Negrón howled as a ragged outcropping with cathedral spires, six feet high, hovered straight ahead on the top of a rise. As he cranked the wheel, the jeep did a fast sideways slither down the dip. The tires spun, then caught, and they topped the slope some twelve feet from the rocks.

The first rifle shot must have slammed into the left front tire, the second certainly splintered the windshield. One second they were in the air about to bounce down on rubber, the next they were crashing on a metal rim. The vehicle flopped resoundingly on its left side, the headlights uselessly slashing the sky.

Balthazar realized he was moving his mouth, but no sounds came out. He grabbed for breath, feeling as if the seat belt were constricting his lungs. He managed, "You okay? We got to get out. Turn off the lights."

"Get off me!" Negrón croaked, fumbling frantically until he found the switch. He clicked the radio twice and furiously threw the useless microphone at the dash.

Groping for his buckle, willing his eyes to adjust to the sudden darkness, Balthazar pushed at the door handle and swung his good left leg over to smash the door open, rolled over to land on the ground on his right arm. He rolled again as he heard Negrón pitching after him.

The third bullet whanged against the upflung jeep door. Five feet to his left, Balthazar made out a gravestone-size boulder and scrambled crabwise to it. Negrón almost beat him there.

"He must have a night scope," Balthazar gasped.

Scrunching as flat as he could, his head next to the rock, Negrón hissed, "Typical gringo info. Prompt, accurate, and totally worthless!"

"Try this," Balthazar threw back bitterly. "If we'd gotten to the house earlier, we'd both be dead on the patio." Half strangled by the alkalines of anger and fear, he swallowed. Then he added more calmly, "We wait here. He knows we can't follow him. He'll get tired and take off."

"Or," Negrón bit out, "he circles around, picks us off easily from the side."

Instantly, they both breathed more quietly, as if that would help. Stretched out flat, Balthazar slowly turned his head to the dark trees rustling to his left. "For once, you got a point," he whispered back. On the far side of the jeep, the tall rocks pricked the night sky and, as far as he remembered, they afforded some side protection as well.

"Do it now." Negrón echoed his thoughts.

"We should wait, give him a chance to get nervous and move off. I admit he's not the type, but—"

"What do you mean—he's not that type? You don't know who the hell it is!" Negrón rasped. "I'm going *now*." Before Balthazar could protest, he'd raised up on all fours, then on feet and hands, head down, and scurried off, a few loose rocks marking his progress in the quiet. Just as Balthazar decided he must have reached safety, another shot burst out. He heard Negrón's surprised, agonized cough, almost felt him fall.

Before he could even decide to move, he heard something odd. A far-off fireworks thud. Then the field lit up with a thousand blue noons. Screeching from the trees, a disgruntled flock of birds rose from the nearby trees, then cawed off overhead. The magnesium flares drifted down. In their harshness, he could see Negrón face down just before the rocks, and without thinking he raised up slightly, saw the lean figure of the killer on a distant knoll, rifle dangling, with his back toward him, staring out to sea. One unburdened horse was rearing up, tethered; there was no sign of the other.

Before he realized he was in motion, he was behind the jeep, and then pulling Negrón backwards by his shoulders, roughly, clumsily. He almost blessed the second round of flares, waiting for the burst of supernatural light before rolling the Puerto Rican over. The glare made the blood spurting from his right thigh an ill-omened black. At first he thought Negrón unconscious, but then he saw his eyes were open, the upper teeth jamming into the lower lip. Grabbing at his own shirt buttons, Balthazar yanked it off his shoulders, stripped off his belt, jamming his gun butt into the elastic of his shorts. Wadding the shirt, he managed to strap it over the thigh before the light faded. But that was followed by the heavy concussion of the booming artillery. He thought confusedly that the shells really did whistle before they landed. The earth rocked beneath his feet.

"You got to sit up," he shrieked in the wounded man's ear. "I can pull you back all the way in." The streaking shell flashes blinded, rather than illuminated, and he slid his hands under the unmoving shoulders, pushing without effect upward. Negrón might have been screaming in agony, he thought, but he couldn't hear over the guns' thunder. At last he felt him lift slightly and he tugged ferociously until he could prop him up in a sitting position.

Rubbing his palms on his pants legs got rid of the wetness, but not the stickiness, and he stopped, leaned a trembling forearm against the rock's pitted abrasiveness. Then he almost leaped off the ground as a heavy shell exploded somewhere in front of their protective cover. Fine earth rained over his face, and the gunpowder smell of charred logs and sulphur scoured his nostrils and then his throat. Instinctively throwing his hands over his head, he squatted down. In his imagination, the next shell blew the rocks and them away. He had no idea of how long he crouched there.

The pounding in his ears stopped after the cannons did. In the absolute silence, he took in Negrón's helpless, guttural curses. Reaching over, he lightly touched the thigh, horrified at the soaked bandage. "You got to take off your shirt." He tried to sound matter-of-fact.

"Your fucking navy—" Negron screamed.

"Shut up and give me your shirt," he roared back. The slippery belt buckle finally yielded to Balthazar's shaking fingers. His only coherent thought as he pressed on the second shirt, retightened the belt, trying not to listen to the pain wheezing through Negrón's teeth, was that the man was surely going to bleed to death. And even if the shelling stopped now, if there was no second barrage, he could think of no way to get him out. No one would come in. Gusto might be on the road, but he would wait for their return. He himself could run. Well, do a fast hobble. But even with two good legs, he couldn't carry Negrón. And even if he did the four-minute mile, Negrón couldn't wait, at the rate the blood was gushing out of his leg, until help arrived. *Think, think,* he urged himself.

At some unconscious level, Balthazar knew what the sound coming toward them was, but it took a few seconds before he identified the scrabbling hoofbeats. Over them, there was the thunk of a flare. And another. The second barrage would begin. In the new light, he found a small rock ledge, peered through an arrow slit near the top. After the cannons' authentic roar, the rifle had lost its authoritative crack, and the repeated shots riffled like popping corn. But a shoreward settling flare backlighted the marksman. He was aiming out to sea, emptying his gun at a distant cruiser.

Balthazar could distinguish the man's fury and frustration in his hunched shoulders, in the way he jerked the gun, firing again and again. Then the next minute he disappeared in a volcanic upthrust of earth. But his loosened riderless horse was running right at their rocks.

If he could get those loose reins, *if* he could, but he'd have to wait until the last second to spring out or the panicked horse would bolt in another direction. Right. He couldn't imagine doing that, couldn't conceive of it, until he found one sweating hand around a leather strip. The small horse reared in a circle as he clutched the single rein, its flailing legs aimed at his chest. In reckless fear, he struck out, bashing his balled fist against the horse's jaw. They were both astounded. The dazed horse put four quiet feet on the ground. With the last shred of light he got the second rein. In the silent darkness, he jerked the horse's face next to his, felt its hot breath almost scorch his cheek, its chest muscles heaving next to those of his bare arm. He decided he loved the animal.

"Get up, Negrón," he almost whispered.

"No! You crazy? I can't."

"Get up *now*," he snarled quietly, "or the horse will step on your leg." The scuffling, the ragged moans as he scraped to his feet caused the horse to dance, and Balthazar prayed fiercely for one minute more of quiet from the guns. One minute. No, two minutes. And three more flares, too. He inched the horse into the encircling rocks, backed it up, shoving its rump against them, until he stood between it and the injured man.

"There's a ledge by my feet," Balthazar was still

whispering. "Put all your weight on me, then try to hop up on the ledge with your left foot."

The Puerto Rican made no movement, and his clenched moan sounded negative. This time Balthazar thought about it. He transferred the reins securely to his left hand. He would no doubt regret it forever, but it was surely the time, the place. When his right fist clipped Negrón's chin, he felt the grate of the beard. Then he thought his knuckles would fall off.

Thick enraged fingers, cold with sweat, clumped on Balthazar's shoulders. The nails dug into his flesh at the base of his throat, then loosened.

"Forget the ledge, get on my back, get your left leg over the goddamned horse, idiot!" Bare chest thumped against his back and he staggered sideways, brutalized by the burden, the searing pain in his right knee. Miraculously, it lifted as Negrón threw one arm, one leg and then dragged his bulk onto the horse. As a life preserver, Balthazar considered, anger was right up there.

Tossing its head upward, the horse was trying to swallow, or at least chew through the bit, but the heft of someone in the saddle seemed to reassure it. Even if that person, as Balthazar now realized, was quite unconscious. He fumbled for his left hand, found the fingers knotted in the mane, and slipped the Puerto Rican's unresisting left foot into the stirrup. Quietly he inched the reins over the animal's ears, remembering that the last time he'd done that was when he was four and forced to pose for a picture. After sliding them over the slumped body of Negrón, he wound them tightly in his right hand. Patting the horse's perspiring rump, he wondered if it could possibly carry them both. Felt solid.

Before he could make his decision, the navy did. The whump of artillery sent the horse's front legs straight up, and Balthazar jumped on behind Negrón. Their combined weight had one good effect. The horse hadn't the strength to rear, and it jogged sideways but, with clamor and fear as a spur, more or less ahead.

As they slithered and stumbled down the slope behind the rocks, the New Yorker kept his left arm crooked around Negrón's waist, his naked forearm melding clammily to the other man's skin. His own eyes teared from the pungent smoke, Balthazar begged the horse to see. Just to the buffer zone, he pleaded silently, just get there, and we'll make it.

Later, he remembered thinking that there was an unusual slightly sweet smell that lingered after the explosion of so much gunpowder, but he was never sure.

23

"THE FOOTPRINTS—behind Clay's house—that's when I knew," Balthazar repeated. "Negrón apparently was too much in a hurry to look at them closely." Except for intermittent metallic squalls, the phone line was so clear that he could hear a two-fingered typist somewhere behind Sixto at headquarters. "Something New was noticeably pigeon-toed. And what had been bothering me about him was that he'd said he couldn't read. Yet Yung had said he'd noticed him, sitting by himself, grinning at the fortune in his Chinese cookie."

Sixto whistled appreciatively into the receiver. "Good catch, *Baltasar*!"

"Really a last-minute save. Otherwise, I would have ruled him out. He never overdid that nobody-here-but-us-chickens routine. I think it must have really amused him to Uncle-Tom it like that. And, of course, that whole slightly guilty act was a double-bluff. He had the hand-in-cookie-jar look. Venial sin. But he was committing murder."

Balthazar started to doodle but, because of his bruised knuckles, just grasping the pencil was painful. Wincing, he put it down and got up to unkink his knee. Back pain stabbed him. He settled for perching on the edge of the station's wooden desk chair with his leg outstretched. "You know," he went on, "I'd given the edge to Santo when I heard his last name."

"*Sí, sí*. In Spanish, Reyes means kings, and Richard—" Clicking, as if from a child's hand-held toy cricket, cut off the rest of Sixto's reply.

"If he were the poet, he could have picked Reyes as a little joke. I kept thinking of that odd dedication to *The Sepia Mirror.* Maira had told me that Blaylock's recent work was very poor. After I knew about King, I thought Blaylock, maybe as a way of appeasing his own guilt, was acknowledging in a backhanded fashion that King was the real author. 'Poetry is King. Long live poetry, long live the king.' In French, the king is *le roi.* Blaylock added: 'The first is the last.' But everyone who mentioned that line had a different interpretation. Maira thought that it referred to the writer's view that his art would always rule his life. Joan Blaylock assumed it meant her husband would only love once. But he himself had told her it was a play on words. The man's last name was King. Something New told Yung his first name was Leroy." Balthazar was looking forward to describing this reasoning to Maira that evening. Admiring crackles now came over the phone line from San Juan.

Forgetting about yesterday's whiplash, Balthazar started to tuck the phone against his left shoulder. His neck refused to bend. Propping the phone against his ear with his good left hand, he went on, "And this morning, the Peace Corps confirmed that one of their early volunteers was named Leroy King, a black Harvard graduate with a double major in anthropology and English. He and Douglas Blaylock had gone to Brazil in the sixties. The two had an unusual assignment, almost an undercover mission. They were trying to establish communication with a Stone Age tribe called the Solveyos. King's dossier records that after a few weeks in the jungle he'd become too sick to travel, and his partner went for help. When Blaylock came back in a helicopter, piloted by Chet Luttrell, they found evidence at their former campsite of King's death, or so they reported." Pausing, Balthazar added, in a subdued voice, "I asked for a photo of King and a set of his prints. We retrieved his body—had to use a helicopter as a matter of fact."

"But I do not understand why he was riding around this field with shells in it in any case."

"Me either," Balthazar groaned. "Of course, he didn't expect the late night bombardment. That was a surprise demonstration for the admiral. Big surprise for us, too. In fact, I can only guess about a lot of things. Luttrell and Blaylock must have brought back the Indian bones that Kimble mentioned and sold them to Clay. Gusto found out today that he'd talked the navy into storing some boxes in a climate-controlled warehouse here. Their files just list the contents as 'museum exhibits' belonging to Clay. Probably the Brazilian government could claim them. And I think Clay believed that Mildred Luttrell knew about them, that she might say something and he'd have to return them."

Because someone was crumpling aluminum foil next to the receiver, he could only make out every third word of Sixto's next query. Balthazar responded, "No question that he's the one who attacked her. Clay was strangled. Then his body was tied onto one smart little horse. The minute the shelling started, it headed briskly for home. This morning Gloria's ex-husband went dutifully to the Ridders' and there it was in the pasture, still 'saddled.' Gusto and I found the dog bites on the corpse's ankles and lacerations in the palm from the collar's shell decorations. Coroner here thinks Clay was killed sometime late Sunday. King apparently just left his body in the house until he had time to collect it. Just lucky he didn't collect Negrón and me at the same time.

"And speaking of which, I'm glad Negrón's okay. Anybody been able to talk to him yet?" The line was perfectly clear now, and he could hear Chief Villareal in the background, sounding huffish.

"No, he is still in recovery. He owes you, *Baltasar*," Sixto answered quietly.

"Well, it was good thinking on Gusto's part to have the ambulance out there. And Negrón's tough—he was even conscious when they loaded him on."

"He say anything to you?"

"Sure did. Looked right at me and said. 'Fucking gringo.'"

"Perhaps . . ." Sixto hesitated. "When he is better, he will think about it and express—"

"You're right there," Balthazar interrupted, grinning wryly. "He'll think about it and when he sees me next, he'll express it better. He'll look at me and say, 'Mother-fucking gringo.'"

Sixto's amused agreement was almost drowned by Villareal's voice, now quite near the receiver. Balthazar only caught the last word, which was "tomorrow."

Best to wind up the conversation, he decided. "Again, happy to hear you had a good weekend." Sixto's earlier comments had been brief, but his tone had bordered on the ecstatic. "And mention to the chief for me that, in lieu of combat pay, I'm going to take a few days off, just stay here." He could hear Sixto faithfully relaying the message, but an entire colony of live crickets infested the line. Deciding that must mean Villareal agreed, he hung up.

24

"MILDRED SAYS the lotus is actually a water lily, and since Howard Yung is going to expand the restaurant, she's going to put ponds filled with them in strategic places around the grounds," Maira remarked. Seated at one of the Kimbles' glass-topped poolside tables, she was jotting essay marks in her grade book. Tuesday had cooled into satiny night. Champagne was icing in a glistening bucket, but Maira had insisted it not be opened until she'd finished. Work, she'd said that morning, would be an anodyne and the only possible way she could justify staying until Wednesday.

Floating on his back in the Kimbles' pool, Balthazar decided that the stars were lower here than any place on earth and that the knuckles on his right hand hurt worse than any other part of his body. His right knee and back were close seconds, but the water was definitely helping them. The trade-off was that the chlorine was stinging the cuts and scratches on his arms and chest. He said, "She really seem better? One good thing, her head was a lot harder than I thought."

Shutting the book, tossing the pen on the table, Maira dug her fingertips luxuriously into her loose hair as if thinking had wearied even the roots. "She was still a little trembly on the old pins, so she agreed to go back this morning for a week's recuperation on St. Croix. She handled her sister remarkably well. Impressive—Helen is a natural force. On the flight here, she had mentally moved Mildred and her possessions, excluding Party because Helen's allergic to dogs, to St. Croix permanently. But Mildred just kept repeating that Howard needed help with the landscaping, and good help was hard to get on Vieques, so she'd have to be back soon. Helen was Not Pleased, but Howard certainly was. It's appropriate—in Greek history, eating the lotus put one in a state of dreamy content, made one forget home and family."

"Families are designated, as well as born into," he remarked to the night sky. "But only a few men are really lucky. They meet just the right woman. Also, I find the sheer efficiency of getting both a wife and a son at once very appealing."

In the process of stretching luxuriously, Maira suddenly bent at the waist and let her hair cover her face as she rubbed her neck. Better not reply, she reasoned; she wasn't ready. That he was not the man to drift away when lutes came unstrung or roses were out of season, he'd surely demonstrated that weekend. He was a strong and committed man. A member of the community. But his strength was itself a problem. "Has it occurred to you that nothing happens on this island the way you expect it to?" As if to soften the shameless change of subject, Maira pulled her chair to the edge of the water.

As she sat down, bent forward, he noticed that the shaded pool lantern brushed her delicate cheek bones, turned the edges of her hair into shiny floss. Standing before her in the shallow end, he had only to reach out to cup her face, tangle his fingers in the silken hair.

"This weekend, for example," she elaborated, "I had planned to grade papers, of course, but also to relax and lie about a great deal. A few days of laborious idleness. Hmm. Now that I think of it, 'laborious idleness' is an oxymoron: one word contradicts the other. Vieques is an oxymoronic island. A bombarded paradise."

"Where," he waggled his hand in the water, hoping for a beneficent effect, "we all eat jumbo shrimp. And, along these lines, where a yarnball-size dog and a horse were the weekend's real heroes."

"No," she said firmly, "they weren't. And if you'll get out of the pool, I'll smear ointment on your battle scars which I can see gleaming redly all over your skin."

Handing him a towel, she commented ruefully, "Your body has had a hard weekend—hardly an unscarred inch."

"True," he said, marching to the table, "and when the going gets tough, the tough open the champagne. Ooof. Unfortunately, the tough have only one working hand."

"Luckily for us, we have three altogether." Smiling, Maira took the bottle, untwisted the wire from the top, and pressing her thumbs on the side, sent the cork plopping into the pool. Then she giggled. "Normally, of course, I don't approve of litter. Private joke, which will be explained at time and date to be announced."

The liquid sparkled over her fingers and then into the glasses. Handing him one, she said, "Here. And for the outer man, the antibiotic lotion. Turn around—this first-aid cream is fairly nonstinging." Squirting a length of it like toothpaste in her palm, she stroked it on the torn skin across his shoulder blade. "The dog and horse were just acting on instinct, whereas you were genuinely brave. Sit still. I haven't finished with your back."

His hair was drying into spikes, and she thought that, despite the broad shoulders, he looked much like her nephew after his bath—all bruises, scrapes and vulnerabilty. With an effort, she restrained herself from kissing the small scratch on the side of his neck. She fumbled for more lotion. "You know," she went on, "talking to Mildred when she first arrived, I kept thinking that she should stop worrying about every little thing. But I had to admit to myself that I'm a fearful person. If a man is weak, that scares me. If he's strong, that frightens me, too."

Reaching over her shoulder, he caught her wrist tightly. "Wait! I think you should come around here and tell me what you mean."

Wiping her fingers on a towel, she picked up her glass and slid into the chair next to him. "Waiting for the ferry to come here, something happened. What was important about it was the way I reacted afterward. Let me tell you." When she'd recounted the incident on the dock, she concluded, "So, although I wasn't at all hurt, all I could think of was that I *needed* you."

"Say *wanted*. Wanting is good." His eyes, on hers,

were wholly serious. "You certainly didn't need me. But if you had, what's wrong with that?"

"I don't like the idea that somehow I expect you to take care of me. That's not the way I want to feel. Perhaps it has something to do with your genuine abilities, or perhaps it's the way we met in January. That was... archetypal. Hero rescuing naive fair maiden from villain. It's set up dependency-thinking on my part."

"I see no sign of that." He pulled his chair closer, would not let her drop her glance. "You were obviously always self-reliant. Getting a job, taking on the responsibility for your nephew. And what's more, you took care of that purse-snatcher handily." He ran an anxious hand through his hair. "But it does worry me. What if he hadn't been knocked out, went for you?"

"Well, I did have a plan B. Jump in the ocean, and purse-strap clenched between teeth, swim toward ferry." She grinned over the top of the wineglass.

"I've never met fair maiden who was less helpless. I don't see—"

Setting the thin glass on the table, she clasped her hands between her knees, leaned toward him. Her voice was passionately earnest. "Zar, it's just that I don't want to love you because I *need* you. I want to need you because I love you. Wait a minute," she splayed her fingers over her eyes. "Did I say that right? Love, need, yes. Because otherwise it is just dependency. You have to be very clear about this at the beginning of a long relationship. Because that gets mixed up as you go. Then you both need each other. Do you understand?"

"Not really. I *need* you. For all the reasons, beginning with a reason to live." His voice vibrated with urgency. "I *want* you. Your incredible face, body, and alphabetized spice rack. I love you, Maira. *Do* you love me?"

"Yes. Oh, yes. I'm just trying to be clear about—"

Jumping up, he pulled her to her feet. "Tomorrow, definitely, we can talk about the reasons. I will stop being an archetype. I will rescue only if requested. Just say that again."

"I love you, Zar."

Kinsey Millhone is . . .

"The best new private eye." —*The Detroit News*

"A tough-cookie with a soft center." —*Newsweek*

"A stand-out specimen of the new female operatives."
—*Philadelphia Inquirer*

Sue Grafton is . . .

The Shamus and Anthony Award winning creator of Kinsey Millhone and quite simply one of the hottest new mystery writers around.

Bantam is . . .

The proud publisher of Sue Grafton's Kinsey Millhone mysteries:

- ☐ 26563 "A" IS FOR ALIBI $3.50
- ☐ 28034 "B" IS FOR BURGLAR $3.95
- ☐ 28036 "C" IS FOR CORPSE $3.95
- ☐ 27163 "D" IS FOR DEADBEAT $3.95

- -

Bantam Books, Dept. BD26, 414 East Golf Road, Des Plaines, IL 60016

Please send me the books I have checked above. I am enclosing $_____ (please add $2.00 to cover postage and handling). Send check or money order—no cash or C.O.D.s please.

Mr/Ms _____

Address _____

City/State _____ Zip _____

BD26—4/89

Please allow four to six weeks for delivery. This offer expires 10/89. Prices and availability subject to change without notice.

NERO WOLFE STEPS OUT

Every Wolfe Watcher knows that the world's largest detective wouldn't dream of leaving the brownstone on 35th street, with Fritz's three star meals, his beloved orchids and the only chair that actually suits him. But when an ultra-conservative college professor winds up dead and Archie winds up in jail, Wolfe is forced to brave the wilds of upstate New York to find a murderer.

THE BLOODIED IVY
by Robert Goldsborough
A Bantam Hardcover
05281 $15.95

and don't miss these other Nero Wolfe mysteries by Robert Goldsborough:

☐ 27024 **DEATH ON DEADLINE** $3.95
            —FINALLY IN PAPERBACK!
☐ 27938 **MURDER IN E MINOR** $3.95

            "A Smashing Success"
                —*Chicago Sun-Times*

And Bantam still offers you a whole series of Nero Wolfe mysteries by his creator, Rex Stout

☐ 27819 **FER-DE-LANCE** $3.50
☐ 27828 **DEATH TIMES THREE** $3.95
☐ 27291 **THE BLACK MOUNTAIN** $3.50
☐ 27776 **IN THE BEST FAMILIES** $3.50
☐ 25550 **THE RUBBER BAND** $2.95
☐ 27290 **TOO MANY COOKS** $3.50

Look for them at your bookstore or use this page to order:

Bantam Books, Dept. BD17, 414 East Golf Road, Des Plaines, IL 60016

Please send me the books I have checked above. I am enclosing $_____
(please add $2.00 to cover postage and handling). Send check or money order—
no cash or C.O.D.s please.

Mr/Ms _____

Address _____

City/State _____ Zip _____
                                                        BD17—4/89
Please allow four to six weeks for delivery. This offer expires 10/89.
Prices and availability subject to change without notice.

THE MYSTERIOUS WORLD OF AGATHA CHRISTIE

Acknowledged as the world's most popular mystery writer of all time, Dame Agatha Christie's books have thrilled millions of readers for generations. With her care and attention to characters, the intriguing situations and the breathtaking final deduction, it's no wonder that Agatha Christie is the world's best-selling mystery writer.

☐ 25678	**SLEEPING MURDER**	$3.50
☐ 26795	**A HOLIDAY FOR MURDER**	$3.50
☐ 27001	**POIROT INVESTIGATES**	$3.50
☐ 26477	**THE SECRET ADVERSARY**	$3.50
☐ 26138	**DEATH ON THE NILE**	$3.50
☐ 26547	**THE MYSTERIOUS AFFAIR AT STYLES**	$3.50
☐ 25493	**THE POSTERN OF FATE**	$3.50
☐ 26896	**THE SEVEN DIALS MYSTERY**	$3.50

<u>Prices and availability subject to change without notice.</u>

Buy them at your local bookstore or use this page to order.

Bantam Books, Dept. AC, 414 East Golf Road, Des Plaines, IL 60016

Please send me the books I have checked above. I am enclosing $_____ (please add $2.00 to cover postage and handling). Send check or money order—no cash or C.O.D.s please.

Mr/Ms _____

Address _____

City/State _____ Zip _____

AC—5/89

Please allow four to six weeks for delivery. This offer expires 11/89.

Special Offer
Buy a Bantam Book
for only 50¢.

Now you can have Bantam's catalog filled with hundreds of titles plus take advantage of our unique and exciting bonus book offer. A special offer which gives you the opportunity to purchase a Bantam book for only 50¢. Here's how!

By ordering any five books at the regular price per order, you can also choose any other single book listed (up to a $5.95 value) for just 50¢. Some restrictions do apply, but for further details why not send for Bantam's catalog of titles today!

Just send us your name and address and we will send you a catalog!

BANTAM BOOKS, INC.
P.O. Box 1006, South Holland, Ill. 60473

Mr./Mrs./Ms. _____
(please print)

Address _____

City _____ State _____ Zip _____

FC(A)—10/87

Please allow four to six weeks for delivery.